Zahryn's Light

Across the Waters

JANIS CONSTABLE

RESOURCE *Publications* • Eugene, Oregon

ZAHRYN'S LIGHT
Across the Waters

Resource Publications
An Imprint of Wipf and Stock Publishers
199 W. 8th Ave., Suite 3
Eugene, OR 97401

www.wipfandstock.com

PAPERBACK ISBN: 979-8-3852-3930-6
HARDCOVER ISBN: 979-8-3852-3931-3
EBOOK ISBN: 979-8-3852-3932-0

03/11/25

Zahryn's Light

—ACROSS THE WATERS—

"Across the Waters" is a dynamic mindset,
a way of seeing, a way of being.
It is a true liberation
of body mind and spirit.

Fresh new thinking. Revelation.
No limits, boundaries, or restrictions.
No hoop jumping
or brick walls blocking the way.
Unbridled consciousness.
Freedom and happy place—
and happy dance too!

Place yourself in the heights, on the edge, at the precipice,
looking out into the open—the oceanic wide, wide openness.
Open yourself. Re-invent yourself.
Re-imagine yourself in Wholehearted Living.

Gazing, dreaming,
yearning, learning,
visioning, envisioning.

Longing, belonging,
connecting, disconnecting,
part of, more of,
reaching out, stepping out.

Emboldening, empowering,
being, becoming,
present, graced, One.

Issues, sentiments,
questions, conundrums
bubble and churn
in random and nebulous chaos
and emerge with clarity
in Light-bearing truths.

Faith opens. Hope arises.
Healing begins. Transformation wells and swells.

Light into Light—Across the Waters.

Open the eyes of my soul to see
within, beyond, and through—
the Sacred, the Holy, the real,
the true.

May I be open and spacious,
expansive and free.
With fresh hope arising,
the new dawn is calling ME
into the truth, into the now,
into the spaces of life and matter—
into the vastness, across the water.

Across the waters
I am. I delight. I shall ever be
shimmering, shining, I shall rest—be free.
Light into Light—so let it be.
Amen.

To my big sister—my redheaded angel of a sister, Brenda—BJ—
who taught me firsthand all about glass-half-full living
and about perseverance.

Like the lyrical blackbird,
she took her broken wings and made them fly
all through her darkest nights.

Hers was an enlivened spirit—
and daily, she sparkled with her very own *joie de vivre*.

She lived and breathed the fullest meaning of the words,
"Happiness is homemade."
She had an insight into humanity that was inborn.
She saw into people's souls and understood their hearts.
Brenda simply knew people.

Brenda always lived her best life—
she lived and embodied the Wholehearted Life.
Brenda knew inlonracance intimately.

Brenda, was Light.

God bless you, Red.
May your Light shine ever brightly.

Contents

PART THREE
BE THE LOVE—UNCONDITIONALLY

EPILOGUE

A New Word

INLONRACANCE

Pronounced	in—LAHN—rahk—ahnse
Category	Noun
Origins	in (interior) lonrach (Irish word for shimmer) ance (act of being, or process of being)

Meaning

1   An interior feeling of an all-encompassing joy arising within the self in response to a current life-circumstance, or personal circumstance. Simply, a joyful state of being, not outwardly expressed.

2   A sense of inner glow, or radiance, or shimmer caused by overwhelming joy in the moment.

3   That exquisite human interior experience of joy, as a shimmering light arising within.

Whereas *exuberance* is an external expression of joy arising, *inlonracance* is an internal shimmer of joy arising, which is delightfully suffusive and personal.

The Irish word for shimmer is lonrach (LAHN-rahk). Add a prefix of "in" to make it inner, inward or interior. Add a suffix of "ance" to make it "the act of" or "the process of."

See also	inlonracancy (noun) inlonracant(adjective)

Author's Note

EVER HAD THE FEELING that you were glowing from within—that you were so blessed, so overjoyed, so radiantly and exquisitely happy—but you had no word, no single word, to describe your interior exuberance and your volcano of erupting joy? Your perfect inner shimmer moment?

Well, that is me, right here, right now! I'm inwardly shimmering with joy! So, what is stopping me from making up a word that means exactly what I'm feeling? Nothing is stopping me!

Drumroll, please! My hot-off-the-press, newly-minted pseudo-portmanteau is *inlonracance*!

I am in complete, full-blown inlonracance, for only me to sense, for only me to experience. In this moment, I am all lit up in my own glowing, in my own inlonracance. Sigh. Wow!

Have you known inlonracance? Have you felt it? Have you cherished the moment? What do you call your inner joyful shimmering? Say it! Use the word! Appreciate its depth and texture and color! And its internal densities, translucencies and dimensions!

Inlonracance!

Pronunciation Key

Zahryn	ZAHR—in
Padraig	PAH—dreg
Tagyn	TAY—ghin
Gaelan	GAY—lan
Saorise	SUR—shuh
Aoife	EE—fuh
Maevyn	MAY—ev—in
Rose	Rows
Connor	CON—nar
Sully	SUH—lee
Delaney	Duh—LANE—ee
Erinn	air—RHINN
Paige	Page
Enya	EN—yah
Noémi	Nho-eh-MEE
Saana	Sah-NAH
Madoh	Ma—DOH

Prologue

"ACROSS THE WATERS" IS metaphor, yes. But it is, in fact, real. It is *something*. Something new, more, or unknown. Something bigger than the here and now. And, quite possibly, something better.

Across the waters lies a hope, a vision, a dream. Tangible. Intangible. Attainable—or maybe not. Across the waters is a mindset—it is an attitude of awareness, a life perspective, an energy arising from within. Across the waters is synonymous with visionary living—with transcendent being—with acknowledging the Sacred sage of the soul, deep within.

Psychotherapists, rapid transformation therapists (RTTs), life coaches, parish nurses, and spiritual companions all talk about glass-half-full living. Positivity. Optimism. Celtic Christians talk about seeing the Light in the dark. Seeing the Light within. Seeing the Sacred within. Lay people talk about living the good life—living their best life. They speak about knowing self and finding self. About knowing God and finding God. They all share words—theories, testimonials, and stories—of living in gratitude, of giving back, of being whole, being one.

"Across the waters" is all of this, when you're ready, for this.

AT THE DAWN OF November 1, 2022, Zahryn drove her hand-control-equipped UTV up the mountain trail to the precipice. She was alone. As was her habit, she stopped right at the edge and took in a really big breath. Her heart was not racing with exhilaration. Rather, it had slowed to a barely palpable pulse. Lup—Dup—Pause—Lup—Dup—Longer Pause. Repeat.

An aura of Light enveloped Zahryn's fragile silhouette. The November sunrise was only one hour ago, and it seemed that the dawn could carry on forever in her heart. She gazed with contentment across the waters in a southerly direction, across the Celtic Sea. She lifted her eyes up to the sun, to the Light of the morning, and beyond.

From her vantage point on the mountains of the Ben Lonrach, the vista was breathtaking. Sparkling. Shining. Shimmering. How apropos! "Ben Lonrach" translated from Gaelic as the Shimmering Mountains. No matter the weather, no matter the season, no matter the time of day, these mountains had their own Light, their own energy, their own timeless legends and truths, if one were only open to see.

Zahryn's story is dark, but she herself is Light. Her parents, Connor and Rose, were in their early-twenties when they married in the autumn of 1986. Soon after their honeymoon, they conceived. They instantly fell in love with the idea of becoming parents. They both had had wonderful upbringings in their mid-century, rural-town, British Isle lives in the mountains of the Southshore Islands—the Ben Lonrach mountains. In the months before Zahryn was born, they had vowed to raise their child in a household of love—of unconditional love—in a world of honesty and truth, in a wholesome frame of Living Faith. Their Celtic Christian roots were strong, deep, and daily they acknowledged the Sacred in all life and living.

Sadly, Zahryn's mother died in childbirth, leaving her father to raise their daughter all by himself. Then Zahryn developed polio as a toddler. She recovered very well after a few years, left with only the aggravation of a chronic lung problem. And later, in 1997 when Zahryn was age ten, her father died of cancer, only four days after his diagnosis. She was, needless to say, devastated. Broken. Life was dark, indeed.

Her mom's sister, Auntie Tagyn, came to live in Zahryn's home in the Ben Lonrach, in a small town called Moonstone Cove, to raise her niece into adulthood. Zahryn went away to university in Scotland, and returned after graduating to live with her aunt. Gloom and doom flirted once again, at age twenty-five, when Zahryn was diagnosed with post-polio syndrome (PPS)—a progressive neuromuscular weakness that would lead her, soon enough, to a life in a wheelchair.

Throughout her life, Zahryn was resilient, adaptive, optimistic. She moved forward with grace, with tenacity, with hope. She looked for the Light in the darkness, always. She looked out, with hope and vision, across the waters.

AT 8 A.M. ON November 1, 2022, Zahryn's dear friend Gaelan approached the precipice quietly. He walked with stealth, with ease, on the mountain ridge trail, as in Solomon's Springtime Rhapsody where the nimble

mountain gazelle comes surely nearer, leaping in the mountains and bounding through the hills, seeking his beloved.

Gaelan's heart was in his throat, and a fearsome grip seemed to be slowly tightening, banding him, deep in his chest. Something Zahryn had said to him the evening before on the phone did not sit well with him overnight. The words of the song she sang to him were lyrical, yet foreboding. He was restless and he did not sleep at all. His concern for her grew. It consumed him.

At home at daybreak, he'd had his coffee and only a protein bar for breakfast. He really wasn't hungry. He just wanted to know, *to see* that Zahryn was okay. He set out at sunrise to find her. When she wasn't at home, he instinctively knew where to look.

He hiked for forty-five minutes, up the zigzagging rocky mountain trail, into the heights. He paused at the edge of a clearing, at a lookout named Crag Misneach. He could see Zahryn up ahead by the edge, seated in stillness on her hot yellow UTV, in her all-time-favorite place. This was a precipice facing the south, overlooking the grand Celtic Sea. Except for a few rocky outcrops rising out of the depths offshore, the waters stretched out far and away as if into eternity. No land mass was visible on any horizon whatsoever. He knew that Zahryn loved this place. It was freeing and invitational. Full of hope and empowering energy, it beckoned. It held all the potentials of raw and real emotions. It was a Celtic Thin Place, translucent and so close to God.

True to any other moment there at the edge, Zahryn was full of Light. The mountain was full of Light. Light arose and emanated, freely.

Gaelan called out softly to Zahryn, but she did not respond. She was facing away, across the waters, seemingly mesmerized. The wind was fierce. It was always fierce at the edge. Onshore winds and vertical updrafts arising made for gusty breezes at the best of times. Zahryn's long auburn curls and tresses were lifted in the wind, ringlets forming in the dampness, blowing and whipping wildly behind her. The blackbirds—the lennons—circled, high in the sky.

Zahryn was wearing her favorite cape, a thick Merino wool in a weathered tartan weave, in sage, claret, navy, and teal. Warm and cozy, yes, but she wore it mostly to block the incessant and chilling wind.

Gaelan approached her from her right side. The clear plastic oxygen tubing graced her nostrils and traveled up over her ears and down onto her chest toward the portable tank by her side. Her eyes were closed. She was peaceful. Her long arms were relaxed and her hands were crossed in her lap. She appeared at ease. Her long, slim legs were clad in black leggings and strapped in securely. Her body harness was locked in place. Her freckled countenance had a pallor, despite her glowing Light. Her head was tilted back, as if she was communing—meditating—praying.

Gaelan called out softly, "Hey, Red!"

When she didn't answer, he spoke louder above the sound of the wind. When still she remained silent, he shouted, "Hey, Red!"

Silence howled in the wind.

Gaelan reached forward to touch her. She was icy cold. Her lips were dusky, but they had been off-colored for as long as he could remember. He spoke again, this time with great hope in his voice. "Hey, Red! Can I have this dance?"

His heart was sinking, tumbling off the cliff. She was gone. His girl was gone. Zahryn was dead. That precious life, that precious glowing Light, in that very moment was leaving her. In one final flicker, one final showing, it was gone. That incredible Light which so uniquely defined Zahryn—that energy—that spark—that iridescent aura—would shine no more. It would sparkle and blaze no more. It would simply be, no more. Snuffed out like a candle in the winds, in the early hour of morn.

Gaelan broke into a sobbing despair. His sorrow hurtled loudly into the wind. His angst chilled him and his wretchedness overwhelmed him. Shaking, shivering, quaking, he fell to his knees and placed both of her hands in his.

Through his tears, he gazed up at her. His spirit was momentarily attuning to her peacefulness. Her eyes were gently closed. She had the most contented visage—an expression of fullness, wholeness, complete-ness, oneness.

Then the weight of his emotions gave way. And without holding back, Gaelan lifted his voice to the heavens and wrenched out his aching desperation in a single word. His unrequited love bellowed out, into the rawness of the wind, into the celestial vastness, into the whole of eternity, across the waters, "NOOOOOOOOOOO . . . NOOOOOOOOOOO . . . NOOOOOOOOOOO. . . . " There were no echoes.

PART ONE

Be the River—Go with the Flow

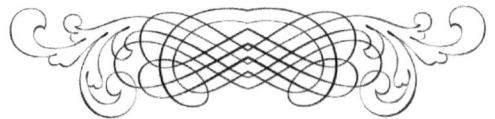

Sad, Sad News

JUNE 8, 2022

DR. PADRAIG GORDON CAME into his office, closed the door, and walked around the desk to sit in his oversized leather desk chair. His tie was loosened, and his shirtsleeves were comfortably rolled up. With his elbows resting on the grand mahogany desk, he leaned forward. He interlocked all of his fingers tightly, his knuckles blanching white.

He spoke in earnest to Zahryn in her wheelchair. Auntie Tagyn was beside her, pale with worry. "Zahryn, I'm afraid it's not good news," he said. "Your post-polio syndrome is advancing significantly, where your lungs are concerned. The PPS has started to limit your lung capacity. I have the results of your pulmonary function tests, and there is already a marked decline. No wonder you're tired and short of breath at rest. Your lungs have taken a beating for thirty-five years, and the wear and tear is finally showing.

"I don't want to frighten you, but it is very important that you do all you can to prevent any infections—any respiratory illness. Avoid choking. You could easily aspirate food or fluids and then you would get a pneumonia that you would have trouble clearing. Developing pneumonia could surely be fatal for you. I know you're up to date on all of your Covid vaccines, but still, the Covid virus would be the end for you. You must be careful. You must stay safe and protect yourself."

Tagyn reached over to hold Zahryn's hand. It was icy cold. Zahryn's facial color was pale, but of late, that was her normal. Her lips looked sickly dark, a purplish blue.

Zahryn, ever-hopeful, spoke slowly. "Will oxygen help?"

Dr. Gordon nodded. "Yes. Your numbers are low enough now, Zahryn, that we should be getting you set up with an oxygen condenser in the home and portable oxygen for when you're out and about in town. The portables are quite sleek and lightweight. You can easily manage them with your wheelchair.

"And you can likely still use your UTV. I know you love being outdoors and getting around with it. I've heard you say that your UTV is your freedom dance."

Zahryn smiled at his knowing comment, and she spoke again, bravely. "How much time do I have, Dr. Gordon? Like, should I be getting my affairs in order? Should I be telling my friends? What should I be telling them? What should I expect? What should they expect?"

She stopped her barrage of questions. She didn't need all of the answers right then and there. She just needed to visualize her new reality. She needed time to settle into a new normal with lots of unknowns, with fewer tomorrows, and with no room for meaningless pursuits. It was time to make each day count—time to make each moment count.

Dr. Gordon looked down for a moment to collect his thoughts. He spoke slowly, surely. "It's not easy for me to answer you, Zahryn. Yes, you should get things in order. Yes, all your friends should know, and you should have meaningful conversations with all of them. Clear the air. Say what needs to be said. Forgive what needs to be forgiven. Live in gratitude. But, most of all, live in hope. So long as there is time Zahryn, there is hope."

He went on. "You might have six months. You might have four months. You'll have a lot less time if you happen to get any respiratory illness or experience a bad episode of choking or aspiration. I do not have a crystal ball, but I can tell you that your lungs are steadily growing weaker, and they cannot do all the work of breathing that they need to.

"At the right time, you'll have the palliative care nurses come to your home to walk you through your care needs. Hospice care is available in-home and at the hospice centers. But, that's all down the road. Right now, I want you to tell me how you're feeling about all of this. Is there anything I can help you with, in your understanding?"

Their eyes locked. Dr. Gordon had known Zahryn for thirteen years, ever since she came home from university at age twenty-two. He had only ever had one post-polio syndrome patient in his whole family practice, and that was Zahryn. PPS was a rare condition in these times and he had delighted in being her go-to healthcare provider for all those years. She had literally thrived.

Zahryn, calm and collected, was taking all of this in stride. She spoke almost casually. "I'm okay Dr. Gordon. Really. I've known for my entire life that my lungs were my weakest link, and I've known for the last ten years that my PPS would eventually seriously affect my lungs. And, that all my muscles would waste away and weaken.

"It's kind of like a biblical prophecy coming into reality. It had been spoken. It was truth. It is now real. I've had a lot of years to prepare for this, to accept my pathway. No use in my fighting it. I know that my kicking, yelling, and screaming won't get me anywhere. And I do know that grace and hope will move me forward.

"My glass is by no means half-empty. I am living and breathing and full of life, and I will be, until I'm not. I have a plan. I will surround myself with those who love me. I'll spend my time nurturing my spirit. And I'll live in gratitude for all the joys my life has brought me. Like the river, I'll flow on." She stopped to catch her breath. She lifted her chin and spoke to her doctor-friend. "How's that for how I'm feeling?"

She turned and looked at her Auntie Tagyn by her side. Over the years, these two women had shared many similar conversations about facing Zahryn's mortality when the time came. And the time was now.

Auntie Tagyn reached over again to hold Zahryn's hand. She knew that her niece was so self-aware, so fully attuned to her needs, and so accepting of her limitations in life and living. She offered a smile of encouragement to Zahryn, who in turn smiled back.

Dr. Gordon leaned back. He raised both arms and ran both hands through his shock of thick, red-brown curls. He looked relieved. But more than this, he was filled with a rush of awe. Zahryn was resilient. Zahryn's body was failing but she was whole in mind and in spirit. His wise-beyond-her-years patient was full of insight into her illness and she was capable of facing anything that life or death could bring. He knew that she was strong. She was Light.

Auntie Tagyn spoke calmly. "Zahryn, we'll be here for you, honey. We'll all be here for you, always. Let me take you outside now, maybe to the park, and we can sort things out. We don't have to do anything right this minute, right Doctor? Can we go and just let all of this sink in?"

"Yes, Tagyn. Yes." He stood up and walked around his desk to Zahryn. He got down on both knees and held out his hands to her. She threw both of her arms around his neck and hugged him. He had been there for her through thick and thin. There, in the moment, her hug—of understanding and trust, of hope and optimism—was all she could do. It spoke volumes. He hugged her back.

Dr. Gordon stood up and stepped back. He inwardly marveled at his complex patient. She had always held him in such high esteem. He knew this and he felt this. He had led her through many health-related storms in her medically-challenged life.

He remembered—his mind was suddenly flooded with beautiful memories—of Zahryn's spoken confidence in him, of her expressed gratitude for him, of her unfailing desire to be as whole and as well as she could be under his teaching, guidance, and care.

He also recalled her profound words from a few years back, comparing his compassion to the light of a lighthouse beaming over treacherous rocks. She had said that his compassion glowed like Light from within him, much like the Ben Lonrach—the shimmering mountains on the shores of the Celtic Sea. Her words—this imagery—he held in his heart.

Zahryn spoke. "Thank you, Paddy, my friend. We knew this day would come, didn't we? We've traveled an uphill road together all these years. The road has been twisty and tortuous, and," she paused as she faced the reality of her own words, "it is going to end. It will dead-end at a shore, or a cliff, or an impassable chasm. It will just stop where it does. And that's okay. The journey together has enriched both of our lives. Uphill or not, we've seen and done and known some moments together that others will never come close to experiencing, or exploring, or engaging in.

"And I thank you for your candor—for your honesty and integrity. You have always been straight with me, and there for me and my Auntie Tagyn. We have appreciated your care more than words can ever say. I've come to look to you like a father figure, in everything that a father says and does. You've put me first on many occasions on this journey. You've befriended me. You've believed in me. You've been frank with me, and expressed your displeasure with me when I was less than compliant with your wishes. You have stepped up for us, beyond the call of duty—far, far, far beyond. 'Thank you' just isn't a big enough word. Another hug?"

They embraced again, in a hold-me-tight-never-let-me-go hug. Tagyn wiped away her own welling tear.

"Okay you pair of mushballs. Break it up! You're making me cry!"

For one more moment, they held each other close. Dr. Gordon pulled away, quiet, moved. He was soft on the inside, strong on the outside.

"Thanks again, Paddy. Thanks for your time. That was not easy news to share, or to receive. I'll go with Auntie now. I'm good. I'm okay. I'll find my way. See you soon."

Dr. Gordon smiled. "Bye Tagyn. Bye Zahryn. Talk soon."

Zahryn skillfully turned her wheelchair on a dime, to face the door. Tagyn knew her cue and reached out to open the wide, swinging door. It led into a well-lit corridor and out to the waiting room. Zahryn and Tagyn left the office together, and out into the freshness of the day.

Secrets Revealed

UPON REACHING THE SIDEWALK, Tagyn said, "It's a sunny day, Zahryn. It's a short walk to the park. Can I take you there and we can just catch up and take a deep breath or two?"

"I'd like that very much, Auntie Tagyn. It is a beautiful day, no matter what Dr. Gordon had to say. It's a perfect day in a beautiful world. Let's go!"

Tagyn wheeled Zahryn along the sidewalks for two short blocks to the park at the edge of town. At the entrance, there was a thick and towering cedar hedge flanking the grand iron gates. The waft of fragrant cedars greeted them graciously on their arrival.

Moving along, they breathed in deeply in the freshening breeze. They passed by the giant gorse bushes that were in full bloom. The coconutty-vanilla scent of its pretty yellow blossoms saturated the air.

They made their way toward the south end of the park, to the pond. They were hoping to find a place to sit near the still waters. And sure enough, there were a few vacant benches. It was a weekday after all, not a busy weekend, so they had their choice of scenery and seating.

They chose a bench that was right beside an ancient footbridge on their path. The rustic mortared stonework gracefully arched over a stream that tumbled down a gentle slope into the calm, deep pond.

The voice of the stream itself was a little more than that of a babbling brook, and a little less than that of a rocky ledge waterfall. More like a gurgling and churning, an energized-and-moving-onward-forward kind of sound—a brisk and confident kind of sound—an optimistic heart-full sound. It was as if the stream was echoing the spirit of the moment.

On the far side of the pond, a similar stream led downhill, away from the still waters toward the shores, onward on its way to meet and co-mingle with the salty seas.

"Let's sit here," said Tagyn "This is a lovely spot." She turned and set Zahryn's wheelchair at ninety degrees to the bench, so that Zahryn could see both the moving and the still waters—so that Zahryn could fully appreciate her time and place on her journey—so that Tagyn and Zahryn could both see each other clearly, in the moment.

Zahryn and Tagyn sat in absolute silence for more than half an hour, communing and simply breathing it all in. They were in a beautiful place together, in body, mind, and spirit. They would soon share what lay across their hearts and minds, together, there in the beauty of Creation.

They remained still, amid the sights and sounds and scents of the moment. Like the streams and the pond, they were interconnected as one. Their hearts would bond most fully in the moments ahead, as their words and their emotions gently flowed forth, like the stream. Love was their bridge. Love and hope, like the bridge, like the stream, would lead them on. Their shared Lights were shining ever so brightly.

Tagyn lifted her face into the sunlight, into the breeze. At fifty-five years of age, she was a striking beauty. Her long brown-grey tresses were neatly coiled into a loose bun at the back of her head. She was of medium height and medium build, boasting the longest legs you could ever even imagine. She still enjoyed shorter hemlines, and higher heels. But today, she was dressed for walking. She had known she would be accompanying Zahryn in her wheelchair to and from her appointment, so she had worn sensible flats and Bermuda shorts.

Gazing down at her long, well-muscled legs, she said to her niece in earnest, "Zahryn, honey, I truly wish you could have my strong legs, and my good lungs. I wish that you never had polio, or this darn PPS. It has certainly carved out a life-path for you that has been full of struggle and limitations. If only your legs and lungs could be strong, forever strong. I'd give anything for that, my sweet Zee, anything."

Zahryn turned away from the stream and looked deeply into her auntie's deep green eyes. "Auntie Tagyn, you are one beautiful soul. It means the world to me that you would even think that. Your heart is so special. So giving. So thoughtful and ready to help whoever needs your help. Your heart is so big with love. You never cease to amaze me."

Zahryn noticed Tagyn's eyes tearing up, and her lips drawing in tight. They were quivering. Zahryn spoke softly. "Oh Auntie Tagyn, I didn't mean to upset you. I love you so much and I just want you to know that I love you to the ends of the earth and back. And I always will! What did I say? What has upset you so? Oh my God! Please, please, please, tell me!"

Tagyn collected her words and braved her first sentence. "It's not you Zee. And it's not anything you've just said. It's a very emotional time for me, hearing about your prognosis, and your end-of-life-story. Your time with me is so limited. Your days are now truly numbered, and I need to help you to make the very most of your precious time."

Tagyn drew in a few long breaths. She leaned forward and reached out to hold Zahryn's hands. "I've dreamed of this moment for a really long time, Zee. I have something to tell you, that you need to know, and there's no time like the present to tell you."

Zahryn was still gazing into Tagyn's eyes, and she gave full attention to her auntie, as her curiosity was rapidly piquing. She smiled warmly at Tagyn, encouraging her to go on.

Tagyn said, "So, let me begin. You've been told all along about your mom, Rose, my older sister, who died in childbirth while delivering you. I am younger than Rose by one year. Your dad Connor, and your mom Rose, got married and before they knew it, they were happily expecting you. This part is true, the rest, not so much. I need to tell you a secret—the real story about your parents—your real parents."

Zahryn tucked her chin in and leaned back quickly. Her eyes grew wide with surprise.

The anticipation in the moment was palpable. It's not every day that an older woman who has borne a lifelong secret, chooses to share that lifelong secret. It's not every day that a woman willingly opens up and shares a story so steeped in mystery, in vulnerability, in complexity.

Tagyn continued, "Zahryn, what you don't know are the many little details. The pieces of a puzzle. These will be life-changing for you.

"Your father, Connor—his own parents moved away to London when he was just eighteen, when he went away to university in Scotland. His mother would receive complex continuing medical care there. At first she had had some strokes, and then she had daily seizures, for years and years.

"Connor understood the reason for their move, but, he still felt so abandoned, so lonely, and very alone. He just needed to be needed, to be wanted and loved. Some evenings, he used to sit with ol' man Sully in the bar, here in Moonstone Cove. It was here that Sully would tell Connor of his own shenanigans as a traveling salesman all over the UK. Sully had fathered a lot of illegitimate sons and daughters, and he only ever spoke of his willful, lustful ways to listeners that he could trust.

"Your father, Connor, was one good listener. Connor looked up to Sully and affectionately called him "The Travelin' Man." Well, Connor's work as a salesman was beginning to take him on the road all over the southern UK. His sales territory was big enough to keep him away from home for one or two nights at a time. Like Ol' Sully, in his loneliness and his extreme need to feel needed, Connor turned to strangers, young women, for company and pleasure. Connor was becoming the new Sully.

"This alone, Zee, must be so hard for you to hear. You loved your daddy so much. And learning at this stage in your life that he was a player, well, that must hurt you, something fierce."

Zahryn sat up a little taller, and spoke with a steady voice. "I've heard some hints of stories and rumors over the years, but no one ever came out and told me to my face. Maybe they were protecting me. Yes, this is hard to hear, but please, tell me more. I want to know all you can tell me."

Tagyn continued. "So yes, I'll go on. We were all living in rented spaces in the Ben Lonrach. Connor and Rose moved into a cottage in a little village called Pearl Haven, and I was in a tiny flat. Just before your parents got married, I spent a little time with Connor. Oh, this is so hard to say. My guilt, my shame, my sin, has been hidden all these years, and now I'm spilling my beans to you."

Zahryn held her breath, and braced herself.

Tagyn paused, choosing her words carefully. "Connor and I, we fooled around just days before Connor married Rose. I'm not proud of this, but that's what happened. And after they came back from their honeymoon, it was like Connor and I couldn't keep our hands off of each other. We were so attracted to each other. It was lust. Pure lust.

"And in three months' time, Connor and Rose announced their pregnancy at the same time I was confirming my own pregnancy. Believe it or not, Rose's due date and mine were just days apart. We were sisters, impregnated by the same man, Rose's husband, your father, Connor.

"I was shocked! Overwhelmed. I was pregnant! I couldn't believe my bad luck—I couldn't believe that it had happened to me! Bad luck happened to other girls but never to me! I was single and unattached, and I was dumbstruck. I knew I had to move away, right away, so as to not be tempted any further by Connor. I kept my own pregnancy a secret from my family—from anyone who knew me—and I moved far away from Pearl Haven.

"I rented a place in a small town in the Ben Lonrach called Shinever Rock. Well, it came time to deliver, for both Rose and for me. And then all hell broke loose. Literally."

Zahryn was almost holding her breath, taking in every minute detail of her auntie's compelling story.

"On a Thursday, I went into labor three weeks early, in Shinever Rock. I delivered a baby girl, and I planned to stay a few days in hospital while they got the adoption all set up. And no one in my family knew anything of this. In those days, women stayed a few days in hospital after delivering.

"On the very next day, Friday, Rose—God bless her—she began hemorrhaging at home in Pearl Haven, and by the time the paramedics got her to the hospital in town, both Rose and the little baby girl had died.

"It was a horrible, messy bloodbath in Connor's home—like a horror scene in the movies. All of the white carpets and the white furniture, and the bedroom. Ohhhh. It was just awful. And Connor came home to it all, with no wife and with no child in his arms. Aching empty arms they were, and blood everywhere.

"He totally lost it. He drove for hours, bawling his eyes out. He drove around, out of town, to just get away from the mess, from the ugliness, from his grief.

"He called me when he got down the mountain to the shore, to Moonstone Cove, to tell me of the death of my sister, Rose, and, the death of his baby girl.

"By the end of that conversation, we had a plan. We completely shifted gears. He told no one else about the death of his baby girl. I was no longer making plans to give my baby up for adoption at the hospital. I knew what I had to do.

"And here comes the big secret, Zee. I drove to Moonstone Cove that night, and I secretly gave my baby girl to Connor to raise. He was the natural father and I had absolutely no means to support a child. You, Zahryn, are my baby girl!"

Seeing Zahryn's absolute look of shock, Tagyn kept on talking hurriedly, hoping to share as much detail as possible in as few words as possible.

"You have been raised by your father all of these years, believing that you are my niece, but in reality, you are my daughter. You are Connor's daughter. The secret was born the minute I brought you to Connor in Moonstone. No one in that town knew him, or the story of his wife and baby's tragic death. No one knew the truth and no one asked. His own parents didn't even know the whole truth. They were only told that Rose had died. They were never told that Rose's baby died as well. And Connor had to face burying his and Rose's baby secretly, alone, with no funeral. It was all so very sad.

Tagyn watched Zahryn closely as she spoke. In the moment, Zahryn offered no words, no questions, as she was still blown away with the news.

Tagyn continued, "Living so far away in London, and what with Connor's mom's fragile health, they never got to meet their wee granddaughter, you, Zahryn. Never, ever. Not even to this day.

"Connor's own older sister, Claire—you remember your Auntie Claire? She lived in Moonstone Cove, and she helped Connor an awful lot with you as a baby and as a toddler. She became your daytime babysitter and your pre-school daycare provider until you entered school, in Primary One. Claire was a godsend, a precious gift, to both you and Connor. Then she got married to an Aussie and moved away, down under."

Zahryn was still absorbing all of the minutiae and the complexities of her auntie's story. She had lots of questions but remained notably silent. Her self-restraint was incredible. She simply allowed the story to flow on like a wide river into freshly opened sluice gates in the downstream dam—into the new watercourse that is life. She was eager to hear more of the mountains of secrets that had been guarded, protected, held safe by her loving Auntie Tagyn for all of these years.

And Tagyn continued. "I went back home to Shinever Rock without you, Zahryn. I packed up and moved far away again, this time to the village of Opalon, still in the Ben Lonrach Mountains, to try and get my life started over again."

Zahryn's words finally caught up with her and she voiced her first thoughts. "Auntie Tagyn, Oh my God! I've known you all of my life and you have been there for me through thick and thin, mothering me with unconditional love. You have been the very best auntie, and a stand-in mom when my dad died—but you have actually been my very own mom all this time! This is *unbelievable!* All along I have felt amazingly close to you. So connected to you. So very much a part of you, and now I know why!

"How did you manage to hold onto this secret for all of these years? You must be one strong woman to have done that. Of course, you were protecting my dad and me from all of the small-town gossip and scorn. You selflessly put our needs ahead of your own, for thirty-five years! Auntie Tagyn, you are so special!"

Zahryn stopped and took a breath. And then more words spilled out in her rapid-fire questions. "Oh, this is amazing, Auntie Tagyn! Oh! Should I call you Mom? Or maybe I shouldn't? Oh, what to do? Can I just hug you?"

Then, the hug evolved. It started as a tight embrace. It became a neck-nuzzle. Then a waterfall of tears, an epic explosion of released emotions. The hug ultimately sealed their bond.

There were no words for a few moments. No words to distract the two women from the endearing moment. Their streamside, pondside hug was a perfect and pure juxtaposition. Moving water meets still water. Stream meets pond. Daughter meets mother. Past meets present. Truth meets untruth. Sunlight and breeze. Birds and bees. Love and mystery. What-was-told, versus what-was-real. What was then, and what is, now.

Then Zahryn pulled away from the hug. She pulled away with a questioning heart. "My mind is working overtime, Auntie Tagyn. Why on earth did you and dad not get together to raise me? To be my parents, together? It makes perfect sense to me! Why did you leave? Oh, if only you two had stayed together!"

Tagyn collected herself. This, more than "the secret," was going to be even harder to put into words that Zahryn could understand and accept, and feel good about. Words that would not diminish Zahryn's parents or her spirit.

"We couldn't be together, honey. We just couldn't. Had his or my parents and our families found out about our sexual affair—our betrayals—they would have disowned us. Both of us.

"They were pretty upstanding folks and they never would have accepted us as a couple, if they knew the truth. The cold hard truth—how my parents would have seen it—is that a brother-in-law and a sister-in-law had had a torrid affair and a baby, but their own daughter and grandbaby died tragically in the midst of it all. We couldn't put them through any of that. We just couldn't. They already had enough to deal with. So, your daddy raised you alone. And when he died so suddenly when you were ten years old, I knew again what I had to do. I packed up and moved to Moonstone, to raise you myself. I was your auntie and you were my niece."

Zahryn's heart was racing. It was so full of emotions. Her mind was in overdrive, and it pushed her into a bit of an adrenaline rush. She only wanted to soak this all in, every detail. Take it all in stride. Flow freely in the stream. No need to rise to senseless anger when she was simply powerless to change the story. No need to resist the truth, when the outcome actually connected her to her own birth mother. No room in her heart for hurting, as it was quickly filling up with a river of love.

All of her life she had secretly dreamed of having a mom to share her life with. Her very own birth mom. And her dream had just come true! Her birthmother was sitting right beside her, sharing her life-story, loving her, caring for her, encouraging her. What more could she ask for in the moment?

"Okay, now you're making me cry, Auntie Tagyn! I am overwhelmed, yes, but more than that, I am overjoyed! I have a mom! My own mom! I've never ever had a mom! I've always longed for, and yearned for my mom. And you—you have been with me all along!

"I have a tough road ahead of me, Auntie, and I'm so glad you told me all of this now. You have no idea how much this means to me—how much stronger I feel, just in knowing I have a mom! I am not alone! This is beyond my wildest dreams. This is pure bliss. This is out-of-this-world-amazing!"

Tagyn's tears were full on flowing, flooding, freefalling. They were releasing a lifetime of pent-up angst, doubt, guilt, sorrow, sin, and shame. Her daughter was accepting her. With wide-open arms. With a wide-open heart. Her daughter wanted her, and needed her, despite knowing the deep, dark secret. Tagyn gathered Zahryn into another loving hug, and quietly thanked God for the beauty of the moment. They rivered on, in love.

Her Song of Songs

OCTOBER 31, 2022

NEVER DID METAPHORS HOLD more power, more slant, more Light.

Solomon's Song of Songs delights in the union, the intimacy, and the depth of relationships rooted in love. When songs are sung, deep calls to deep, loudly, fervently, revealing love's passion, desire, and need.

And tonight, as the evening twilight grows in the moonless skies, the tides recede into the night. The sun is setting only to rise again, to bring the coming dawn. And the Day of All Saints will soon follow the sun.

Zahryn spoke quietly into the phone. She was at home, almost ready for bed. She kept her oxygen tubing on, but her face was finally free from the N95 mask. Her energy was low, and she was trying to conserve her strength and breath. "Hi Gaelan, my friend. How are you doing?"

Gaelan, at home reading a book, was so glad to receive her call. "Hey Zee, hey Red, I'm fine. Really, I'm fine. But I should be asking you that. You've got a lot going on, for sure."

Zahryn said, "Yes, Gaelan, you know me so well. Life is pretty complicated, but it's not like I've never had to deal with complicated before." Her voice trailed off. A warming silence befriended them.

Zahryn continued. "The palliative care nurses visited a few days ago, here in my home. Auntie Tagyn was with me, and I'm grateful for that." Zahryn paused again.

Gaelan's heart felt the weight of Zahryn's changing world. He said, "It must be hard having conversations with those nurses. I wish I had known. I could have been there with you, like, just to be there with you."

"It's okay, Gaelan," Zahryn replied. "I'm okay. I've known for a few months now that this day would come. I've actually looked forward to meeting them and to making some final plans through them. They were super-helpful. They are great teachers and go-to people. I have a lot less unknowns now, because of them."

Zahryn took some more intentional deep breaths before continuing. "They left us a medication kit, and a lot of written instructions for the use of the meds for pain, anxiety, or restlessness, and for trouble breathing. They spent a long time with us, teaching us what to expect, and how to manage my symptoms.

"They actually called the medicine kit a 'symptom relief kit.' They addressed the medical management of my final days in a very friendly—not scary—and matter of fact way. They also said that my name was now on the list for a bed in Hospice, either here in Moonstone or just up the road, in the town of Pearl Haven. A bed might come available in another week, or so."

She paused again, this time to catch her breath. Gaelan remained silent. He was so acutely aware of Zahryn's state of heart. She was speaking so calmly about managing her final days, her final moments, her final breaths. He marveled that she was so articulate, and so comfortable, in voicing these details. He heard no fear. No angst. Just overt comprehension, acceptance, and readiness.

Zahryn went on. "Gaelan, you and I, you know, we have something really, really special." Inwardly, she reminded herself *I know that Gaelan is my brother—and he does not know this. And I also know that this is not my secret to share.* She said, "It's like we know each other's hearts—each other's souls. We understand each other so well. And, how important is that, to have a friend always by your side, who not only likes and loves you, but who also 'gets you' completely? It's like we're connected somehow!"

As Gaelan's silence persisted, she went on. "The Irish talk about a term, *Anam Cara,* a friendship bond that simply enfolds two hearts, two souls, two beings into one. Saorise, my best friend, is my Anam Cara, and Gaelan, you should be too. You shouldn't be just my guy-friend, but my forever Anam Cara—my soul friend. Not just through our shared life experiences but also through our faith journey, through our moral compasses, and through our very own shared Light—our Light within. Our Lights merge together, and shine as one."

Gaelan listened intently. He loved hearing Zahryn voice her feelings about their relationship so openly, so freely. He too had felt the power of their shared bond. In his own emotional immaturity, he believed that what he was feeling was an unrequited love. He had never been able to name his true feelings for her. He had tried to bend his head and his heart around the words, love, puppy love, lust, adoration, deepest respect, compassion, true love, first love, unconditional love. Quite possibly, he felt all of these.

He sensed a vibe, a connection with Zahryn that ran deeper than emotion. Perhaps it was spiritual—perhaps it was ancestral from way, way back in time. But then again, maybe it was simply his confusing, previously latent, now manifest male hormones. He only knew that the power and the intensity of his feelings for her were all-encompassing and overwhelming. It often left him tongue-tied and fearful of the very depth of his feelings.

And, not only could he not name his feelings, neither could he express them to Zahryn. He simply could not put into words what his heart was experiencing. He wished he had the confidence and simple ability to tell Zahryn how he felt about her so that she could finally, after all these years, know the depth of his feelings.

"Gaelan." Zahryn changed the subject abruptly. Her tone got his attention right away. "Do you remember when a bunch of our friends were at the pub earlier in the summer, and we all got to talking about Medical Assistance in Dying? MAID they called it."

Gaelan nodded into the phone and simply answered, "Yes, I do." He hadn't forgotten. This was a sensitive matter for him and he had never, ever voiced his opinions about it publicly. He wasn't sure how he really felt about someone ending their life, on their terms, on their timeline, even on their own turf. In his mind, this was simply suicide. Giving up. An overt expression of hopelessness, of surrendering. He didn't understand how folks could speak of MAID as being genuine acceptance, of coming to terms, of readiness, and being finally at peace. He questioned—he wrestled—with knowing whether theirs would be an everlasting Holy rest in heaven, if they lived out their own will, not God's.

He knew in his heart that there was a time and a place for such decisions, but the whole idea frightened him. Gaelan valued all life and living. He valued his faith and his God. He knew that this was such a personal and faith-based matter. He was just not prepared to even talk about this on any level, with anyone. Not yet anyway.

Zahryn continued, acutely aware of his hesitance to voice his feelings. "Well, "truth be told, I've thought about it a lot. If death becomes the only pathway for the terminally ill, and suffering is a sure thing as part of that pathway, then, why should they have to suffer? If they are of sound mind and judgment, why can't they just say farewell when the time is right, and be allowed to move along into eternity, to slip away blissfully with a little help from science, medicine, and technology?

"And you know, on that note, people then might not actually live their whole lives in fear of dying, if they knew that their death could be facilitated—that it could be a beautiful transition—that death on their own terms could be peaceful, and freeing. It does not need to be frowned upon as being wrongful or sinful, or cowardly. No one should be scorned for choosing this humane assistance, this proactive decision making, at the right time."

Gaelan still didn't speak, choosing to honor his feelings. His discomfort remained unspoken, in the moment.

In the weighted pause, Zahryn shifted gears. She summoned her lung power. She started humming and then began singing softly. Gaelan appreciated her change of focus and he attuned to her stirring voice. Her breathing was labored but he heard the words of her song so very clearly:

> *Oh blackbird of the open skies, on broken wings no more.*
> *In life, in death, in every breath, you lift on high to soar.*
> *Time like the ever-running waves casts all its cares away.*
> *Sweet flight transcends upon the winds and rests at dawn of day.*

Her voice had a wee lilt as she sang the ancient English folk tune. Gaelan had heard her sweet voice many times before, but this time it was different. He listened eagerly.

Haunting, and uplifting, her song carried him in the moment. Her dulcet tones drew him in to her peacefulness. The riddle-esque lyrics played into a growing sense of mystery. As pretty as the verse was, its fullest meaning was still veiled—it was yet to be revealed.

A profound silence nestled itself between them in the phone call. Their souls received comfort, together, as one. Time seemed to stop. They felt they were part of something greater than a telephone call between friends—part of the mystery and wider interconnectedness of all life and living. Truly part of each other in the moment.

Zahryn was now audibly short of breath at rest, but she managed a lingering, wistful sigh. Gaelan, noticing her labored respirations, broke the special silence.

"I know you're tired, Zahryn. Your energy is fading, I can tell. You need to rest. I'll drop by to see you tomorrow. I want you to know that I'll always be here for you. Whatever. Wherever. However. I'll be here. Okay?"

"Thanks, Gaelan. So much. Hugs for you. See ya. Light into Light, Gaelan. Across the waters." She sent a breathy sigh once again into the phone and hung up, knowing that Gaelan was still holding on to her ethereal words. She only ever said what she meant. She only ever said what she felt. And in that moment, her feelings were totally summed up in the words "Light into Light. Across the waters."

Cookies, Comfort, and Camaraderie

NOVEMBER 1, 1998

AT 2 P.M., THE doorbell rang and Tagyn went to the front door to see who was there. Eleven-year-old Saorise was standing on the veranda wearing her winter coat, her neck bundled by a thick woolen scarf wrapped around and around again. She was holding a cookie tin with a pretty pink oversized bow that matched her woolen scarf and mittens. Her soft, waist-length golden ringlets billowed in the breeze.

Best friends since preschool, Zahryn and Saorise had grown close. Their shared times in school, in Sunday school, and in the neighborhood had fostered their beautiful bond of friendship.

"Hello, Miss Saorise McGrath!" said Tagyn. "Your mom called and said you'd be here after church. Come on in. I haven't told Zahryn yet. It's cold out isn't it? I can see your frosty breath and your pink cheeks!"

"Thanks Auntie Tagyn. You don't mind if I call you Auntie?"

Tagyn smiled and nodded.

"I hope Zahryn will want to see me," said Saorise. "I know what today is. I know her dad died a year ago today, and she wasn't in Sunday School today. So, I still wanted to see her. These cookies are for her. They're her favorite. Oatmeal!"

"Ahhhh, Saorise, you're so sweet and thoughtful. Did you and your mommy bake these together?"

"Yes! We made them yesterday. Mom only supervised though. She says it's time that I was able to bake things all by myself. She only helps me turn the oven on or off. And she watches me measure. But I do all the rest by myself!"

"That's great, Saorise! You're a little baker woman! That's a skill you'll use for most of your life. No time like the present to learn how to bake and to do it well!"

"Can I go up to Zahryn's room and take these cookies to her to surprise her?"

"Of course you can, sweetie. Let me take your coat and scarf—there—off you go!"

Saorise kicked off her boots and bounced up the staircase and turned immediately to the right at the top of the stairs. The door to Zahryn's room was wide open. Zahryn was lying on her bed, headphones on, listening to tunes on her Sony Walkman. Her tiny little puppy was fast asleep beside her. Master Madigan, was a teacup-size West Highland Terrier. He was just a pup, three months old. Auntie Tagyn had recently brought him home to Zahryn, hoping to lift her niece's spirits as she grieved the loss of her father. Madoh was one of his nicknames. Zahryn and Madoh had quickly become fast friends.

Zahryn was staring straight up at the ceiling when Saorise arrived. Zahryn saw her out of the corner of her eye, and she slowly sat up, taking off her headphones.

"Hi," Zahryn said, with a dull voice.

"Hi," Saorise echoed. "I baked you some cookies. Oatmeal! I thought maybe they'd help cheer you up."

Zahryn smiled. "Thanks Saorise. Come here and sit with me. Thanks for the cookies. You know they are my fav!"

Saorise bounded over to the bedside and sat right beside her buddy. Master Madigan did not move a muscle. He was having his midday nap, as wee puppies do.

Saorise's bestie was hurting. She gently laid the cookie tin on Zahryn's lap and then twisted herself to reach out with both arms, encircling Zahryn in a BFF hug. A long, warm hug. Zahryn leaned sideways into the hug, inclining her ear to Saorise's neck and shoulder.

Saorise spoke first. "I know you miss your dad. Big time. I liked him a lot. He was really nice to me. I wish he was still here. You wouldn't be sad all of the time if he were still here." She tightened her hug a little more.

Zahryn shifted and remained quiet. Her emotional filters were simply spent. They gave way, they let go, and her sadness overflowed, bursting the proverbial dam. Her shoulders heaved and she began to sob uncontrollably. Her tears were hot on her cheeks, and they flowed and flowed like deep, swift rivers. She leaned heavily onto Saorise.

Auntie Tagyn was standing in the bedroom doorway, watching her niece break down. Neither Auntie Tagyn nor Saorise had any words. Zahryn just needed to feel safe enough to just let her emotions go and flow and get it all out of her system.

Zahryn had had a rough year after losing her dad. She hadn't missed any school—she loved school. But she was often distracted in class. She found her mind wandered as she reminisced about the good times and her wonderful father-daughter shenanigans.

They were close. They were everything to each other. His cancer story was so short, so unexpected. There were only four days from his diagnosis of stage-four pancreatic cancer to the day he died. He was hospitalized immediately due to the severity of his pain, and he was then sedated heavily. Zahryn hardly had a chance to talk to her dad during those four grueling days. He slipped away peacefully at the dawning of the fourth day.

Zahryn was only ten years of age when her daddy died. At that time, she had had a few burning questions. They were mostly related to "Why?" and "How come?" The age-appropriate angry words, "It's just not fair!" had crossed her lips many, many times.

Zahryn, now eleven, didn't need her questions answered. She just needed her dad. She wanted her daddy back—healthy, happy, and full of daddy-love and snuggles. She missed the comfort of his big, strong arms around her and his giant man-hands holding hers. She missed him terribly.

When Auntie Tagyn had learned of her brother-in-law's sudden hospitalization, she immediately came to Moonstone Cove to look after Zahryn. No one had anticipated his death would be so soon. Not even the doctors. Tagyn was in shock when he died. She told Zahryn that no matter what, she would step in and move into Zahryn's home to care for her. Tagyn would have to quit her job in Opalon and sell her house there, but all of that didn't matter.

What did matter was that Zahryn would have a close family member looking after her. It mattered that Zahryn could stay in her own home, her own school, her own community and church where she was so well known and loved. Moonstone Cove was a lovely town where neighbors helped each other out and supported each other when bad things happened.

Eventually Zahryn stopped sobbing and her breathing settled back to normal. Her tears stopped in their own time, and she blew her nose. Tagyn stepped away and walked down the hall, leaving the two friends together.

Saorise said, "I feel helpless, Zee. I don't know what to do."

Zahryn spoke through her sniffles. "Thanks for coming over, Saorise. I'm glad you're here. I need a friend. I have Madoh here with me, but I need you. I can't tell you what I need or what to do because I don't know myself. But I do know that I'm happy you're here. Sorry I bawled my eyes out. I couldn't help it."

Zahryn pulled away from the hug, and then drew her long legs up to sit cross-legged on the bed. She pulled sleepyhead Madoh into her lap and he snuggled in.

Saorise too sat cross-legged, facing her friend. Auburn tresses and golden locks flowed freely behind them—love and friendship flowed freely between them. They were bonded by something far greater than oatmeal cookies or pretty pink ribbons. Zahryn reached for the cookie tin and she placed it between them but did not open the lid. She then reached over to her bedside table to pick up her youth edition Bible.

She looked directly at Saorise and said, "My dad told me a long time ago to always look at Psalm 23 when I'm sad or afraid, or lonely."

Saorise reacted quickly. "So, do you? I mean, it's been a year. Do you read Psalm 23? Does it help you?"

Zahryn answered quickly, "Yes! I keep it right by my bed. I can read it before school, after school, and before bed. I like what it says. It calms me down." Her voice trailed off for a few seconds.

"I like to picture myself lying down in the green grass, by the still water. It feels good and calm and somehow right. And then somehow, I don't feel so sad, or so angry. It's like I'm not alone anymore, there by the water. I feel good."

Saorise said, "Your dad was smart to teach you that. I remember having to memorize Psalm 23 in Sunday School. It helped me to picture it too." She smiled. "What does your green grass look like?"

Zahryn smiled for the first time. "It is a meadow with tall, tall grasses. No sheep have been there for a really long time." She looked slyly at her friend and then chuckled. They both chuckled. The thought of accidentally lying down in some fresh sheep manure was all too distracting in the moment, and they burst out laughing. Each knew what the other was thinking!

Saorise said, "My grass is not like yours at all. It's short and thick and dark green, and, there are definitely no sheep around!" They giggled their silly-girl giggles.

Zahryn continued. "Mine is a wide, wide-open meadow that meets up with a still pond. The water is very dark, and I can see the sun and the clouds reflected in it. It's really very pretty. I like looking into the still, dark waters and thinking about things. I guess when my dad told me to think about the 23rd Psalm, he knew it would make me feel good. And it does." She held her sage green, leather-bound Bible close to her heart.

She turned her head to look out the window. "I miss my dad. I really miss him. He was funny and he always made me laugh. He always wanted to ride bikes with me. And he helped me with my homework most of the time.

"He was tough on me with Math, though. He said he knew that I was smart enough and that it was probably best for me to learn by figuring it out myself. That's what Math is. Figuring things out. He'd always check my work though. I learned to like Math because of him. He taught me 'to figure it out,' and I did!"

"Yeah, I remember your dad," Saorise piped up. "He never let you come out to play right after supper—not until your homework was all done. Just like my dad. Pretty strict. But you were quick and you always got it done, and you came out to play with all of us when you were done. Same rules at my house. I guess our parents are smart. They know what we need. We're both lucky to have dads that really care."

The girls sat quietly. They were both eyeing the cookie tin. Zahryn broke first and lifted the metal lid and her hand dove into the cookie tin. Then, ditto for Saorise. They chomped into their yummy treasures, and looked again into each other's eyes.

"Yum!" they said in complete synchronicity, with their mouths full of cookie. They smiled. They were friends from way back in their nursery school days. They would probably be friends for life. One day, they would come to know the ancient Celtic term, Anam Cara, which means Soul Friend. They were indeed, in the moment, Anam Cara in the making.

Meeting of Mystical Minds

By the time Zahryn was in her twenties, she was beginning to face some significant mobility issues. In 2012, she turned twenty-five and her post-polio syndrome had advanced enough that she now needed to use a wheelchair. Always adaptable and proactive, she had an UTV fitted with hand controls so she could still venture into the outdoors, to the mountains, to the waterways, to the shores. She still wanted to—she needed to—access her special Thin Places.

It was a sunny Saturday morning and Zahryn was restless. She knew she needed to get outside, to be outside, to feel free. After breakfast, she went to the garage, where she transferred herself from her wheelchair to her hot yellow UTV. She could still stand up independently, and take a step to transfer, but her legs were wobbly. She fastened the straps over her legs, and securely buckled herself into the chest harness. Also strapped in on the passenger seat was a sturdy storage container, large enough to hold a small picnic basket or a day-tripping knapsack and, once in a while, some good books and a blanket. She was ready.

Today, she'd packed a protein bar, an apple, a bottle of water, a wool sweater, and her cell phone in her knapsack. She had put her heavy wool cape in the very bottom. The forecast gave no suggestion of rain. She closed her garage door behind her, using the remote, and she was off.

She took a peripheral route around Moonstone Cove. She wanted to be alone with her thoughts, and she could likely avoid all people and superficial conversations by traveling this route today.

Eventually she arrived at the entrance to the Ben Lonrach mountain trails. Her UTV was well suited to this region. The trails zigged and zagged back and forth into the heights at a safe incline for the broad wheel base of the machine. The trails were good and wide and free of debris. Zahryn simply loved being out there—traveling independently, up to the mountain and sea view places that she held so dear—on her own time, on her own schedule.

There were scenic moments and little lookouts along the way, offering breathtaking seascapes and vistas to hikers and to trail riders alike. A fast-flowing stream came close to the edge of the trail at one point, and an ancient stone arch stood in one of the clearings, higher up the way. The arch dated way back to the Roman times. Zahryn was drawn to its ancientness, and often she would ponder over its symbolism, its cultural backstory, its place in time. But, she rode onward, not stopping at any of these curious locations. She knew just where she wanted to go. Another thirty minutes and she would be there.

On the trail up ahead was a lone female hiker. A rugged canvas sack crossed her shoulder and rested on her opposite hip. Her long legs were darkly tanned and well-muscled. She looked fit. Her short, curly blonde bob glistened in the sunlight. The hiker turned when she heard Zahryn's UTV approaching and she hailed out, "Hello!"

Zahryn answered back. "Hi! Great day for a hike, yes?"

"It is!" said the hiker. "That's one fancy machine you have—I've seen you a couple of times, riding about in town."

"Yup. I like to get out and about, as much as I can, on my own." Zahryn looked at the hiker who was noticing her leg straps and harness. She answered the hiker's questions before she even asked them.

"I had polio as a child and I recovered well, and then two years ago, I was diagnosed with post-polio syndrome. My legs are getting weaker. I bought myself these hot yellow wheels with all of the hand controls and harnesses so I can still get out here, in the mountains, safely. My name is Zahryn, by the way. What's yours?"

"Hi, Zahryn. Yes. I'm Aoife. Aoife Stewart. So sorry to hear about your legs, but you look like you're well equipped to still enjoy the Ben Lonrach! I'm so impressed!"

"Are you from around here, Aoife? I know a lot of the folks in town, but I'm not sure that I've seen you before. You say you've seen me."

"I'm from Portree, Skye, in the Western Hebrides, the islands on the west coast of Scotland. I went to the mainland to go to university to study journalism, and then I spent three years working on the Isle of Iona. It was an incredible time in my life!"

Zahryn sat up a little taller. "I've heard a lot about Iona. Some call it the Holy Isle of Scotland. Is it true? Is it Holy? Did you actually feel something unique or special while you were there? They say that folks who spend time there come away forever changed. Did that happen to you?"

"Oh my, Zahryn. You seem to know a lot about Iona! Yes, it is a Sacred place, and, mystery and mysticism are there, everywhere. In the earth. In the rocks. On the shores. In the air!"

She paused. "But, I can take lots of time, and tell you all about Iona some other day, when you're ready. For now, shall we hike together? Hike and ride together?" She smiled with encouragement.

Zahryn said, "That would be really nice. I thought I was wanting to journey alone today, but, how nice is this to meet you, Aoife, and to hear part of your interesting story! We all have a story, don't we?"

Aoife answered, "Yes, we do. All of us."

They both smiled and continued together, upward on the trail. The UTV engine noise made for difficult conversation, so they traveled together, without speaking.

After about half an hour of steady uphill going, Zahryn suggested "There's a lovely lookout with a gorgeous view just up ahead. Do you want to stop there and rest a while? Have a bite? Have a wee chat and get to know each other more?"

"Sounds lovely!" said Aoife. "Lead on!"

In just a few more minutes, they arrived at the lookout. They were just in time to see a whole flock of large blackbirds, lennons, take off into the wind, over the sea. Their broad wingspans gracefully reached out wide, wider—wider still—catching the currents of the rising air in the updrafts at the cliff.

This blackbird visual stirred something deep within Aoife. She stepped willingly into her own stream of consciousness. Words arose. They drifted and sifted through her mind, gifting her with new colorful images, new contexts, and new Light.

She whispered quietly into the wind "Arising. Soaring. Borne. Me. Unbroken. Unbridled. Ever-free. Blackbirds high. Blackbird sky. Love abounds—it's all around." In that time, in that place, vicariously, she too had soared.

Zahryn was driving her UTV up close to the precipice. She could not hear Aoife's poetic affirmation over the noise of her wheels. She was about one meter away from the rocky edge of the cliff, which towered some two hundred meters above the sea. Aoife called out, "Oh, Zahryn, you're awfully close to the edge!"

Zahryn said, "Yes, I am, but it's okay. This is all solid rock—not like other rock faces with scree at the bases. This is safe right here. Welcome to Crag Misneach. Rock of Hope. My very own name for this craggy cliff. I feel strong like a rock here. Grounded. Open. Free. If you've lived on Iona, you'll know what a Thin Place is. And this place is truly thin. I feel the presence of God here. I feel connected, body, mind, and spirit."

"Oh, yes," Aoife responded. "The wonder of Thin Places." She sighed, remembering fondly.

"There's no raised rock or bench for you to sit on, Aoife. I have my cape here with me. You can sit on it like a tarp. Here, take this." Zahryn lifted the lid of the storage bin beside her, unzipped her knapsack, and pulled out the woolen cape from the bottom of the sack.

When she handed it to Aoife, their eyes met. They shared a knowing gaze, a moment of grace. Theirs was a space of welcome, of wonder, of great anticipation.

Aoife partly unfolded the cape on the ground, and plunked herself down on it. "Thanks, Zahryn. What—a—view! There's a high hill on Iona that has a view just like this. I just love looking out into the wide-open sea, into the vastness. I feel amazing when I can just 'be' in the midst of Creation's greatness."

Zahryn spoke quietly. "I think we have a lot in common, Aoife. How nice for us to meet up here, where we're both so comfortable, where we share a lot of similar thoughts and perspectives.

"I love to gaze out across the waters, too. I make plans. I dream. I have visions. Hope abounds. And the vastness of the open waters is a perfect backdrop to frame my thoughts. I lose all of my doubts and fears, and I open my heart and my mind, and I can see life in a whole different way, out here."

Aoife nodded, listening intently. Zahryn's words were compelling.

Zahryn continued, "Whether I'm contemplating global or personal viewpoints—social justice issues or family relationship issues—it doesn't matter. This view across the waters echoes my spirit, it echoes nature, it echoes the rhythm of my soul. It calls me to a 'place of being' that is indescribably open and freeing. Even visionary.

"And, it gives me a whole new approach to life. Not only is all life more vast than my simple self—I come to see myself as the Celtic folks did, as 'part of' Creation. God is in me. God is in Creation. I am OF God and Creation is OF God. In this knowing, in this understanding, I approach all life and living with reverence, with respect, with awe and wonder. This is the Celtic way of seeing all life and living *as Sacred*. Sacredness matters."

Aoife released a slow and breathy "Wow . . . . That's so real."

Zahryn smiled and spoke with conviction. "The ancient Celtic people have always held an unequivocal awareness of the Sacred essence of all form—of all living and being. The ground we walk on is Holy, as are the trees, and oceans, and skies, and all of Creation. We are invited, through the wonders of the ancient Celtic Wisdom to attune to and acknowledge this Sacredness in all things."

She looked over at Aoife, who was taking in her every word. "Oh, sorry, Aoife! That was pretty heavy stuff! Pretty deep. You probably didn't need to hear *all* of that."

Aoife answered quickly. "Oh no, Zahryn. No, no, no! I want to hear you! I heard your every word! I do love to listen. I learned a lot about deep listening, as a skill, in my journalism studies when we were learning about interviewing—about the art of revealing or uncovering the heart of the matter of the story. I learned that my writing will only ever be as good as my own heart can listen. It's so true! Story, real good story, begins in the heart!"

Zahryn's eyes opened wide. "Wow, Aoife! I like that! Your words are stirring, and rich with deeper meaning. They are epic!"

Aoife spoke quietly as she continued. "They also taught us that truth will emerge, be heard, and find its place, only when we are open. We can seek truth all we want, but we will only find it when we open ourselves fully to the vastness of it all.

"So here we are, both seekers, and dare I say we are both modern day spiritual seers. We are both open, both present in the wide-openness of the great Celtic Sea. I think we are in a very good place and time for truth to unfold. Let's just hold onto this thought and see what truths will open before us."

Zahryn looked again into Aoife's eyes for an elastic moment. There, Zahryn saw wisdom, and integrity, and an openness beyond all words. She sensed both Aoife's textbook smarts, and her mystical ways. Aoife was a whole lot of contrasts—temporal but spiritual. Grounded yet spacious. Earthy yet ethereal. Aoife had depth. She was definitely down to earth.

Zahryn chose her words carefully. "Aoife, I am really enjoying listening to you. I am drawn to your words, to your mindset, to your very being. Let's plan to meet again, maybe at the coffee shop someday. I do want to hear more. I want to feel your thinking. I want to experience your perspectives. I want to grow, to be formed, to become, through your unique ways of thinking. I think you'll be really good for me. Ours, I believe, will be formative times. Meaningful times."

Aoife answered, "A teatime visit would be great. Let's do this! And yes, we'll have lots to talk about. I'm glad to have met you here on the mountain. What a lovely chance meeting!" She continued, "And Zahryn! You give me way too much credit. *I* need to learn from *you!* You have a way about you. A conquering spirit. Here you are in the middle of nowhere with your physical challenges. You are sharing your strength, your will, and your resilience with me. *You* are hope. You have no idea how much I've come to admire you here, in our short time together. I'm the one who stands to grow, in coming to know more about you!"

Their mutual admiration was palpable. Their friendship was kindling. The mountain was aglow—luminescent with Light—shimmering and iridescent Light. Their Lights, all of them together, sparkled across the waters and beyond.

The Door Opens Slowly

JANUARY 4 AND 5, 2005

CHRISTMAS BREAK WAS OVER once again and winter term was just starting at Moonstone Cove Secondary School. Zahryn was in her final year, Senior 3. She arrived in her homeroom class and sat in her usual seat. She was ready and eager to see what 2005—her graduating year—would bring.

Mr. Grady spoke out clearly. "Okay class. You've heard the bell. We have a whole ten minutes to get this homeroom organized before you move to first class.

"First of all, welcome back. I hope you had a great break over Christmas, and some good times with your families. I know that some of you are starting to receive your early acceptances to university, and that's fantastic! Congrats to those who have already heard, and, good luck to those of you who are still waiting. Just a reminder to those undecided few, applications will still be accepted at most universities, colleges, and trade schools until the first of April this year. No pun intended! That's the final deadline.

"Second, I want to change the seating plan in this homeroom. It will be alphabetical, for my sake. Please pick up your things and get ready to move. Starting at your front left and going down the rows. I'll call your names and walk down each aisle, and you can move to the desk I point to when I call your name."

The Secondary Senior 3 homeroom teacher did roll call, and the students moved to their new places. They were all reseated alphabetically in three minutes flat.

"Third," Mr. Grady continued, "I'm passing around a form letter for you to take home. It contains information for your parents about some upcoming school events that they might want to be part of.

"And last, the rest of this time is yours until the first class bell. Thanks!"

Maevyn had transferred to Moonstone Cove Secondary School at the beginning of her senior year. She had mostly kept to herself in the fall, as she had a recent past that she was not willing to talk about to strangers. Fellow students thought she was either ultra-shy, or, a bit of a snob, since she barely ever spoke to anyone.

Maevyn was petite. Long, dark, wispy hair. Dark eyes. Striking in her appearance. Hers was a comical laugh, but sadly, no one ever even saw her smile. She was still working through her recent story, her recent past.

Maevyn had arrived at her new seat, directly behind Zahryn. Alphabetically, Zahryn Walker-Inglis and Maevyn Watt. Zahryn had already plunked herself down in her new seat, and she immediately turned around to face Maevyn, when Maevyn sat down.

"Hey you! I've seen you around but we've never met! I'm Zahryn." She looked directly into Maevyn's dark eyes.

"Hi, I'm Maevyn. Nice to meet you." Maevyn said flatly while averting her eyes.

Zahryn spoke again. "Someone said you came to Moonstone from Opalon. My aunt—I live with my aunt here in Moonstone—she lived in Opalon for ten years or so, a while back. Maybe you know her? Tagyn Walker?"

Maevyn stared at the floor. *Oh here we go,* she thought. *Sharing. Details. I don't need to talk to anyone. Not yet anyway. But Zahryn seems nice enough. Everybody seems to like her. Maybe I could try to be a bit friendly but still keep my secret safe.*

Maevyn spoke cautiously. "Yeah. I know the name. At least I've heard it before." The school bell rang to move to first class.

Zahryn asked, "What class are you going to first? I'm going to English Lit."

Maevyn answered, "I'm going to Urban Geography. See ya sometime." The girls collected their things and moved on.

The next day in homeroom, Zahryn saw Maevyn when she first arrived in class, two minutes before the nine o'clock bell. She hailed out, "Hi again!"

"Hi," said Maevyn quietly.

"I've got first spare today. When's yours?" said Zahryn, in her fresh and breezy voice and manner.

"Mine's first period too," said Maevyn. *Yikes. Now what do I do? Zahryn is gonna wanna talk and get to know more about me. Damn it! Why did I say I have a spare? I coulda just lied!*

Zahryn was quick to speak again, to get some momentum going. "Look, I see that you're not so talkative, and that's okay. We can go to spare and just do our work, or, since there are hardly any assignments yet, we could just sit together. I don't want to make you uncomfortable, but if you'd like a new friend, I'm here." She smiled with encouragement at Maevyn, who seemed to appreciate the offer.

Maevyn mustered, "Ok. See you at spare. But, I need to make a phone call first. So, see you there."

Zahryn said, "Great! See ya soon!" The homeroom bell rang, and Zahryn turned her attention to Mr. Grady.

AT 9:15 A.M., MAEVYN entered the spare room and she took in a long, slow breath. She thought, *Here goes nothin'.*

Maevyn saw Zahryn on the long sofa in the corner and walked over to her. Without a word, she sat down and put both feet up on the coffee table. Zahryn smiled.

Maevyn spoke quietly, despite the noise of multiple student conversations nearby and around the room. "You all seem to know each other pretty well. And it's nice to see. I knew everyone at my old school in Opalon."

Zahryn smiled again. She liked hearing Maevyn offer a little something about herself. "Did you have a close friend or a best friend there?" she asked gently. "Do you stay in touch with your old friends?"

"Well, that's a loaded question or two. I did have some friends—girls and guys I thought were great fun, but then, when I went through some stuff, they all backed off. Whatever. Maybe they really weren't friends after all. Maybe we all walked a bit on the wild side. And when things all went kinda sideways, they were gone. Not one of them stuck around as a friend. Huh. Some friends, eh?"

Zahryn's attention was piqued. "Walked on the wild side? What do you mean? Or, maybe you'd rather not say? But, I am curious. I've led a pretty sheltered life and my own little wild-side adventures are probably pretty tame. You know, there's a little tiny part of me that just wants to rebel, or speak out, or do something dangerous, *just because I can!* I *think* these things, but I never do anything out of line. Someday, I'll get my nerve, and

I'll step out. I won't break the law or intentionally hurt anyone or anything, but I will find my wild side. My badass. Hey. Maybe us together! We'll be a little bad! Raise a little hell!"

Zahryn blushed at the sound of her own tough talk. She questioned herself as to why she was saying this to a complete stranger. She knew in her heart that she didn't need to show off or prove anything. She concluded that she was just trying to show that they could be friends.

Maevyn shrugged. "I'm done with wild. For now, anyway. But, I am really like you, sort of. I want what you've got. You want what I've got. You're nice. Everyone likes you. You're settled. You seem to like yourself and your life. I want that. All of that. I think we both want what the other has. You know—the grass is greener, or somethin'."

Zahryn sat back. "Wow! Maeve! Can I call you Maeve? That's big! Maybe we can spend some time together—maybe we can go a little wild. And you know what? I've never, ever, smoked a joint. And, I'd like to! Maybe someday we can do this together, just for fun? Or, maybe I'm being a bit presumptuous?"

Maevyn nodded and offered a little smile. "Cool." was all she said.

Zahryn went on. "And, maybe you could meet some of my friends and maybe you'll get to feel like you're part of the class? You've seemed so alone since you arrived in the fall. I can help!"

Maevyn looked right at Zahryn. "Yeah, that would be good. But I'm still working through stuff and I don't need everybody's questions, or gossip, or pity. It's bad enough as it is." She looked away and sighed a heavy sigh.

Zahryn spoke tenderly. "Maevyn, I'm not going to ask about your story, or your stuff. Down the road, if you trust me enough, you can tell me, but only if you want to. Some stuff is really no one else's business. Including your stuff. So, for now, we're friends. This conversation is private and anything you have just shared is safe with me. Okay?"

Maevyn looked deeply into Zahryn's sage green eyes for the first time during the spare. Their faces showed genuine care and concern for the other. They literally glowed with the flickering Light of hope. They were newfound friends. They could build a trust. They would build a trust. They wanted, and needed, each other's friendship. All was well in the moment, there in the spare, in their worlds.

The Mild and the Wild

JANUARY 21, 2005

MAEVYN WALKED TO THE Moonstone Cove Secondary School on what was the coldest day yet in January 2005. Although the sun was shining brightly, making the snowdrifts sparkle and gleam, the north wind drove hard and fast through the town. Her woolen scarf was wrapped twice around her neck, and she had it pulled up to cover both her mouth and nose. Her small rectangular-frame glasses barely blocked her eyes from the wind. Her eyes ran with tears from the cold. She pulled her coat hood up over her wool hat, and leaned forward, bracing into the wind.

Maevyn was ready to talk to Zahryn, in earnest, about her darkest days. She had met with her quite a few times in the first two weeks of January and had really taken a liking to her. Zahryn was so easy to talk to. She felt she could confide in Zahryn, and that her story would be safe with her. Maevyn had carried the burden of her own story alone for long enough. It was time for her to lighten her load and share it with her new friend—her new confidante.

Maevyn met up with Zahryn at the front steps of the high school. She whispered into Zahryn's ear "C'mon Zahryn, let's skip school today. The classrooms will be freezing cold. Let's go where we can chat and be toasty warm!"

Zahryn was totally caught off guard at this suggestion and it showed in her facial expression. Up went her eyebrows. She gasped, "What? Skip? Today? Now? Just like that? I've never done that before! Ever!"

Maevyn spoke with encouragement. "It's easy. Grady takes attendance for statistics sake, but for Senior 3 students, he's not obliged to report absences. I guess they figure we're mature enough by now to decide to be present or absent from class. As long as you keep up with your term work, you'll be okay. C'mon! You in?"

Zahryn was intrigued. The idea of playing hooky was tugging at her. She said, "Yeah! Why not? Once won't hurt. Let's go! Let's do this!"

Maevyn held out her hand to Zahryn and they turned and walked away, emboldened and happy, with the wind at their backs.

Maevyn said, "Let's go to my place. We have a coffee machine and a kettle for tea. My Aunt Paige is away all this week with her friends in County Waterford. I think there's an event they're going to at Lismore Castle. Anyway, Auntie is away—us mice can play!"

Zahryn said, "Ha! I'm just skipping school, but I feel like I am breaking the law!"

Maevyn laughed. "You'll get over it. It's no big deal. It's not like we're hurting anyone. We're just making a choice!"

Zahryn had always thought she was a pretty free and easy person, even though rules and schedules had always been her boundaries, and she respected boundaries. That's why skipping delighted her so. She wanted to holler loudly into the high winds at the top of her lungs, but she kept her exuberance to herself, except for her giant Cheshire-cat-grin.

When the girls arrived at Paige's flat, Maevyn unlocked the door. She let Zahryn in and said, "I'll put the kettle on." She moved down the hall to the wee galley kitchen.

The flat was nice and warm. Toasty warm. Zahryn could see into a bedroom—a mattress on the floor with blankets and sheets all tossed onto the far side. She presumed this was Maeve's temporary bedroom.

Maevyn called from down the hall, "I have black tea. That's all. That okay?"

Zahryn said, "Yeah. Black tea is great. Thanks!"

Maevyn emerged in a few minutes with a large mug of coffee—a reheat in the microwave—and a large mug of freshly boiled hot water, teabag in, string and tag dangling down over the side of the mug.

"Pick a seat and I'll hand you your tea," she said to Zahryn who was standing by the window.

Zahryn chose a cool purple plaid beanbag chair, plunked herself down into it, and received her tea. "Thanks, Maeve. This is one great chair!"

Maevyn smiled. It was time to come clean. Tell her story. They were alone. They were safe. They were as warm as they could be on the coldest day.

She began, "Zahryn, thanks for saying yes to skipping class. I've got stuff in my head and I'm kinda restless and if it's okay with you, it's time for me to tell you my stuff. I've done some things that didn't end well. And, well, it's all in the past now, but I'm still dealing with it. Is it okay if I just start talking?"

Zahryn felt warm inside. She liked Maevyn. She could tell that Maevyn was troubled, and if Maevyn was choosing today as the right time to open up, then so be it. She wouldn't get in the way.

Zahryn quietly said, "Whatever it is Maeve, you'll feel better just talking about it. What gets said today stays here. Your story is yours to tell—not mine to blab or broadcast. I'm here to listen—not to question, not to judge, not to fix. I'm all ears." She sipped slowly. The tea was very hot.

Maevyn took in a long slow breath. "I wasn't always a walk-on-the-wild-side kind of person. Actually, I was pretty normal. But things changed when I was fifteen. I was raised by my mom. She was a single mom. Her name is Enya. We lived in Opalon. She's a teacher. Primary school. She loves little kids.

"I had asked her a number of times, who my dad was. And she said things like 'He didn't stick around,' or, 'He didn't live here.' Once, she even said 'Oh, you probably wouldn't like him very much.' She never gave me more than a one sentence answer. And then she'd always change the subject.

"Then one day when I was fifteen, her older sister, my Auntie Paige, came to stay with us for a week. She and I stayed up late one night. I think she had had a few drinks, wine I guess, with dinner, and she let a few things slip. She said some things that she didn't know that I didn't know. She mentioned some things that my mom had never told me.

"She talked about the bar where she worked in Moonstone, called 'Pints.' There was a regular customer there, an older guy, probably in his sixties. His name was Jack Sullivan, but everyone there just called him Sully."

Zahryn was listening intently, wondering where all of this would lead.

"Well," Maevyn continued, "Ol' Sully was known as a travelin' man. A salesman of sorts. Not married. Took his sales pitches all over the Southshore Islands and the South Coast. He liked his drink and he liked his women. Auntie Paige described him as tall, lean, dark-haired and dark-eyed. Clean-shaven but a strong mustache.

"And," Maevyn laughed, "she said his looks were true to his name. Apparently, the name 'Sullivan' in ancient Ireland meant 'the dark-eyed one.'" Maevyn laughed again. "Auntie Paige had actually said a few times before to me, when I was just a little kid, 'Maevyn, my sweet May-vee, just watch out for the dark-eyed boys. They're trouble!'"

Maevyn took a sip of her coffee. She was beginning to relax into her storytelling. "Long story made short, Ol' Sully fathered a lot of kids over the years. So say the townsfolk. And, later in his life, another younger dude named Connor started coming to the bar regularly to meet with him. The new guy was twenty-something, and they'd always sit in the Snug, this private booth with padded bench seats and a round table. It was back in the corner of the pub.

"Auntie Paige would serve them their whiskey or their beers, right up until closing time. They were a pair. They kept to themselves a lot. Whispered stuff. Told stories. Laughed loudly, egging the other on. And at times, they were downright serious. Like they were figuring stuff out, together.

"So, Auntie Paige let it slip that my mom and the younger guy, Connor, had once had a one-night-fling and that he was my dad."

Zahryn had been listening to all of the bar room details and she sat up straight, white as a ghost, after hearing the younger man's name. "Did you say the younger man in Moonstone, Ol' Sully's pal, was called Connor?" Her eyes were wide open and her heart was racing.

"Yes I did, Zahryn. Connor. He was a man on the road a lot, a salesman, like Sully. Auntie Paige even hinted that Ol' Sully was Connor's dad—you know—both being dark-eyed and such." Maevyn stopped when she noticed Zahryn's shocked look, and her fright.

Zahryn was cool and collected on the outside, but she was wildly disturbed on the inside. She intentionally held back her words. She thought about the dad she knew and loved, could this be him? Was she learning something she never knew about her own dad? Her mind was racing a mile a minute. Her thoughts were tumbling over and over and over each other. This was a lot to process all at once. She forced herself to settle her wild thoughts, and concentrate on listening to Maevyn's story.

Maevyn watched her closely. "You're probably wondering why I told you all of this. Well, when I found out who my dad was, I was suddenly mad at the world. My mom had sheltered me, protected me, as long as she could about who my father was, and now Auntie Paige had just told me what I needed to know. I felt hurt and mad, and betrayed.

"I kinda lost it. I started acting out. Smoking. Drinking at fifteen. Drugs. I skipped school a lot. And then at sixteen, my mom kicked me out because I got pregnant. We fought like cats and dogs about the pregnancy. She tried to shame me, but then I told her what I knew about my dad and her, and she got even madder. She sent me to live here in Moonstone, with Auntie Paige, because she just couldn't deal. And so, here I am!"

Zahryn was still listening, in shock and overwhelmed. But she did not react at all to Maevyn. Maevyn needed to share her story, dark as it was, and Zahryn had said she would listen. And she did just that, hard as it was to hear. She knew that eventually, down the road, she would need to find her own place in Maevyn's story.

Maevyn continued, "So I had the baby last July. July 31. They say that my delivery went well, but God, that hurt! Two hours labor and done. I'll never forget that day. I told the nurses that I did not want to see the baby, or even hold her. They were to have her adopted. I just signed the papers. I came home, here, to Auntie Paige's flat, and I've been a mess ever since."

Maevyn stopped talking. She needed to collect her thoughts. She sighed and shifted about in her lime green plaid beany chair. After a bit, she continued. "I need to believe that my little girl was adopted into a good home—one that wanted a little baby. I want to believe it and I need to believe it. It's the only thing that keeps me going, believing that my little girl is wanted, loved, and provided for. Cared for by someone who has means. I sure didn't. I was just a kid in school and I didn't even have a part-time job."

Zahryn realized she had hardly said anything, throughout Maeve's storytelling. She then said, "Oh Maeve. You just told me so much. You opened up and told me a huge story. I'm so glad you got it off your chest. You've finally freed yourself by sharing your darkness—your truth—with me."

Maevyn took a long minute. There were tears in her eyes that needed to overflow. Indeed, she had finally shared her story. Her dark story. She had put herself out there to Zahryn, and the weight of her story was then carried by two.

Zahryn had no magical answers or quick fixes or do-over suggestions. She saw deeply into Maevyn's hurting soul and she reached out simply to be with her in her emotional pain and vulnerability and shame.

Zahryn's very presence and her listening ears were enough for Maevyn to lighten up just a little in the moment. She smiled through her tears and said, "I need a hug."

In her haste to get out of the beany chair, Zahryn nearly knocked over her own mug of tea. "Of course I'll give you a hug! You need a hug!" she said.

And the two girls kneeled on the area rug, in a full-on body hug that sealed their friendship. It was the first hug of many more seasons of hugs to come over the next seventeen years. They were friends. They might be sisters. Theirs was a connection born on the coldest day in January.

Zahryn broke first from the hug and said, "Let's bake some cookies. And we can talk more after. We need a break. Do you have any oatmeal? Or chocolate chips?"

Maevyn answered, "Yup! Sure. I don't bake much, but my aunt does. She has lots of baking stuff. But, I have another idea. An invitation to you, Zee. Can I call you that? I like that name for you."

"You sure can, Maeve. What's up? What're you thinking?"

They plunked themselves down again on the beanbag chairs and curled up. Maevyn's eyes were dancing. She continued, "You said you've never smoked a joint. Right?"

"Right," said Zahryn, instantly intrigued.

And you don't smoke, right?"

"Right." she said again.

"So, I have a recipe for pot brownies. I've only made them once before, but they're great. Yummy! Wanna try some? Bake them and try some? We're not going anywhere. You don't have to be anywhere until dinnertime tonight. So . . . are you in? Are you with me Zee? I checked out the pantry and Aunt Paige has all of the ingredients here. Plus, I have my stash."

Zahryn burst out in nervous laughter. "That's hilarious!" Her whole face lit up at the very thought of ingesting her first-ever edible weed. And she chuckled some more. "First you make me skip school today, and now I'm gonna mellow out and weed away with you? Who'da thought? Yeah, sure! Why not?"

The girls got busy in the kitchen, setting out utensils and bowls, and finding ingredients. Maevyn searched for and found her recipe that she had hidden in her biology textbook. Then came the busy work. Measuring. Mashing. Mixing. Pressing into pans. Making a mess.

The girls sat down over tea and coffee again while the goodies baked in the oven. Zahryn had lots of questions about the pot, and all the steps Maevyn had shown her in preparing the brownie mixture. Zahryn rattled on, still anxious. "Remember, Maeve, I've never done any weed—any pot—before! Is your stuff . . . safe? Where did you buy it—some random guy or someone you know and trust?"

"Whoa, slow down Zee! This isn't my first rodeo! I buy from the same woman, Sami-Leigh, all the time. I trust her. Her mom and my mom worked together for a really long time. Her stuff is good. We're good. But I know you've never had it before, so we'll just go slow."

"Good to know," said Zahryn. "You know I'm going on blind trust here!"

"No problem. All good. The brownies won't be done for another few minutes. We can just hang until they are done."

When the oven buzzer buzzed loudly, Maevyn turned off the timer and the oven. With both hands mitted in oversized oven gloves, she brought the pans out onto the rack on the counter. "We should let them cool a bit."

Maevyn returned to her chair.

Zahryn was mesmerized at the thought of consuming the pot brownies. She said, "Maeve, were you scared when you first tried it?"

"A little, but it's no big deal. Just let it take over and let yourself go. It's not euphoric or even hallucinogenic. It's a good feeling all over. Mellow. Chill. Cool. It's not immediate. Maybe an hour or so."

When Maevyn finished her coffee, she got up and reached for a knife. She cut the brownies in the pan into twelve square pieces. She said to Zahryn, "Since this is your first, I'll cut one in half for you. That okay?"

Zahryn nodded. A gentle smile curled her lips. Anticipation. Allure. Adventure into the unknown.

Maevyn brought a half brownie to Zahryn, and placed it in her hand. Unceremoniously, Zahryn immediately popped it into her mouth, giggling as she chewed. "Yum!" she said, with her mouth full.

Maevyn laughed with her. She took a bite, enjoying the tasty treat. Without swallowing yet, she said, "Let's get those dishes done while we wait. This will be fun!"

LATER THAT DAY, AROUND 3 p.m., Zahryn was quite enjoying her little adventure. "Okay Maeve, this is good. I kinda like being here. I feel safe. I'm feeling fine. I'm glad you're with me though. I'm not sure how clear my head is or isn't. I have a good blur goin' on right now."

Maeve giggled. "Well, good for you! You did it! No regrets? You sound like you're enjoying it."

Zahryn answered, "Yeah, I'm good. Real good. Thanks, Maeve." She leaned forward as she continued, "But I'm not finished with our earlier conversation. Is it okay if I ask you a few more things?"

Maeve said, "Sure. Ask away. I might not know the answer, and by the way I'm feeling right now—kinda free—maybe I can make up some answers—maybe we can both invent some stories of our own! Haha! See where our crazy fantasy and imaginations can take us!"

Zahryn laughed. She knew exactly what Maevyn was alluding to. She too felt free, beyond chatty. Rather loose in her tongue! Ready to speak out whatever came to mind. Maybe, just maybe, she could just let go and confabulate in the moment. She opened with "You said something about your dad earlier, Connor. Did you say that Ol' Sully was his dad?"

"No. No proof. But maybe. They were really close friends though, despite their age differences. Aunt Paige says Sully's whole name is Jack Sullivan, and that his parents used to live on the mountain at the crossroads—in a little hamlet called Sullivan's Gate. Whatever. I'm sure the town name has some historic significance but I don't know anything about it. Everything around here seems to get named for a reason."

Zahryn persisted with her line of questioning. "So tell me what you know about the young guy—about Connor. My dad's name is Connor, and he lived with me here in Moonstone, and he was a salesman, and he was on the road a lot until he died."

Maevyn returned to her serious voice, and spoke with some caution. "Wellllll, it's not my story to tell for sure, but I think you are putting two and two together, like I am. This is all true. This is what I do know. Connor is my dad. Fact. My mom Enya confirmed this. His last name was Inglis. And I know your last name is Walker-Inglis, because we sit alphabetically in homeroom. Walker-Inglis followed by Watt. Watt is my mom's last name. She never married. So, Zahryn, I think that makes us sisters. Half-sisters anyway. Sisters by another mother. I can't prove it, but this is pretty big."

Zahryn felt high. Not high as a kite, but high enough to be buoyed up, enlivened. This was a magical moment. She had just learned—confirmed—for the very first time in her life, that she had a sister. That was life-changing! Zahryn had lived all these years without any siblings, and was now discovering that maybe—that likely—she had a sister! In her expansive and spacious mindset of the moment she was so open to the possibility—the very likely possibility—of having a sister!

She held her arms wide, in invitation. "Come here sister—now I need a hug!" And this time, their hug collapsed onto the floor and they tumbled like two puppies or kittens frolicking in play—for the sake of childlike exuberant expression. Sisters. Connected. Together. And the mystery of the moment was still to unfold with more secrets and in more living truths.

Maevyn sat up. Her dark eyes were dancing with excitement. She had one more secret to literally set free.

"Zahryn, I have something else to tell you, and there's no better time than now. Sit up and hear me. This is only hearsay, but you might as well know what I know."

Zahryn sat up, cross-legged, a little dizzy in the moment. She noted an unusual sense of fullness in her cheeks and face, yet, an uncanny lightness of her head. The air around her felt thin and free. She herself felt unrestricted, unbridled, wide open. The brownies were doing their thing in her time and space. "What?" she asked. "Have you got more dark family skeletons in the closet? Haha! I'll shut up. Sorry. You look serious, Em!"

"Yeah, well, I kinda am." Her voice trailed off. "I have no proof, only what Auntie Paige has told me. And, if you and I play our cards right, we can maybe find out more."

Zahryn took the bait. "Ok! Spill!"

Maevyn went on. "Remember what I said, that Ol' Sully had fathered a lot of illegitimate kids on his travels, in his lifetime, and that Connor, who looked up to him, was proudly walking in the old guy's shoes? I mean, he too was with a lot of different women in so many different towns on the islands, and on the mainland. I'm sorry if this upsets you to hear—if this Connor is your dad and all—but please hear me out."

"It's okay, Maeve. Just tell me."

"Auntie Paige let something else slip. She overheard the two of them talking one night, in the Snug, maybe ten years ago or so. Sully and Connor were laughing loudly about their travels in the UK, sowing their wild oats. Comparing notes and notches on their belts, so to speak.

"And Connor had boasted that night saying, 'And my farthest and greatest conquest for sure is Doran's Brook, in the Hebrides. My son there, Gaelan, is one smart little boy. I talk to his mom once in a while, but I never get to see the little guy. At eight years old now, he's already talking about conquering the world with Math.

" 'The little lad told his mom just last week "Numbers rule, Mom! Numbers are everything! Everything in this world can be counted, measured, calculated and predicted and produced, by numbers and number systems!" His mom, Kelly, said his IQ was measured and it was way high up there, off the charts. I bet he'll go to university and take over the Commerce or Math departments. Maybe someday, his numbers-smarts will make him a rich and a happy man!'

"So, Zahryn, we have some clues about a potential brother of ours. I bet if we try, we can find him and find out more!"

"So now, my sweet Em, you're telling me that I have a brother too! Haha! There's some really good stuff in these brownies! May-vee! This is crazy!"

Zahryn was still fuzzy, and she guffawed—loudly. She was almost shouting in her own current state of disinhibition. "Just re-capping here, okay? So, you want me to go away to some random university, and find all the dark-eyed Gaelans whose mother's names are Kelly, who lives in the Hebrides, in Doran's Brook specifically, who studies Math or the like. And, just how many colleges and universities do I have to go to, to find my bro? Our bro?"

They laughed again, hysterically. Maevyn piped in, "Wellllll, if you ev-vvvvver just happen to find yourself in the Hebrides . . . ." and they laughed at the absolute craziness—the absurdity of the suggestion. As if anyone, EVER, "just happens" to be in the remote western islands of Scotland!

It's a well-known fact that no one—absolutely no one—arrives in the Hebrides unintentionally or by sheer happenstance. It takes intentional travel plans—train, ferry, bus, and another ferry just to get to the tiny islands.

And Zahryn spoke out in a silly voice, "Like, a 'chance arrival' in Doran's Brook—a chance meeting with a Kelly AND a Gaelan in Doran's Brook—would seem as far out there as us seeing a Scottish unicorn choir singing the national anthem under a rainbow, in the enchanted forest, with

Tiny Tim conducting—with inquisitive faeries and leprechauns all watching from behind the magical trees!"

The girls threw their heads back and rocked with laughter. Tears came to their eyes. Then they got the silly giggles. Maevyn accidentally snorted while laughing so hard and they broke out again.

And Maevyn said after a beat, "Hey, Zee, just to add some more fun to this story—the name of the town, Doran's Brook, has a little mystery to it too! 'Doran' is an ancient Irish name which means 'stranger, or wanderer'— those who are unafraid to pave their own path. And 'Brook,' you know, is a wandering stream—it eventually moves on to bigger waters. What a cool name for a town! I'd like to go there someday and see what it's all about. Cool people, I bet! Those sound like my kind of people. Strong, hardy, and finding their way in life!" Her voice trailed away, into the corners of silence.

She spoke once more, this time in a quieter, more serious tone. "Zee, I think we should keep all of this to ourselves. For now, anyway. People don't need to know we're siblings. No one needs to know that we know. Maybe some of them know already. Most of them won't have a clue. But, let's play it safe. For now, don't even tell your Auntie Tagyn. Okay? Secret?" She pinched her lips between her thumb and first finger, and looked to Zahryn for affirmation.

Zahryn said quietly, "My lips are sealed, Sistah!" And she motioned to zip her lips.

Like two teenage girls, skipping school and lightly weeded out on a Friday afternoon, they were in a space, in a place, in a moment where they were open to anything, preposterous or not. The sisterhood was born. Life was good.

When Visions of Motherlove Danced

JUNE 21, 1974

As a child, Rose Walker lived in the quiet village of Pearl Haven, in the Ben Lonrach Mountains. A roadside sign at the entrance to the village paraphrased their 1 Corinthians-based core value. Love is everywhere. Love is forever. There was a strong sense of community and all of the neighbors worked hard at fostering goodness, kindness, and peaceful living. Life in Pearl Haven was pretty idyllic.

A precocious and happy-go-lucky Rose stepped forward on stage in the school auditorium. She stood facing a mic on a boom stand. When she adjusted the height of the mic, it made a really loud feedback sound. Some of the students covered their ears.

Rose threw her arms out wide, and stepped back from the mic. "Whoa!" she called out loudly, startled. "Sorry! That was loud!"

Rose took a deep breath, stepped up to the mic again, and continued. "Okay. First of all, I'd like to say thank you to the staff at Pearl Haven Primary School, for hosting this annual public speaking contest. It gives us kids a chance to think about something important, and then, to tell our friends—to tell an audience—why it is important.

"These two-minute speeches are hard to do, but, they really make you think about WHAT you want to say, and, WHY it is important to you. So, here I go!

"My name is Rose Walker. I am ten years old. I am in Primary Four. And, I am the happiest girl! I—love—summer! And school is almost out for summer! Yay!

"But, my speech is not about summer at all! The title I chose for my speech is "I Want to Be a Mommy!" I chose this because I have a really great mother. And someday, I want to be just like her. She loves me. And I know she loves me. All the time. I'm a pretty good kid most of the time, but my mom loves me even when I mess up. She might not like what I just did, or, how I did it, or, she might get mad because I forgot to do something. But, even when she's mad, I know she loves me.

"Like, the time I left the bathwater running and it flooded the bathroom floor. Like, the time I didn't close the back door of the house and our bird, Joey, flew away. He never came back. And, then there was the time when I was three years old and I painted mom's red nail polish all over the piano keys! Yikes! She was very mad at me! She yelled at me!"

Rose stopped for a moment to listen to the laughter in the audience. They were really enjoying her story. She continued, "But, she never stopped loving me. One day, she told me that love, was like a magic braided carpet underneath me, everywhere I go. In the storms. In the dark. In the noise and the confusion. If I got lost. It was always her love that was plaited into my magic braided carpet and it would go with me everywhere, all the time— forever and always. My mom uses a really big word for this. I think she says love is 'unconditional.'

"I love my mommy. And when I grow up, I want to be just like her. I want to love like she does. I want to teach my children about the magic braided carpet of love. I want to have lots of children, and I want them all to know what love is. And that is why 'I Want to Be a Mommy!' If I ever get to be a mommy, I will be the best mommy ever. Because I know what love is. Thank You!"

Young Rose stepped back from the mic and heard applause. Some of the parents in the very back rows were on their feet, clapping loudly. Rose's primary class teacher, Mrs. Avery, in the wings of stage left, beckoned to Rose. Rose walked off the stage toward her, into the wings.

Emcee Mr. Lowden strode toward center stage. Raising the mic on the boom, he said, "Good afternoon students and staff and parents! This concludes the formal speeches portion of our public speaking contest. The judges are just finalizing their scores. Wow! What a high note to end on! The innocent word of a child meets the power of love. On a magic braided carpet made of love! Let's hear it again one more time for Rose."

The whole audience cheered and whistled.

"Why don't we change things up a bit now, and let's give it up now for our mothers. We all have one. Let's all show our appreciation for our mothers."

And the clapping erupted again. The audience was so responsive, so receptive, so expressive of their joy. This was small-town Pearl Haven in the 1970's, where peace and love were main themes in the songs and pop-culture of post-war life. Love was a cool thing. "Peace, Love and Rock and Roll" was a popular mantra of the day.

When the uproar had almost died down again, Mr. Lowden began to speak. But he stopped when he heard a commotion in the back rows. A few

of the parents had become a little vocal, lyrically speaking. They were singing the chorus of a beloved chart-topper from the '60s. The Youngbloods'
lyrics, *Get Together*, arose into the crowd, and became increasingly louder as
more and more voices joined in.

Once, twice, three times they sang the chorus through. They called
out for love. Their singing was totally impromptu, unrehearsed, unbridled,
in the moment and free. Their passion spoke out the need—the universal
need—to love. The beautiful lyrical sentiments lifted up, up and away in
song, and were heard clearly throughout the auditorium.

There was a shared moment in the auditorium, that was vibrant and
rich and colorful—full of meaning—a message in the moment.

Mr. Lowden started again. "I don't know what to say! Thank you to
all you beautiful people—especially to the parents in the back row. This is
an afternoon to remember. And, as this year draws to a close, it is most
certainly the highlight of my school year!" The audience cheered again.

"And now, I think the judges are ready. He looked across the stage—to
stage right—and the judges nodded. One judge emerged from the wings
carrying a sealed white envelope. He gave it to Mr. Lowden and then returned to the wings.

Slowly, Mr. Lowden opened the envelope. He paused and smiled as he
looked at the name. He took a giant step backward while taking a moment
to unbutton his sport coat. He stretched both arms up and out—high and
wide in the body language of victory. He said with a full and resounding
voice, "And the winner is . . . Rose Walker!"

Wide-eyed in the wings, Rose gasped loudly as both of her hands flew
up to cover her wide-open mouth. She was shocked. Her gasp was completely lost amid the thunderous applause. Inwardly she knew she really liked
her speech topic, and she thought she had spoken pretty well. But she had
absolutely no thoughts that she could be a winner. And she was! The winner!

Mrs. Avery took her by the hand and walked with her back out to join
Mr. Lowden, at center stage.

The room broke out again with a fervor that was beyond understanding and beyond explanation. A ten-year-old's words had gathered them in,
and touched their hearts. It had bonded them, in love. Love was known.
Love was wanted. Love was needed. Folks needed to be mothered and they
needed to mother well. Folks needed to express their gratitude for the universal mothering spirit, and for the ever-enduring mothering heart of love.
And Rose's speech did just that. It reminded them of their own mother's love,
individually, collectively and communally. This town—this village—knew
love. And so did little Rose. Love lived—love was alive—in Pearl Haven.

Be the River, Be the Light,
Be the Love

JULY 10, 2007

ZAHRYN HAD ALREADY BEEN home for two months in the spring from university, and she found herself feeling restless and scrambled. Lately, she had been fidgety and uncertain.

She stood in front of the mirror, brushing her hair and trying to decide how to calm the mini-tornado of swirling thoughts inside her. *I need to stop in my tracks and isolate all of these words and feelings, and try to make sense of them*, she reflected.

If there was one thing Zahryn didn't like, it was chaos and uncertainty. She paced in her bedroom and went to the window, looking down at the quiet street and searching her soul for the source of her unrest.

I need direction and purpose and meaning. I need to name some important things in my life, my priorities and goals. I need to put words to my feelings, she thought. *I need to define me—name me—understand me—in a clear and succinct way.*

Zahryn knew that this wasn't the kind of thing that talking to a friend would solve. She needed to talk to God, but first she wanted to do the work of laying her cards on the table and organizing her thoughts.

Zahryn spoke inwardly, with conviction. *So, I need to go to a peaceful place. No interruptions. No distractions. Somewhere inspirational and thought-provoking.* And she knew just the place. Riley's Beach. She could go past the pond and follow the little brook in the park down the hill to the shore—to the ocean—to the rock-strewn beach where the brook meets the sea. *Yup. That's just where I need to be.*

Zahryn called out to her aunt in the room down the hall. "Auntie Tagyn, can I borrow the car for an hour or more? I want to go to the shore."

Tagyn answered clearly from her study, "Sure, Zahryn. I'll see you at home for supper, yes?"

"Of course! Earlier than that. And, I'll help you cook!"

"No need," Tagyn called out. "I'm just reheating the stew tonight—the lovely lamb stew from the weekend. Go and take some time for yourself—catch your breath. You always keep such a busy schedule. Downtime will do you some good. Supper will be ready at six. Have a great afternoon! Love you sweetie!"

Zahryn didn't pass up on this moment. She walked into the study where her aunt was sitting at her desk, with her back to Zahryn. Niece approached auntie, giving her a surprise hug from behind. It was a warm hug, full of gratitude. Tagyn reached back to stroke Zahryn's face.

Zahryn turned and walked toward the hallway. "Okay. I'm gone. See you at supper! Love you too!" And with that, Zahryn strode out of the room, picking up the keys from the key rack in the hall.

Upon opening the front door to the world, she paused and took in one long deep breath. It was a little cool for July, but still very pleasant. Fresh. Salt air filled her nostrils. Zahryn never got tired of her hometown salt-air wafts and whiffs. Home. Moonstone Cove—home sweet home by the sea. Home sweet home on the island. Home sweet home on the mountain. Ben Lonrach Mountains—islands in the sea. Shimmering. Shining. Light-bearing. After one more long breath, she sighed and moved on.

She drove just a few blocks to the outskirts of town, and then into the park. She parked in the lot near the entrance, and hopped out of the car, setting out with a long-stride-pace over to the brook. The path beside the brook would lead her down a gentle rocky slope to the shore. The name of the beach, Riley's Beach, was truly a misnomer. Not a sandy beach at all, but rocky and pebbly. It was covered with layers of palm-sized grey-white-pink round rocks, shaped through the eons by the waves, the weather, and the wind. Their edges were softened by time and eternity, together.

Zahryn paused at the shore. There was something very grounding, very centering, very deep, at the shores. The ancient Celtic people spoke of the Thin Places—places in time and space and in being, where the Human and the Divine were so very close—so palpably close. The metaphorical veil that separated them was said to be thin, translucent, barely there.

"Okay! I'm here!" she called out, to no one there. The sky was bright blue with little puff clouds drifting slowly by. She noted a windless waterscape with small, perpetual, running waves lapping on the shores. No crashing waves. No distant echoes of drones or groans of the sea. Gentle breeze. Salt-air breeze. Peace.

She strolled over, sat down on the rocks, and nestled in to get comfortable, about two meters from the shoreline. She folded her tall, lanky frame, pretzel-like, cross-legged, and content on the shore. She felt the sun-warmed rocks under her thighs. Riley's Beach was wide open to all of the elements, and, wide open to her thoughts and her musings. For twenty minutes, Zahryn sat staring, emptying herself into the vastness, readying herself for her contemplative inquiry.

"Okay. Where do I start?" she spoke again to no one there. "I think I need a mantra. A daily mantra. A life mantra. A self-defining mantra. I think I need to reflect on all of these swirling ideas that are deeply meaningful to me. And then, I could use these words daily with my affirmations, as a mantra, to keep me strong, to keep me centered, to keep me positive and hopeful and mindful. This mantra would enliven my spirit. It would engage me. It would articulate the very essence of me. Not only who I am, but who I want to be—who I want to become. I would feel connected, like I was part of something greater through this mantra—something far greater than my single self. Hmmmmm . . . ."

Zahryn reached for her knapsack. She always kept a coil-bound notebook with her, for moments like this. She had something to say and she knew that the words and images and phrases would soon begin to tumble rapidly in her contemplative mind—in her expansive mindset.

She turned her gaze to the incessant running waves on the shore. And then, it happened! It was like her pencil became a channel from another source, from another realm, from another being. She put her pencil to paper and out fell these words . . . .

Be the River. Be the Light. Be the Love. Across the waters.

Her pencil fell out of her hand onto the rocks, when she wrote the last word. She stopped and stared at the simple words. She knew that SHE had physically written them—it was HER handwriting for sure. But, she also knew that the words DID NOT come from HER. She knew what her restless thoughts and words were, and she knew of her discomfort with such random and nebulous and scattered thinking. And here, without any effort on her part, she had written down what appeared to be a mantra—almost in riddle form. It was a life-giving, Light-bearing mantra with her personhood written all over it.

She already knew in her heart, she intuited the deeper meaning of each phrase and image. And, she knew the power and the clarity of the commanding yet encouraging word, "Be." For someone wise had already written "Be the Love" in their own mystical prose, many, many years ago.

Zahryn knew instantly that this mantra was hers. It was given to her. It arose out of months and months of self-discovery and self-reflection, and out of years of her innocence, her contemplative thinking, and her inquiring spirit. These words defined her as she questioned her very being and her becoming. These words compelled her, led her, and called her. They spoke to her, creating powerful images in her mind's eye.

"Dear God," she spoke quietly on the shore. "In 'being the river' I will journey on, undaunted, with conviction, with purpose. No back paddling. No hesitation. No dramatic or resistive behaviors. *Forward, onward, toward life and living.* Like a river 'just goes and flows' around the bend, over and around the boulders. And even over the cliff in the magnificent escarpment-waterfalls-of-life. 'Be the River' is a mindset. It will be my mindset and my approach in all life and living. It is a positive and move-forward-at-all-costs approach. It will mold me, shape me, form me, into the person I long to be—into the person that you long for me to be. I can do this!

"And God, 'Be the Light' is already 'me.' Through my faith, through my church, through my own lived experience, I have understood what it means to be the Light for those in need. Of course, 'Be the Light' needs to be part of my mantra, part of my life!

"And I already understand 'Be the Love' through You, God, and through my family and community and friends. Life has been hard for me, God, but I have been loved—I have known what it means to be loved unconditionally, all of my life.

"'Be the River. Be the Light. Be the Love' is written across my heart, and it is snuggling in with my soul. These words are colorful yet so very plain. These words are poetic yet so very real. These words are full of life and Light. They will most certainly bring Light to the fuzzy shadows and into the darkness, and into the depths of the night.

"But for the words 'Across the Waters,' God, I'm going to have to do some thinking here. They too are poetic, but they are much less concrete—much more vague, and much more mystical. There is mystery and curiosity and intrigue in 'Across the Waters.' I'll love to spend time in these words and discover their meaning for me—discover their relevance in my life and in my living.

"These words, this mantra, are gifts to me, God, and I believe you gave them to me! You are leading me. You are always leading me, and for this I give thanks. I am humbled. I set out with questions and you supplied the answers. You know my needs. You know my heart. You know me inside and out God, and I am comforted in this knowing. Thank you, God. Amen."

Zahryn stood up slowly. Her load had lifted. Her mind was clear. No more weighted burdens on her shoulders and no angst churning in her gut. She felt whole. She felt strong. She had a broadening sense of self and a solid sense of personhood. She felt as if a warmth was emanating from her depths, there on the shores, affirming, inspiring, life-giving. It was inner joy. *Inlonracance.* She breathed in deeply, looking up to the skies. She clasped both of her hands in front of her heart and spoke with passion, with conviction, with delight, to no one there.

Raising both of her hands high over her head, she called out loudly into the vastness, across the waters, out to the distant horizon, "Be the River. Be the Light. Be the Love. Across the Waters."

"Who are you talking to, Zahryn?" a kind voice spoke softly from behind her.

Zahryn nearly jumped out of her skin and into the Celtic Sea. She turned around sharply, to see who was there.

"Auntie Tagyn!!! Oh my God! I didn't expect to see you out here! How'd you get here? How long have you been here? They stood in an embrace that molded the two into one.

Auntie Tagyn spoke first. "I needed a break too, honey, and I walked over. I left home right after you did. And I've been here only a few minutes, watching you sitting at the shore. It's always therapeutic to come to the shore. There is healing here.

"You were so deep in thought," Tagyn continued. "And I didn't want to disturb you. But then I saw you raising your arms and talking out loud to the skies and I got a little worried. Are you okay?"

Zahryn held onto this moment of beautiful care and concern. She didn't say anything, but held her auntie closer in their sweet shoreside hug.

"Are you okay, Zahryn?" Tagyn repeated her question. "I thought maybe you might need a sounding board, or a helping heart, or a new perspective or two. Have you had enough time by yourself? I can leave if you want. You just tell me what you'd like me to do."

Zahryn pulled Tagyn in close again. They shared a bond of love, Auntie and niece. Inseparable in heart and spirit. They were knowing, loving, together on the journey of life, bound by a power, a mystery, an ancestral drumbeat of life and living.

Zahryn spoke with conviction. "Auntie Tagyn, you know that there are some times and some things that just cannot be explained."

Tagyn stepped back, still holding her hands on Zahryn's shoulders. "Yes . . . go on . . . ." Tagyn sat down on the rocks, beckoning Zahryn to join her. They both gazed out into the beyond, into oblivion.

Zahryn sat and was quiet for a few minutes. "You know, Auntie, sometimes things are too new, and too fresh, and too big for words. They need to be processed. I have a story. A really big story that is too incredible to even articulate fully, right now.

"This is a Thin Place. I can say that God's presence has been made known to me, here and now. And I will say that I've received a gift from God that has transformed me—and it is going to change my life. I have always known about the Thin Places, and it is going to take me a long time to un-pack what just happened to me here at the shore. All I can say right now is that God knows me well and He is with me. God is good. Omni-good!"

Tagyn put her arm around Zahryn's shoulders and together, they in-clined their heads. They were so connected, there on the shore. Theirs was peace. Theirs was grace. Theirs was love. Across the Waters.

PART TWO

Be the Light—Shine Brightly

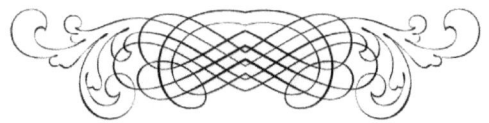

Anam Cara

DECEMBER 18, 2005

CHRISTMASTIME IN GLASGOW IS festive! Ancient buildings and cobblestone courtyards come alive in the evenings. Holiday trees glisten with garlands and bows. Wynds and narrow closes glow in the snow under pretty white lights. So many lights! Church bells toll in the frosty air, in the frosty nights. And Christmas simply lights up the faces of all those attending services, symphonies, pageants and choral concerts alike. Christmas is love, and Glasgow glows with love and Light.

"Well! That was totally exhilarating!" Saorise flopped down on the sofa in the church reception hall. The high-ceilinged room was elegantly appointed. It was 9 p.m., just after the Sunday evening choral Christmas concert, at the Glasgow Church of Scotland—the Glasgow Cathedral—the High Kirk of Glasgow. Some guests were lingering in small groups, others were collecting coats and getting ready to depart. It was noisy and busy and the hype in the air was supercharged.

Zahryn dropped down dramatically on the sofa beside Saorise. "No kidding!" Zahryn said. "All of those Thursday night choir rehearsals this fall were so worth it. We got to meet some really cool musicians—choristers— people who love to share their faith through song. I'm so glad we didn't do a modern cantata. I really prefer singing the Sacred classics and the traditional Christmas carols.

"What a rush!" Zahryn continued. "The organ was amazing. The trumpets and tympani were like icing on the cake! And those soprano descants nearly blew the roof right off!"

Saorise said, "You know, Zahryn, we were probably the youngest voices up there in the choir. It felt so good to be simply surrounded by all of those amazing voices. They've all been singing in church choirs all of their lives and they know how to blend their voices so well. Maybe we were forty voices or so, up there? But all together, all of us, we sounded like just 'one voice' in the unison sections. Surround-sound at it's finest!"

55

She went on. "Zee, let's get outta here! It's way too noisy. The sanctuary is probably empty by now and we can just sit there quietly and chat, or maybe, back in the chancel, up in the choir loft? What do you think?"

"Don't have to ask me twice. Let's go!"

They jumped up off of the sofa. They were, without a doubt, feeling at ease in the big old stone church. Saorise reached out for Zahryn's hand. In their sheer exuberance, the two tall young women ran together freely, hand in hand, like little children, their gorgeous tresses flowing behind them. They ran out of the reception room, down the grand hallway, and out in to the lofty, arched sanctuary.

Breathless in exhilaration they stopped in their tracks. They found themselves at the foot of the red-carpeted stairs going up to the altar. Silently, they each took in some deep breaths. They just gazed, and listened. It was quiet. Not truly silent, but quiet, as with a reverence—with a hush. They were filled with a sense of breathtaking awe as they shifted gears and took in the grandeur of the moment.

The concert-going, shoulder-to-shoulder crowds of early evening had all gone home. The tall stained-glass windows stretched high into the space above them. The windows were softly backlit in the evenings to enhance their beauty. The vibrant glass was alive with story, truth, and Light. Stone columns stood steadfast, rising up into high arches and domes—up into the arching, wood-adorned ceilings.

Saorise and Zahryn raised their eyes to survey the architecture and the art of the ages. Awe simply found them and graced them. Every breath they drew was reverent. Every heartbeat was Sacred. And every blessed thought crossing their minds was Holy.

Saorise slipped her arm around Zahryn's waist and whispered, "Let's sit down in the transepts. It's a smaller space. It's private. There's something I want to share with you."

Without answering, Zahryn walked with Saorise to a ribbed stone pillar, encircled by a ring of cloth-covered chairs. Rising directly in front of these chairs in the transept was an oversized stained-glass window—a modern rendering of the biblical Tree of Jesse. The highly symbolic scarlet thread twisted itself boldly throughout the vibrant red glass inlay, evoking deeper questions and posing colorful themes to wide-eyed daytime onlookers. But the onlookers had all gone home. All but Saorise and Zahryn.

Saorise said, "We can talk here."

Zahryn sat down with Saorise, still looking up. She wondered what Saorise wanted to say. She said nothing and let Saorise open the conversation.

"Zee, I have something really nice to say to you but first I have to tell you some backstory—something interesting that I've been learning in my Ancient Celtic Studies class at Glasgow U this fall.

"Recently, we learned about the term, Anam Cara. I've heard it many times in the past, but I've only loosely known its meaning. My course has helped me not only to know the meaning, but honestly, I think I can now embody it. We can embody it. You and me.

"They say an Anam Cara is a soul friend." She pulled out a folded-up piece of paper from her pocket and opened it up. "I love how this lovely author put it." She began to read the contemplative prose.

"Soul friends—Anam Cara—
friends connected uniquely and deeply by the Light of life,
by their shared experience,
by a depth of faith inherent in their very being,
by an intangible knowing and understanding
of each other's heart.
They hold each other accountable on their faith journeys—
on their journeys of life.

They allow wanderings for curiosity and creativity and such,
but admonish when poor paths are chosen
and when the way is lost.

They love with honorable love.
And they hold each other in utmost respect and regard.
They encourage and support and comfort each other,
through all the curves of life.
Their Lights broaden together.
Their rivers-running-deep are a blessed confluence of souls,
meandering through all time and eternity.
Truly, they know each other's heart,
as surely as God knows their hearts."

"Doesn't that sound like us Zee? We've known each other our whole lives. We're on the same wavelength, and the same pathway, where life, faith, and humanity are concerned. You have a Light that shines and so do I. We are one, bonded by faith, by friendship, by our Light, through all eternity.

"This is special Zahryn, and . . . Sacred. I want to—I need to—name you as my Anam Cara."

The girls sat facing each other, under the massive glass art window, The Tree of Jesse. The ancestral lineage of Jesus was creatively depicted in color, design, and form in a simple whimsical tree. The two girls had a connection—a strong bond of friendship and faith that anchored them, as would sturdy roots anchor a tree. The branches of the tree reached outward, much like Saorise's and Zahryn's Lights reached outward to the world around them, shining there for anyone to see, if they were open to see it. The symbolic scarlet thread of their own Living Faith drew them in close.

Zahryn had taken in every word that Saorise had just offered. She understood. She too felt the meaning of Anam Cara, deep within her being. She had already intuited this bond, and had pondered it many times. Their beautiful bond grew in strength as they named each other Anam Cara.

"Saorise, yes, for sure, you are my Anam Cara, and I am yours. I'm honored that you feel this way about us, and it's even more special that you told me here, in this place. This is a Holy Place, and our bond is a Holy Bond. And I want it to be this way for always."

"Zahryn, of course! We're friends for life. Anam Cara for life. No matter where we are in our lives, we are soul friends. I hope this conversation wasn't too out there for you. Like, too deep. I meant every word!"

"Saorise, it was perfect. You and me—Anam Cara—done!"

It was drawing close to the hour when the cathedral doors would be locked for the night. Time to go home.

They walked toward the massive main cathedral doors. They walked under arch after arch after arch with an ineffable sense of God's Presence with them. God was indeed smiling, beaming, at his two beautiful children—his daughters. And he blessed their every step.

Once out of the church proper, they stood on level ground, on a wide-open gathering space—an ancient cobblestone square. It was aptly named Cathedral Square.

There were some people still around, but no crowds. It was a dark sky, and the lamplights gave good light to their feet. They felt sure. They felt safe. They were not alone.

As the young women walked, they talked about their classes and what the rest of the week would hold. Then Saorise said, "Oh! Zahryn! I've been meaning to tell you—my cousin, Gaelan, from Doran's Brook is here at Glasgow U. He's a really nice guy. He's here in first year too, studying Commerce. You probably met him a long time ago when we were little. He came to visit for my fifth birthday and I think you were there too, at my birthday party. You were at all of my parties, it seems!"

Zahryn couldn't believe her ears! She stumbled with her words. "Uh, I really don't remember. Yikes! Saorise, that was a really long time ago!"

Saorise chuckled. "Doesn't matter if you remember or not. He's here, He's smart. He's nice. You should look him up. Maybe we could all do some stuff together?"

Zahryn's wheels were instantly turning. *Oh my God! Gaelan from Doran's Brook sounds so familiar! So does Commerce! Wait! That's it! That's what Maevyn was saying back in January about our possible brother! Born to Kelly—and to Connor—and raised by his single mom, Kelly, in Doran's Brook, in the Hebrides. OMG! Saorise's aunt's name is Kelly! Auntie Kelly! Yikes! This can't be! That was way too easy! I could be on the brink of meeting my brother, if Maevyn's details are correct. I'll keep my mouth shut just in case I'm way wrong!*

Zahryn hid her true panic and said, "Sure. We could meet. I'm not in any hurry though. I'm still settling in to life here on campus. Maybe in the spring? Or the fall? Let's see what happens. I'd like to meet him, down the road!"

Saorise said, "Okay. But don't wait too long. He's a catch. Shy, but really nice. I think you two would be great together!"

"Oh! So now you are matchmaking! Did someone put you up to this? Your mom? Your aunt? You're my Anam Cara. And now, you're playing Cupid—making sure my heart will be well taken care of too! Thanks, Saorise! You crack me up. I love you too!"

They walked arm in arm, across the cobblestones, across the ancient square, into the December night. Two souls. Two Lights shining as one. All was well. And all would be well. Amen.

Sowing Seeds

SEPTEMBER 14 AND SEPTEMBER 19, 2006

PROFESSOR DAVID GOVAN SPOKE out loud and clear at the front of the class. He was a seasoned professor in Statistics and was looking forward to his first day back in class on campus. Glasgow University was a good academic center for higher learning.

"Heads up now, class. Let's get started. It's a new year and a new day and Statistics is a compulsory course for every university student who plans on writing a thesis to complete their degree in their graduating year. Some of you will just love Stats. You will find your niche here. Some of you will strongly dislike it. And then, there are the few who will actually dread it! I'd like to keep this number to a minimum, if possible!" A few chuckles and groans audibly swelled and lifted up into the vaulted academic theater space.

Professor Govan continued. "Honestly though, statistics is a broad-spectrum course that provides grounding, develops critical thinking, and carries curriculum content that is applicable to all realms of study. Like in the Sciences, the Arts, Humanities, Medicine, Engineering, Computer Science—all of these programs need a solid working knowledge of statistical analysis and statistical application.

"I love Stats. I have fun with Stats. I see the need, the place, the time, and the overall relevance of Stats. And I want you to see this too. Hopefully, by the time this course is finished in the spring, you'll agree with me. You need Stats. You like Stats. You want Stats!"

The students in the classroom were notably attentive. Professor Govan's pep talk was meant to be energizing and rally-like for them, but like every other year, there were some skeptics in the room. Doubters. Some who really, truly, dreaded the thought of the mandatory STA220 class. It was Govan's hope, his mission, his will, to at least get these doubters to make passing grades.

Gaelan was a good student, in his second year at university. For a moment or two, during Govan's address, he found his attention drifting. He was in an elevated lecture theater where there was no such thing as a bad seat. As each row of theater chairs rose two steps higher than those in front, every seat had an unobstructed sightline to the prof, to the rotating whiteboards, and to the screens for PowerPoint slides.

Gaelan's gaze had wandered to the young woman sitting in front of him. She had arrived in class shortly after he had, and she'd chosen to sit directly in front of him. She sat tall in her chair and her gorgeous auburn tresses cascaded down her back in a mass of unruly waves and curls. Two skinny braids were nestled in her curls on the left side.

He was awestruck. He wondered if she was Scottish, or Irish. Maybe freckled? He let his imagination run with the possibilities. He had seen many statuesque redheads on the mainland campus throughout his first year, but for some reason, he was intensely drawn in to the wonders of this auburn beauty's silhouette.

The sound waves of Govan's voice bounced back into Gaelan's auditory field. "I am going to leave the room for five minutes to get set up for some course handouts. While I'm gone, please make a point of introducing yourself to at least two other classmates, and please exchange your contact info. Then later on in the term, if you have questions about the course, the assignments, or the exam, you can talk to each other before contacting me. Learn to help each other and ask for help when you need it. You all know way more than you think, so get to it! Meet two people you don't know. Go!"

Much to Gaelan's surprise, the autumn tresses rose to their full 180 cm height, and turned 180 degrees to stand and face Gaelan.

"Hello! My name is Zahryn! What's yours?"

Gaelan tried to hide his shock and he bluntly said, "Gaelan. My name is Gaelan Kennett." He looked into her sage green eyes for the first time and saw a friendly soul—an open-hearted and breezy young woman with a smile that was so broad he believed her freckles were grinning at him as well!

Zahryn piped up, "I'm studying Social Sciences. You?"

Gaelan replied quickly. "Commerce. You know—the boring number-cruncher geek squad." He regretted saying that immediately. Here he was, full-on-self-deprecating in his first thirty seconds of conversation.

After sensing his misgiving in his last comment, Zahryn kept the conversation light. She chose to move beyond his negative words. She went on. "Commerce! Great! So . . . . Math, math, and more math! Economics—and Computers too? Oh, and Stats, of course!"

He gave her a shy smile and nodded. "Yup. You got it, Zahryn. That's my program, in a nutshell." Gaelan was thankful that Zahryn had graciously skipped over his remark and had zoomed in on the core of his curriculum.

She continued, "That's a hefty course load, Gaelan. I hope you have some good profs. They can make or break a course. Some can really inspire you. Others, not so much.

"By the way, here's my email. We can talk more after class. I'll give you my cell number, down the road, if I find I can trust you! How's that?!"

Gaelan, wide-eyed, said, "Wow! Great! Thanks! And here's mine." He quickly scribbled on the corner of his notepad and handed it to her. Their eyes met again. This time Gaelan saw more of Zahryn. She twinkled. Her eyes actually did a little twinkle dance as she smiled at him.

She reached for the torn notepaper and neatly folded it into her handbag. "Thanks, Gaelan. Great to meet you!" With that, she turned right around and tapped the shoulder of the female student in front of her.

Gaelan felt suddenly paralyzed. He had just had the easiest conversation with a female student to whom he felt strangely drawn. And he had been given the chance to stay in touch. He glowed from within.

A tap on his shoulder broke the moment. Gaelan turned to his left to face directly to the student beside him. A guy. Medium height. Slim. Gaelan inwardly surmised *Probably athletic.* The student on his left said, "Hi! My name is Neil. I'm a Math major. You?"

And Gaelan shared, "Gaelan. Commerce. Good to meet you!"

Neil asked, "Where's home for you, Gaelan?"

"Well, I'm staying off campus in a flat, with some guys from the Hebrides. I'm from there, too. Doran's Brook. What about you?"

"I'm from here. Glaswegian to the core. And I'm living with my folks for now. Oh! Prof's back. Here's my email."

Gaelan quickly scribbled his email and handed it to Neil, nodding in appreciation.

For the next two hours, Govan outlined his detailed curriculum and highlighted the assignment schedules. He stressed the importance of the term work and the final exam—a 70/30 split with the heavier emphasis being on the term work.

Govan closed his class with a funny animated video that left his class in stitches. Two cartoon lab mice wearing white lab coats were sitting on the lab bench. They were arguing loudly about the methodology of the experiment that they were conducting on humans in cages behind them, in the research lab. The ominous threat of failure to graduate if they submitted shoddy thesis work was delivered loud and clear. No quality work—no cheese!

The lights came up. Class was dismissed. Books closed as students stood up, preparing to leave. Gaelan had only one thing on his mind. *I need to speak to Zahryn!*

And Zahryn made it easy. She stood up and turned around and said, "Walk with me, Gaelan?"

Gaelan beamed. *This is too good to be true!* "Of course!" he said.

Zahryn and Gaelan strode out of class into the warm September air. Sounds of traffic seemed far, far way. They walked across the campus greens toward the north side. Gaelan said, "I'm heading this way home. Stop for coffee? Tea? Bite to eat?"

Zahryn said, "I'd love a cuppa tea. But, not today. Sorry, Gaelan. Gotta run. Rain check? After class next week?"

"Yeah," was all Gaelan got out.

Zahryn smiled and turned to the west. "See ya, Gaelan!" And with that, she strode off. The late afternoon sun was facing Zahryn. To Gaelan, she was walking away from him, darkly silhouetted in the golden light. *She is special,* he thought to himself. *She's so friendly.* He couldn't wait to catch up with her again.

Gaelan walked with a spirited step toward his flat, his home away from home with the guys. He felt different but couldn't name just what he was feeling. He knew he had a good feeling, but he sensed it was way more than that. He wanted to get to know more about the tall auburn lass.

He suddenly felt impatient. *Next Stats class will be Tuesday, next week! Today is only Thursday! Five whole days until I'll see her again! Why am I so taken by her? Am I that guy? Am I really that desperate a guy that I fall for the first woman who speaks to me on the first day of class? Am I that needy? Did she sense that? Did I make a fool of myself? This feels like high school all over again! I need to calm down. Focus! I'll see her soon enough!*

But man, I'm sooooo drawn to her!

ON TUESDAY AFTERNOON, GAELAN intentionally arrived twenty minutes early for class—Stats 220—and sat in the lecture theatre on an aisle seat near the door. Zahryn arrived with five minutes to spare, and he stood up to allow her to step by him to the seat on his right. *Yesssss! We can sit through class together!*

When class was over, Zahryn leaned over to Gaelan. "About teatime—still wanna go?"

Gaelan said quickly, "Let's go! On or off campus?"

Zahryn offered, "There's a nice tearoom downstairs at the library. We can talk there. And it's comfy."

Gaelan said, "Okay." They gathered their things and walked purposefully toward the library. It was an overcast day with a heavy mist.

"Here, Gaelan. Wait. Hold my stuff." She handed over her two textbooks, and proceeded to gather her long, long hair into a messy bun, using a large cotton scrunchie from its home around her wrist. She giggled. "You know. Curls. Mist. Frizz!" She pulled her hood up over her head before reaching out to take back her books from the eager porter.

Gaelan said, "Actually, no, I don't. No curls here or even in my family." His shoulder length jet black hair was pulled back in a straight ponytail, covered up by his favorite hat. "My flatcap will keep me dry if it starts to rain." He handed back her books and they moved on.

They arrived at the tearoom, ordered teas and biscuits, and found two deep-seated chairs in the corner. They sank down, kicked off their footwear and sat facing each other with oversized ceramic mugs in hand. Zahryn let her tresses down and returned her trusted scrunchie to her wrist.

Zahryn spoke first. "Gaelan, where's your home—where does your family live?"

"I was living with my mom and stepdad and younger sister, Grace, in Doran's Brook. I think though, that by the time I graduate, they'll all be moved to the Southshore."

Zahryn brightened broadly, "I'm from the Southshore. From Moonstone Cove!"

Gaelan thought he heard wrong. "Wait! From Moonstone? That's where my stepdad wants to move! He's a geologist and they have just received a really big grant to study rock formations in the Ben Lonrach, and the company is relocating staff and their families to that area!"

Zahryn and Gaelan looked at each other in amazement. Both of their families would soon be calling Moonstone Cove home! "That's such a coincidence," Gaelan said. "Do you have any brothers and sisters in Moonstone?"

Zahryn went quiet. The next part of their conversation would be tough.

"No, Gaelan, no siblings. And I live with my aunt. I lost both of my parents a long time ago. Actually, I never knew my mom. My dad raised me until I was ten, and then he died. So, then my aunt raised me. She's been really good to me."

She stopped for a moment when she saw the sadness in Gaelan's face. Gaelan spoke slowly. "Zahryn, that's awful. No parents. No siblings. Ugggghhhh, that's hard. I'm so sorry. I'm babbling on about family and . . . ."

Zahryn cut in. "Don't be. It's all I ever knew. It's all I've ever known. Everyone else has a mom and a dad, and I had just a dad. And he was the best dad. I had him until I was ten and then out of the blue he got cancer and died. Four days from diagnosis to death.

"His sister-in-law, my mom's sister—my Auntie Tagyn—moved from Opalon to Moonstone Cove to raise me. And you know, she's everything a mom would be for me. She's tough on discipline, but kind-hearted and loving all in the same breath. And, she is fun! She knows how to have a good time!

"She's the one who insisted that I go away to university, to have fun on campus, and to get a degree in whatever I wanted, so that I would end up working at something I loved—at something that would pay well.

"So, here I am! Studying Social Sciences and Humanities. Learning about psychology, social behaviors, and relationships. Social systems and culture, too. I love what I am studying. It's like studying the human mind, heart, and soul. And what makes people tick. I can't wait to get out there and get a job in something that excites me. This world excites me!" Her speech had quickened and her exuberance showed.

Gaelan looked at her and said, "Wow! Wow, Zahryn! You just came alive! I thought you were a people person and now I know it for sure! It's great to see how excited you are about your studies. You have passion for learning.

"I guess I like what I'm studying too, but, wow! Your energy just took on a whole new level when you talked about your courses. I *like* my Calculus and Algebra courses, but you *love* what you're studying."

He paused for a moment, and took a piece of his tea biscuit. He chewed it slowly, pensively, gazing off. *I really appreciate Zahryn's ability to open up to an almost complete stranger,* he thought. *I have a long way to go in being open as such, and I think Zahryn could be really good for me. Maybe she could help me to loosen up, and be more open.*

He swallowed and said to her, "Zahryn, I'm going to enjoy getting to know you. You have a way about you that I like. You like people, and you see people for who they are. You love your life—that is fantastic! I wish there were a lot more people like you. Your energy is contagious! And, my mind is going in twenty different directions right now, all because of you!" He sipped on his tea looking straight at Zahryn.

Zahryn smiled. She was now pretty darn sure that *this* Gaelan was *the* Gaelan that both of her friends had mentioned earlier in the year. She remembered Saorise's words about her shy cousin Gaelan, from a previous conversation. And once upon a time, Maeve had told her not to say anything to anyone, ever, about their possible half-brother, Gaelan, from the Hebrides.

Boldly, Zahryn asked her new friend, "Gaelan, you say you're from Doran's Brook. This is such a long shot. One heck of a long shot, but here goes. My best friend Saorise from Moonstone Cove has a cousin named

Gaelan, from Doran's Brook. And an Aunt Kelly from there, too. Would that Gaelan be you?"

Gaelan looked straight at Zahryn, eyebrows raised and mouth dropping—gaping. "Wow. Zahryn. Yes. My mom is Kelly, and I have a cousin Saorise in Moonstone! This is crazy! Small world. Totally small. Who knew?" He beamed at the very thought of his wonderful cousin, Saorise. She was so nice and so real. And now he was getting to know Saorise's best friend!

His thoughts turned back briefly to how drawn he had been feeling toward Zahryn. And why. He piped up with energy and excitement in his voice, "Have we met once before? Once upon a time?"

Zahryn said, "Well, Saorise seems to think so. A long time ago, at one of her preschool birthday parties. But, I really can't say. I don't remember."

She paused and smiled at Gaelan. They could now name their connection. A real connection. Their shared past in their long-time-ago acquaintance. She sighed. "Just another amazing illustration of 'six degrees of separation' . . . ." Her voice trailed off.

She said with exuding optimism, "I'm looking forward to more good times with you! You're, you know, a great guy!" They met each other's gaze. Both smiling. Both enjoying the moment, the honesty, and the sweetness of a unique relationship.

Zahryn straightened up in her chair, still cradling her warm tea mug in both hands. "Changing the subject, do you prefer city or country stuff to do in your spare time?"

Instantly Gaelan said, "Outdoors. Rural. Country. Shorelines. Mountains. Just being outdoors. We live in a rugged world with a harsh climate and if we spent all of our time hiding away from the weather, we'd be pretty gloomy people! I love doing anything in the outdoors. What about you, Zahryn?"

"Me too! I think most of my spare time has been spent outside. There's so much to explore around where I live, on the mountain, in the Southshore Islands. Places to get to on foot, on mountain trails, on the shores, and by the sea.

"The Celtic Sea is phenomenal. You can look way out there, across the waters, to the horizon, unless a fog rolls in. You can see weather systems moving across the waters in the south. The distant clouds might be dark and dumping rain into the sea, but you're standing on the shore in the brilliant sunshine and feeling the warmth of the sun on your shoulders.

"I love just 'being' outdoors. I feel a release. I feel free and I have renewed energy just by taking in a lungful of the sea air or the mountain air."

She looked away peacefully, through the tiny basement window of the library. "It's still raining outside. Let's get a second tea!"

Gaelan said, "Sorry, Zahryn. It's my night to cook dinner for the guys. Probably burgers and fries. I should go. But, you can stay if you like, and have a second cuppa tea, on me!"

"No, no. It's okay. I'll leave with you. But, we'll do this again, okay?" She looked him in the eye, her eyes dancing. "This was fun!"

At this simple invitation, Gaelan felt all warm inside. He felt a sudden rush. A fervor. A heightened awareness. He blushed and said, "Yeah! For sure! I had fun too!"

And they packed up their things and walked out into the misty campus, lit by their own radiant lights.

Bounty

SUNDAY AUGUST 1, 1993

AUNTIE CLAIRE AND ZAHRYN were seated cross-legged on a blanket in the park on the first Sunday of August, after church. They were at a community gathering in celebration of Lúnasa—the annual rituals of the ancient Celtic Festival of the Harvest. It was a time set aside to acknowledge the good works of the crop farmers, and to look forward to the bounty and the abundance and the yields of the land.

"You're going to be starting school soon, Zahryn. Primary One. You must be so excited, Sweetie!"

"Oh, Auntie Claire! I can't wait to go to school! I'll miss being with you every day, but school sounds like fun!"

"Well, you'll get to meet a lot of new friends, and you'll learn a lot more—way more than your dad or I could ever teach you. You're doing really well already with your letters and numbers, and with your reading. Lots of kids struggle with reading but you are a superstar! You're reading in the big readers already! Smart little girl, you are!"

"Daddy told me once that my mommy used to like to read a lot. Is that true?"

"Oh, Zahryn! Yes! Your mother Rose loved to read! And you are so much like her! Smart. Always happy. Playful. Your mommy likes adventure . . . er, oh, I'm so sorry, Zahryn. I meant to say your mommy liked adventure. And, she was so full of love. Just like you. 'Love' or 'Lovey' should have been your middle name!"

Zahryn laughed out loud. "Does anyone ever name their baby 'Love' ?"

"No, no. At least not in the English language. But some names like Croia, which means 'little heart,' or Lennon, which means 'lover,' or Carys, which means 'to love'—these names all symbolize love. Like, when you see a big flock of blackbirds—lennons—flying high in the sky, you are said to fill up with love!"

"Wow! That's so cool! Neato! I thought blackbirds were scary. Especially big ones in big flocks!"

"Oh no! Just the opposite. They are a sign of love. Wonderful love. Heartwarming love. "Think on this lovely thought next time you see them! Lennons = Love!"

"Auntie Claire, what does my name mean?" Zahryn blurted out.

"It means 'shining.' Bright. Radiance. And you are your name! You shine light, a pretty, pretty light every day, every minute, in every way. Your mom would have loved to watch you grow up and become such a shining light!"

"I wish I could have known her. Everybody loved her. Everybody liked her. I see all the other kids with their moms, and I see them get big hugs from them. And it makes me want a mom too."

"Oh, Zahryn. Of course you would! There is no other love quite like a mother's love. But we are doing our very best, your dad and I, to make you feel surrounded by love. Always. You are so loved, Zahryn!"

Claire, being Connor's only sibling, cared for Zahryn in her own home-daycare while her brother was out working. And Zahryn would also stay overnight with her Auntie Claire when her daddy was away for a night or two on business.

Claire continued on, "And I am so sad that you are missing your mommy. I'm glad that you are telling me this and being honest about your feelings. I hope you will always tell your dad and me how you're feeling. We'll always love you, Zee Zee. You've had a rough start without your mom, but I hope you still know that you are loved, no matter what, till the sheep's wool stops being warm!"

Zahryn smiled. "Yeah, I know. I learn about love at Sunday School. I wish everybody could be loved. Daddy tells me that if we all loved everyone, then there would be no more war, and no enemies, and no strangers. That just sounds really, really nice!"

"And your daddy is right! 'Love makes the world go 'round.' Those words are the title of a famous Gilbert and Sullivan song, and it is so true! If we all held this in our heart, the world would be a better place!"

"So, what's in the picnic basket, Auntie Claire? I'm hungry!"

"Okay! Let's look! What do you think, Zahryn? Will we find bounty in this basket?"

"Yes!" Zahryn smiled knowingly. "And we have bounty in our hearts. We have bounty in love!"

Lumana Rising—Going Deep

OCTOBER 24, 2015

ZAHRYN HAD AGREED TO meet Aoife for tea today, at the Lumana Café, in her hometown village, Moonstone Cove. It had been a few months since their last conversation—a cozy fireside chat over a bottle of wine in Aoife's tiny cottage home in Moonstone.

Zahryn really enjoyed her times spent with Aoife. They were very much alike in spirit and in approach, yet their lived experiences were greatly different. Other than Zahryn's time away at university in Scotland, Zahryn had pretty much lived in one place, in one home, her family home, and she knew her community so very well. She felt content in being home.

Aoife too, had previously been away at university in Scotland, but her studies in journalism and her inborn spirit of inquiry compelled her to up-root herself frequently to find new and intriguing places to discover and call home. Call it writer's wanderlust, call it seeker's will, call it whatever you like, Aoife had the gift of settling in wherever she laid her hat. She knew she was growing, and she was coming to understand herself and her place in the big wide world, each and every day. Wanderlust and wonder-lust were Aoife's middle names! She most surely had a peregrinating spirit.

Auntie Tagyn helped Zahryn out of the car and into her wheelchair. Zahryn was pretty independent, yet Auntie Tagyn still handed Zahryn her purse, and then pulled up and tucked in Zahryn's long sweater, which had draped itself over the wheelchair's oversized wheels. She then closed the car door. Her every move was attentive, helpful, supportive.

And her assistance was welcomed by Zahryn. Auntie Tagyn was always there for her, ready to help out, ready to pitch in, ready to make life's moments easier for Zahryn in any way she could. Her love for Zahryn was expressed in her everyday care, in a million little things, in a million tiny ways. Her love was not icing. It was cake. Fruitcake. Chock full and filling. Delightfully intriguing in flavor, surprising in texture, and most deeply and thoroughly satiating. Auntie Tagyn was love.

"It's 2:30 p.m. now, Auntie Tagyn. Maybe you could pick me up here, say at 5 p.m.? And I'll help you make supper when we get home. Aoife and I tend to have really long, deep conversations, so, two and a half hours should be good. Does that work for you?"

"Five o'clock is perfect. I'll see you then." Auntie Tagyn bent down to embrace Zahryn in a tender hug. "Say hi to Aoife! I'm glad you two have found each other. Kindred spirits . . . ." She let her voice trail off. She meant what she had just said about Aoife and Zahryn's friendship. Though their blooming, newfound friendship was only a year old, it held a depth seldom discovered, even in the oldest of friendships. Auntie Tagyn could see this plain as day.

"I will, Auntie Tagyn. Thanks," Zahryn said as she turned her wheelchair on a dime and rolled toward the café door. "See ya later!"

The popular café in Moonstone was aptly named Lumana. It was warm and inviting, a peaceful place of gathering. Harmony simply nestled therein, feeding and nurturing local souls.

Aoife was already in the café, and she strode over to meet Zahryn at the door. She stepped outside into the brisk, damp autumn air to hold the door open for her friend. Zahryn nodded in appreciation for the gesture. Aoife looked over toward Tagyn at the car. She smiled and waved fondly.

Aoife stepped behind the wheelchair and pushed Zahryn through to the back room. "I got us a table in the back corner, by the rear window. We'll have a lovely time here."

When Aoife stopped pushing the chair, Zahryn reached down to lock both of her wheels. She automatically flipped up her foot pedals, using the tops or her feet to do so. This task was becoming increasingly more difficult for Zahryn to do independently, but as long as she still could, she prided herself in her ability. She did not dwell on her disability.

Zahryn used both of her hands on the armrests of the wheelchair to push herself up to standing. She took two wobbly steps to the tall-back cushioned chair in the corner and sat down gracefully. Her legs were still strong enough to not plop!

Aoife chimed in, "Is it okay if I fold up your chair and move it away, over there?" She pointed at the hallway that led to the loo.

"Perfect. Thanks, Aoife."

The young women settled in, each ordering a pot of their preferred teas when the server, Noémie, came by.

Noémie was well known to Zahryn. She was a thirty-something French Canadian with a barely noticeable accent. Her voice was soft with a cadence, a gentle flow of pure welcome and hospitality. The name, Noémie, means good, pleasant, lovely. Noémie wore her name well.

Zahryn greeted her warmly, "Well Hello, Noémie! How are you today, my friend?"

Noémie's eyes sparkled, lighting up her pretty face. "I'm well. And thank you for asking!"

Zahryn didn't miss a beat in her questioning. "And how are your wee nephews doing? How old are they now?"

Noémie had a really big heart—she led with love in all she said and did. "The twins are three months old now. It's hard to believe! They are getting bigger almost every day. And they are becoming so alert!"

Zahryn continued to engage. "And Sanaa—your sister—she's doing well also?"

Noémie's wavy brown locks were braided into one long braid. She had been stroking and twisting the end of it while she was speaking to Zahryn and Aoife. She slowly lifted it over her shoulder, allowing it to fall away, behind her back. "Yes, Sanaa is so happy. But she is tired—really tired—and I'm happy to help out as much as I can. I go there every night. You know. There's always more laundry, more dishes, more little things that Sanaa needs help with. And, I get to see those sweet boys every night before bed. They are so beautiful. They are gifts from God. So precious."

Aoife was watching both Noémie and Zahryn as they spoke. She could sense a real warmth—a *joie de vivre*—a connection—as the women shared in conversation.

Noémie spoke again. "I'll go and get your teas. One Cardamom and one Earl Grey coming up!"

Noémie walked away with a bounce in her step. Zahryn turned back to face Aoife across the table. "Noémie is such a fine woman. I really like her. I've seen her home. It's neat as a pin. My Auntie Tagyn is friends with her mom, and they like to have tea together. Noémie always has her hands in the dough, making biscuits and braided sweetbreads. And her Christmas cake—her fruitcake—is to die for. It's really super-heavy-weight because it is chock full of candied fruits and nuts and it's totally saturated with brandy. So much brandy!"

Aoife listened to Zahryn's details. Zahryn seemed to know a lot about everyone. About everyone and their dog, their uncle and their neighbor.

Aoife reflected *I guess I'd attribute this to Zahryn's inborn friendliness and her love of the human condition, rather than just Zahryn's being in a small town where literally everybody knows everybody. And Zahryn really cares about the people she knows. She has a real knack for getting know those around her.*

Noémie returned to the table with a pot of cardamom tea for Zahryn and a pot of Earl Grey for Aoife. "The kettle is freshly boiled. Please be careful. The tea is hot. Don't burn your tongue!"

Noémie set the teapots down and placed quilted tartan tea cozies over them. "I'll come back with your teacups." Bowing her head as she nodded to the young ladies, she turned and headed back to the counter.

Zahryn inhaled deeply. The rising steam of both teas was highly aromatic and her nostrils were just then attuning. Savoring. Delighting in the moment.

Zahryn and Aoife had had many previous discussions in their recent past regarding the earthy, grounding, contentment-evoking powers of both cardamom and bergamot in these teas. They had also raised some fun questions about the addictive powers of said spices! Indeed, they lived to question the details of life and living! Even the hidden healing powers of tea!

Zahryn gazed out of the large, almost floor-to-ceiling picture window to her left. Her tea was still steeping. Her long legs barely fit under the small round table. Her feet rested on the creaky wooden floor. Noémie came by with two china teacups and saucers. "Thanks so much, Noémie. So good to see you again! Maybe someday I'll get to meet your nephews. That would be nice! And please say 'Hi' to Sanaa for me. Thanks again for the tea!"

Noémi graciously nodded and left.

Zahryn turned again toward Aoife and opened the conversation. "You know, Aoife," she mused, "if this place could talk. This building is probably at least 150 or 200 years old. Maybe even these floors are original. And that courtyard out there, right behind the café? Well, those stones in the patio and the walls and the arches—even in the little stone nook over there in the corner—they must be even older. Ancient. It makes me wonder about what this property was, five hundred or more years ago. Who used the courtyard? Was there another original building here? Maybe the courtyard was a front court for an ancient home? I've never been back out there to the courtyard or beyond to see if there are any ruins of an old building there." She sighed heavily, wistfully, searching.

"This, what I'm about to say, is not an original thought, but it sure paints a picture of my state of mind right now. 'If only the stones of the courtyard, the boards of the creaky wooden floor, and these old stucco walls—if only they could speak and tell the stories of life and times through the ages.' If only we could open ourselves to learn more from our whereabouts, and from things in our midst. If only we could hear their stories, appreciate them, value them, and hold them as part of our own story! Wouldn't we feel just so connected, and interconnected in place and time?" She sighed again.

"And, hey!" Zahryn's face lit up. "Don't you just love the name for this little café? Lumana!"

Aoife smiled warmly, nodding in agreement, saying, "Yes, I do. It's very right for this space."

Zahryn continued, "It's just a perfect name for its current social niche—for its time and place in the new millennium. It simply means friendship, goodwill and harmony. I like the name, a lot!" She sighed deeply, pensively, as her words simply lifted up and away, into the midst of their moment.

Aoife was watching Zahryn intently during her sensitive musing. She already knew that Zahryn was a deep thinker, that she was a contemplative at heart. But today, she saw something more, and she was interested in watching Zahryn's body language.

Zahryn was literally unfolding. She nestled into—molded into—the comfy cushioned chair. Her shoulders lowered. There was no neck tension or facial tension visible. Zahryn's one hand toyed with the tiny teaspoon on the table. Her other hand was relaxed, with her pale pink fingers turned slightly under, toward her palm, in her lap.

Aoife heard the power of Zahryn's questions, but, she also saw—she witnessed— the absolute ease of questioning. Aoife saw both depth and weight purely juxtaposed with light airy breeziness, in the very same moment. Aoife could see clearly that it was Zahryn's body language speaking out as if to share more of the query, more of the vastness of the question—and more of Zahryn!

Aoife didn't answer for a minute. She sat with the questions before joining Zahryn in her contemplations. "I think so much of life has been witnessed here in this place. I'm only a newcomer to this town, but I know that this gathering place has been here a really long time.

"In my work, my lines of journalistic questioning in this last year have led me into many conversations about this place. The magazine—my employer—loves historical articles—they love stories drawn from our heritage and from local lore.

"You know, this shop used to have other purposes too. The front of the store in the 1920s—that's a hundred years ago!—used to be a small general store for dry goods. People would barter and trade a lot. Times were tough. And back here, by this big window, was just a little room. It was a cozy tearoom for the ladies only a few afternoons a week, and other times it was used by the elder ladies to teach the younger ladies some specialized skills. Stitching. Tatting. Candle making. Preserves. Recipe sharing. This was an honest to goodness sharing place. Women taking care to teach women. They even shared ancestral songs and chants and prayers, until they couldn't—you know, the Clearances and all."

Aoife and Zahryn just looked at each other for a moment, silently wondering what it must have been like to live in a time where your land and possessions, your culture, and your faith were literally taken from you—ripped away from you against your will—burned and bulldozed and banished. The young women cringed in this thinking. Their facial expressions were of deepest care and concern, but they did not venture further in this line of questioning. It was too painful. The Clearances was a horrible time—an ugly scar in their ancestral heritage. Today, in their conversations, they just weren't going there.

Zahryn took her first sip of tea from her bone china cup. The hot fluid traveled from her lips to her tummy, creating an internal warmth, a warming flow. She savored the moment in silence, as her friend was also doing the same, almost mirroring her sip.

"Hey, Zahryn." Aoife settled back against the tall back of her chair, fingers nervously tracing the rim of her saucer. "I have a story to share with you, and now seems as good a time as any." She looked over to Zahryn who simply raised her eyebrows while taking another coveted hot sip of tea.

Aoife went on. "I can't believe it's been a year now since our meeting on the mountain trail. And it's been great getting to know each other. I like having you as a friend here in Moonstone!"

Zahryn and Aoife had found many ways to enjoy each other's company. Teatimes, cozy living room chats, wine and cheese, potluck, good-ol'-fashioned afternoon baking marathons, and more. On occasion, Aoife had even asked Zahryn for her opinion on some unedited articles before she submitted them to the magazine. She valued Zahryn's opinion.

Zahryn piped up, "For sure it has! We've had fun! We make our own fun!"

"So, Zahryn, what I need to tell you, are the stories I've intentionally left out. I don't like secrets, or lying by omission, so, it's time I told you more about me." Aoife drew in a very long, slow breath, watching Zahryn closely.

"Well, go for it, Aoife. Tell me whatever you need to. I haven't ever felt like you were hiding something, withholding, or, holding back. What's up?" Zahryn smiled with her gentle encouraging smile. She now noticed Aoife's hesitancy and discomfort.

"Okay," Aoife said. "Here goes." And she poured her heartfelt story out for Zahryn's listening and receptive ears. Aoife's voice became a little quieter as she spoke.

"I went away to university from 2004 to 2008. And then I lived on Iona from 2008 to 2011. I've not said anything to you about the three years right before I came to live in Moonstone, in 2014. Sooooo . . . here goes.

"While I was away living on the Isle of Iona after graduating from university, I did a lot of soul searching, and with a lot of thinking, communing, researching—and prayer—I made an enormous life-changing decision."

Slowly and surely, Aoife laid the factual groundwork for her story. "I was born a boy. My name, back then, was Evan. I knew all during my childhood and my teenage years that I wasn't a guy. Yes, I had all the physical body parts to prove it, but inside, I felt really different. Disconnected. Mismatched. Like my body and my personhood were two separate beings. I felt that I was absolutely foreign to myself."

Zahryn was wide-eyed, but she did not react overtly. She simply gave time and space for Aoife to lay out her story.

Aoife went on. "Back in my university days, there were a few times when I actually allowed myself to accept myself as a woman. And those were the times I knew peace in my soul. All of my angst completely went away.

"But then, like a bloody yo-yo, I'd crash again, knowing the reality of womanly-me living in a man's body, knowing the falseness of my own reality, sensing the fear of the unknowns in my near and distant futures. Self-loathing became my living hell.

"So, I talked to a few campus physicians and they weren't much help. They suggested a psyche consult. Dr. Google helped more, but it was a rather impersonal approach to a very personal and sensitive matter."

As Aoife reached for her tea, Zahryn spoke for the first time. Her words were carefully selected—sensitive and safe. She spoke softly. "Aoife, this is big. I am listening. Please tell me everything."

Zahryn reached out her hand. They held hands for a moment and the trust between them was palpable. Zahryn's empathy mantled Aoife's vulnerability, and Aoife found the courage to continue sharing her dark story with her Light-bearing friend.

"So, while I was away, working in Iona, I spent most of my off-hours figuring out my life. Literally figuring out my next steps. I left the island in 2011, got the medical and psychological support I needed, and I transitioned in Glasgow in 2012 to 2013. I had my gender-reassignment surgeries—top and bottom surgeries. I will be on hormone therapy for a long, long time.

"And now, thank God, I am fully recovered. I am healthy, with no surgical complications whatsoever. And, I am healed in more ways than you could ever know.

"Affirming myself as a woman is a dream come true. I wrestled with it. I talked to God about it. And after three really good, but long years on Iona, my self-help efforts paid off.

"I like me. The new me. Aoife, the loving, caring, sensitive, nurturing, mystical woman I've always known myself to be. I am proud to be a woman.

Proud to be seen and known as a woman—finally! I am comfortable and wholly at peace with my decision to transition.

"My doubts and fears have been replaced by self-confidence, conviction, and affirmation. And self-love. I couldn't ask for anything more."

Aoife reached for the teapot. She so wanted the comfort and the healing powers of tea. Zahryn filled her own cup as well. Aromatic wafts of cardamom and the Earl graced the space between them.

With encouragement in her voice, Zahryn offered, "Thank you, Aoife, for sharing all of this with me. It must have been so hard keeping your story safe. I am so glad you decided to share it with me. My heart goes out to you.

"Did you confide in anyone? Family? Friends? Teachers? Guidance counselors?" There was no urgency in Zahryn's voice, only genuine empathy. She did not want to sound like she was interrogating her friend.

"That's a whole other story. My parents were not receptive at all. They were hurt. Judgmental. Afraid of what the neighbors would say or think. My sharing of my story with them essentially fractured our family. We broke apart. They know I've transitioned, but we don't talk much at all. They still don't really know what to say."

"Well that's just awful!" Zahryn raised her voice. "Did they not support you at all?"

"Not one bit. I went it all alone. Financially, surgically, and emotionally. Thank God I have my faith. God is a really good listener. No judgment. No back talk or criticism. Just safety and trust and love.

"And you know, as much as I feel that God led me through my self-discovery and my discernment, I think I've come to realize something really big! That God truly let me make my own decisions. I knew and I felt God's unconditional love, all throughout my growing up years. Boy or girl. Man or woman. Didn't matter. I knew God loved me just as I was, and, just as I knew I needed to be.

"You know, for a while after my bottom surgery, I went through some pretty heavy stuff. Guilt. Shame. I actually looked upon my new womanly-self as an imposter. A fake. A pretend woman. I was pretty emotionally raw, and I was damn hard on myself. I never, ever doubted the choices I made, but the imposter feeling was real. Scary real. But, as time went on, those negative thoughts just went away by the wayside. And I began to flourish. Now I am happy and content and whole as a woman. I am NOT a fake. I AM a woman. This IS the real me. Life is good now."

Still missing a few details, Zahryn wanted more. But she did not want to pose any questions to Aoife that would seem offensive. Or, God forbid, she did not want to ask Aoife anything that she was unprepared to answer. Zahryn wanted to respect Aoife's personal privacy in every possible way.

"Aoife, you look happy and you sound happy, and you tell me that you're happy. Please do not read any judgment into my next question! Please, don't think I am judging you or your choices—'cause I am not!"

Aoife raised her eyebrows and braced herself for Zahryn's question.

Zahryn asked plainly, "Do you have any regrets?"

Aoife sighed with relief. This was a question she was comfortable answering. She leaned back in her chair and said with conviction, "No, Zahryn. No. None at all. I am whole. I love myself, my choices, my life, and my womanhood. I am finally at home in my own body. And Zahryn, that is just a fine question. A fair question. I don't feel judged. I do feel heard, and valued and accepted by you. I never, ever, feared your response to my story. I've only ever feared my finding the right time and place and the courage to tell you! But, I've done that now. Loads lifted. You have no idea how free I feel, having just shared my story. Let's vow from now on, to keep a No Secrets Pact for our friendship. That way we can always be there for each other and help each other as needs arise. How's that? Truth and honesty are everything."

"Okay! Pact! Yes!" Zahryn said. As different as their lives were, even more so now in the light of sharing truths, the two young women were so similar in attitudes, in approach, in spirituality, and in their moral matrices.

"Aoife, I am so sorry that you have had such a dark and difficult journey. I completely understand darkness. Believe me, I do. But, you have persevered and your conquering spirit has brought you through to the other side, from darkness to Light. I am so proud of how you managed your journey! Yes! You need to be your own person! Yes! You need to honor your own feelings, and feel good about owning them. You have a basic human right to be who you are and to express yourself freely, whatever that looks like for you. God loves you and will not judge the decisions you needed to make. God is a compassionate God and you are His. You are a child of God. You are blessed and beloved, no matter what."

Zahryn paused and gazed at her friend, in her vibrant femininity—in her vibrant wholeness. Aoife was now so relaxed, settled, and visibly freed of her fears, her burdens. She was smiling!

Zahryn spoke with urgency and excitement. "Can we hug?"

Aoife got up quickly from her chair, took a few steps toward Zahryn, and bent down to hug her friend, right there in her chair. Blonde curly bob meets cascading locks. Long strong arms meet lean lithe body. Woman meets woman. Love meets love. The hug certainly sealed their understanding and their trust. The hug symbolized the strength of their friendship. It was affirming.

Aoife broke away, returning to her own chair, while playfully taunting Zahryn. "Well my friend, aren't you going to ask me the big question? The really big question?" She smiled ever so broadly, with eyes twinkling.

Zahryn bought the invitation. "Okay Aoife! Here goes nothin'! Have you had sex with a man yet?" They both giggled nervously, like two naïve school girls exploring the world of sexuality—finding words for their own bodies and their private pleasures.

"Yes! I mean, yes that IS the big question! But, the answer is in fact, no. If and when I find a guy who I feel totally safe with, and who knows my story, and who'll still want to be with me, then, we'll explore that journey together. I'm still hopeful!"

Zahryn smiled. "Good for you, Aoife! I wish you all the best. Keep me posted!"

Aoife grinned ever so slyly and said, "I will." Then she shifted topics. "So, we still have lots of tea and lots of time. What's next in line to talk about?"

Zahryn started in. "Well, I'm gonna make you talk some more—a lot more! Tell me more about your travels to Iona, Scotland. I know you loved it there. I so want to live there, if only for a short term. Maybe a volunteer work-away term. But, I am limited, you know, by my medical stuff. It's a long way to get off the island to get medical help on the mainland. Ferry, bus, and ferry again, just to get to the mainland.

"Tell me something about Iona that you haven't shared with me yet. Something you learned, or felt, or experienced, or witnessed. Something that someone said that resonated with you. Something that stirred you deeply."

"Well," Aoife paused. "That is a wonderful lead, a beautiful wide-open question. Wow! How do I start to answer that?" She collected her thoughts while she sat with the Earl.

"I arrived to work on Iona after I graduated with my journalism degree in the summer of 2008. I went there for an extended work-away experience. There were students and young people from all over the world choosing to do their work-away time on Iona. Young people from New Zealand. Brazil. Africa. Germany. Norway. Even Canada and Iceland. It was so cross-cultural, so ecumenical and inclusive.

"I traveled there alone, and lived there alone, but over the next three years, I met up with many pilgrims to the island. They'd all come by ferry from mainland Scotland, and they'd stay for a weekend or for a week. Sometimes even two weeks. They'd all go on a nine-mile guided hike around the island. They'd take classes with various poets and scholars of the ancient

Celtic wisdom. They'd all worship in the Abbey, and in Oran Chapel, at varied times throughout the day.

"There are many artists, poets, and writers living on the island. What a beautiful vibrant community who choose to share their artistic and spiritual gifts with all. In real short order—like in just a few weeks—I really came to feel like I was part of the Iona Community. I felt like I truly belonged. I felt the strong ancestral draw of the rugged Hebridean lands. I felt the powerful undercurrent—the call to action for peace and for justice. I felt the wonders and the depth of the ancient Celtic Wisdom, in their overt yet deep-rooted compassion and respect for all life and living. My eyes were opened and my heart grew. I know I became more fully human through my time on Iona by living in their faithful, reverential, peace-loving ways. They indeed opened the eyes of my heart."

Zahryn loved listening to her friend speak about her travels—the people, the places, and the minute details of her story. Zahryn sat back, ready and eager to listen for more story, more meaning, more lessons in life and love.

"Two great stories come to mind now. I'll tell you 'The Communion Story' first." Aoife reached for her cuppa, and sipped a slow and pensive sip. "The communion chalice and plate at the Iona Abbey were ceramic. They were thrown on a pottery wheel by a local artisan there on the island. They were hefty, solid pieces, with curious seafoam and teal-green colored glazes.

"I remember one night walking to the 9 o'clock communion service, in silence, among others who were walking toward the Abbey in silence, too. There is a large, free-standing High Cross—the St John's Cross—just outside the Abbey. It stood tall and stark in the twilight. It was an awe-evoking moment, simply passing by that Cross, knowing and sensing the power of its inherent message over the ages. That moment of awe had put me into a wonderful heartset and mindset. Maybe I'd even stretch my words to say 'faithset.' I was in a spacious and expansive and open state of being, but I hadn't taken this all in. It took me a really long time down the road to unpack my feelings of that moment and of my experience during that particular communion service.

"So, the communion service is Christian, ecumenical, and much of the liturgy, prayers, and songs are written by members of the Iona Community themselves. They have compiled their own Iona Community Hymnbook, which contains both traditional and contemporary hymns. There was an organ instrumental piece being played at the very beginning of the candlelit service, during a time of reflection. The piece played was a well-known score written by J. S. Bach, *Sheep May Safely Graze.*

"The melody was so familiar, so pastoral. It grounded me. The lyrics instantly flooded into my consciousness. I had sung them often in our own hometown church choir as a special anthem for Sunday services. 'Sheep may safely graze and pasture, in a watchful Shepherd's sight.' I repeated these lyrics over and over and over as the organ continued to play the lengthy piece.

"And, I couldn't help but visualize all of the sheep and the tiny little lambs grazing in the barrens out in the wilds of the Hebridean lands, under the watchful care of a gentle loving shepherd. They felt safe. I felt safe. All was well. All was good with the sheep and shepherds. All was well with me.

"But the best is still yet to come. The cumulative, or compounded effect of the silence, the cross in the twilight, the music, the images of the sheep in the safety of their shepherd, the reverence of the moment—all of this was priming me for what was about to happen."

As Aoife spoke, Zahryn began to feel that she too was in the Abbey, in the Sanctuary, in the candlelit pew, with her friend, waiting for communion. Aoife's storytelling was powerful.

Aoife paused. "You know, in some church communion settings, you walk up to the Chancel to receive the bread and wine. But, in the Abbey, in the evenings, their practice was to pass the elements, one person to the other. You receive the plate of bread from the person on your left, and you partake of the bread, praying words that are customary for you. You then take the plate and serve the bread to the person on your right. When that's done, you turn to your left again, and the person on your left then serves you the chalice and the linen, you partake and wipe, and then you serve the person on your right.

"It is upon this moment, the very moment I received the chalice, that this story is centered. When I received, in my two hands, the handmade teal colored ceramic chalice containing the red wine, I gasped immediately. In that moment, the almost half-full chalice WEIGHED A TON! A veritable ton! I wasn't expecting the weight and my hands, forearms, and whole upper arms tensed up so tightly so as not to drop the Sacred cup. I then felt something—something profound—something exquisite settling in my midst. That feeling too, was heavy, but at the same time, lightweight and ethereal. It was a presence. I say it was a Holy Moment. I know that God made his Holy Presence known to me in the simple receiving of the cup.

Aoife continued, speaking freely, comfortably. "This is a communion practice to which I am fully accustomed and with which I am wholly comfortable. It was familiar. This was the first time ever, that God revealed his presence—in the weight and in the thinness—the cup was heavy and the veil was thin as I sat in Sacred Presence—as I communed with God of my heart.

"There is no more to this story than this. In God's time, in a Holy Moment, God gifted me with his Presence. There were no words. He had no verbal message for me. My takeaway message however, was deep, profound beyond words, weightier than my fullest comprehension. I knew—I affirmed in that moment—that God is with me. And I firmly believe that it is always up to me to be open and awakened to his Presence, to seek his Presence, and then to know his Presence. *The thinness—the Thin Place—is all up to me and to my state of being.*

"That evening, I was open. I was open to the Presence of God. And I carry the weight of the chalice, the weight of the symbolism, and the weight of the Holy Moment in my heart, always."

Aoife raised her teacup, and sipped, and simply sat in blissful contentment in the stillness between them.

Zahryn sat quietly by the window. She slowly moved forward to pour more hot tea from her cardamom pot into her empty teacup. She lifted the dainty, wee teacup to her lips with one hand, noting its feather-weight. She tried to imagine just how surprising it would have been to have experienced the unexpected weight—the heavy weight of the chalice, in the mystical, enlightening, Holy manner that Aoife had, so long ago in the Abbey. It was a moment to remember for sure. Aoife had found the Presence of God, in a Holy Moment, during Holy Communion.

A quiet enveloped the young women. Time moved on, yet seemed to pause, to linger. Unrehearsed, they shared a moment attuning to the Sacred in their midst, attuning to the Sacredness of one another, attuning to the Sacredness of all time and Eternity. When Zahryn would later reflect on this time with Aoife, she would acknowledge that this teatime at Lumana too, was truly a Holy Moment.

Zahryn broke the shared silence, saying, "Thank you Aoife. I will recount your story over and over again in my heart. In listening to your story, I felt what what you felt. I was drawn into the Sacredness of your experience. You really need to keep on in your career of storytelling and writing, sharing all that is on your heart. You are a born journalist. You have a gift. You are Sacred."

Aoife responded slowly, "You know, Zahryn, it's not all me. Honestly. Thank you, but not every soul who hears that story responds to it like you just did. You're truly open and receptive to the Sacred in your midst. I've seen this in you before in our conversations. You have an inherent wisdom, a depth, and an insight into humanity that draws me to you. You have a gift."

A thought flashed through Zahryn's mind, and impulsively she decided to share it with Aoife. "You know Aoife, this is going to sound kind of off topic. But, it is truly an extension of what you just said. You already know that blackbirds are full of symbolism. We've talked about this before. And, I've been doing some interesting reading over the past few months. I just learned something else that is so mystical—kind of out there. They say *'a blackbird is a metaphor for an awakening on a deeper level.'* Whether this is truth, or whether the source is Celtic legend or from an ancient sage, or even a lively bard spinning a tall tale, who knows! But I thought of you, Aoife, when I heard about the metaphor."

Aoife replied with great intrigue. "Oh, it's amazing that you should say that! It's so unusual. You know, I am strangely drawn to flocks of blackbirds. They have an energy, a presence. It's palpable. The very sight of a large flock of blackbirds can simply fill you up with love!"

Zahryn spoke softly in agreement. "Yeah, I know! My Auntie Claire once told me that too!"

Aoife was right there on Zahryn's wavelength with her. "I think *you*, *Zahryn*, are so very awakened to people and to energy and to life, on a really deep level, on a whole different plane than most folks. In your awakened-ness, you have a way of responding on a deeper level to people, places and times. Just like you responded now to my communion chalice story."

Zahryn lightened up the moment, smiling broadly. "Did you just call me a blackbird? Haha! Just kidding. I know you're being serious!"

They chuckled as they each took the beautiful blackbird metaphor into their mystical minds to store there, ready for a revisit or reflection someday down the road.

Aoife paused. "I need to stand up and stretch for a moment. I have another special story to share, but let's take a break. Do you want to stand up too? Can I help?"

Zahryn nodded and the two got busy, swinging Zahryn's legs out from under the table. Aoife helped Zahryn to stand tall, steadying her by placing her own two hands on Zahryn's hips.

"Oh that feels good to stand. Get my circulation going. We've been sitting here, in stillness for a while."

A few minutes passed while they stood, stretched, took a few deep breaths, and eventually resettled in their chairs. A seventh inning stretch is always welcomed.

"How's your teapot, Aoife?"

Aoife touched the pot under the tartan tea cozy. "Still good and warm. Still lots. And yours?"

Zahryn made the same checks under the cozy. She lifted the pot to confirm its fullness, and said, "Yup. All good. So, Aoife, you said you have a second story to share. Do we have time to hear it?" She checked her watch.

It was 4:15 p.m. "We've got forty-five minutes. Can we do this? I'd love to hear more about Iona!"

"Yes, I think so. This isn't really a story, per se. It's just some random observations I made while on Iona.

Zahryn smiled. "I'm all ears!"

Aoife began. "So many people go to Iona, longing to find the true meaning of a Thin Place—and perhaps even to come away from the Island having experienced one. It was one of the things that I was open to explore while I was there, and after a while, I came to my own evolving understanding of a Thin Place. And yes, indeed, I experienced this, but not in any way I could ever have imagined."

Zahryn leaned forward, listening attentively. Her curiosity was piquing. "I know a little about Thin Places, but I'm keen to hear your story! I too am evermore and always searching for Thin Places in my life and in my living. Please tell me more!"

Aoife went on. "Well, maybe I can help you feel out a Thin Place in a whole new way, if you'd like—a potential 'hook' for your own experiential learning?"

Zahryn lifted up her words. "I love it! Talk to me! Tell me! Show me!" Her exuberance shimmered like an aura. Aoife saw this and she held the sight of Zahryn's Light in her heart.

"One day on Iona, I walked with a lovely Australian pilgrim. We were virtual strangers, but we had an in-depth conversation as we traversed windswept grassy meadows and climbed rocky hillocks.

"We sat and watched the tide receding. The waves on the shore were rather quiet, despite the howling high winds we encountered in the upper meadows. The perpetual running waves gently lapped upon the shore and then receded into oceanic oblivion.

"In this incredibly rugged place, we talked about some pretty sensitive stuff. Like what love and compassion look like today in a changing world. We talked about mothers, the mothering spirit, and the unconditional-ness of motherlove. We found comfort in hearing each others' stories. We talked about how the sense of our mothers' presence is something like God's presence—always with us. Everpresent."

Aoife stretched both arms up over her head, and took in a long, deliberately slow breath then returned her hands to her lap. "And this—this is the heart of this story, right here. At the end of our hike, just before we reentered the village of Iona, she handed me something. She placed it gently into the palm of my hand. It was a weathered, water-washed, heart-shaped stone that she had picked up along the way! It was grey with concentric rings of rose-gold colored glittering fragments. She said, 'This is my gift to you. You helped me find a Thin Place. You are a Thin Place, Evan! Your heart is a Thin Place! Your love, given freely, is truly a Thin Place for those who are open to see it.'"

Aoife paused, gathering her thoughts. "You know Zahryn, she blew me away with that heart-shaped stone, and with her gratitude, and heartfelt words. I truly think she was a modern-day seer or a sage. I felt something— she touched something way down deep inside of me. Her words and their meanings were solid, but there was an echo, a resonance within them. She was a gift to me, delivering the wisdom and insight I needed to move forward in my own understanding of Thin Places.

"A Thin Place is NOT a geographical place. It is not topographical either. It's relational! It is a state of being—a state of intimate relationship held by one with the Divine. It is a state of openness, readiness, reverence, and oneness, all cultivated by one in the Presence of the Divine. That pilgrim, through our conversations, had developed a really good sense of who I am and the reverence I hold for the Sacred. And, she could see that 'I see with the eyes of my heart'. She was open to this and concluded that I was the Thin Place that she was looking for! Me! She overwhelmed me with these words, and I am still mulling over them today.

"And right here in this moment . . . " Aoife looked straight into Zahryn's eyes. "I'll bring the richness of this insight into our own here and now! You, Zahryn, are the Thin Place! Your heart and your love is the Thin Place, known only to those who seek this. You are Sacred and Holy. I can come into God's Presence through you. You are my Thin Place."

All Zahryn could do was take in Aoife's words. They were loaded and profound. They were gift, music to Zahryn's heart and soul. She knew she needed to spend more time in Aoife's words, wisdom, and exquisite story.

"Aoife, that is incredible!" Zahryn said quietly. That is so powerful— connecting openness and readiness with Thin Place and love. It is an epiphany. It is ancient Celtic Wisdom arising to nurture my open and receptive heart. I have no more words. Can I hug you? Are you tired yet of my hugs?"

Aoife got up again to bend down and hold Zahryn in a warm embrace. It was 5 p.m. Best teatime ever!

A Mother's Love and Lament

TUESDAY AUGUST 1, 2005

LEGENDS TELL US so much about the Ben Lonrach—the Shimmering Mountains. Stories of olde tell of the mountains being aglow by the Light of random precious gemstones found in the region, in the heights throughout all time. The town names of Moonstone Cove, Shinever Rock and Amberleigh come to mind, all alive in their own Light. Celtic legend also says "Souls, impassioned souls, forever light the world."

Enya was at home in Opalon, seated comfortably on a rocker on her wide-open veranda. She was gazing out into the unobstructed vastness, over the Celtic Sea. The blue sky and the horizon were uninterrupted by clouds or boats or outlying rocky islands. Enya was radiant with anticipation as she eagerly awaited the arrival of her houseguest.

A car pulled up in her laneway and she recognized the driver immediately—her older sister! She quickly got up to greet her, noting the warmth of the air—the gently moving summer air. It felt oh so fresh on her face. It was literally a welcomed breeze bringing a welcomed guest.

"Hi Paige! Thanks for coming all the way to Opalon to stay with me. We'll have a nice few days here together, to visit and get all caught up. Girls' Week! I miss you, Sis! It's been pretty quiet around here for a year now, since Maeve moved in with you! Kinda lonely."

She held the door, allowing her sister to enter her home. Paige plunked her suitcase and her handbag down onto the floor in the hallway. The sisters wasted no time. They threw their arms around each other instinctively. Reminiscently. They were close. So very close. And they were so happy to be together.

Enya broke away and moved Paige's suitcase to a bench by the staircase. She then beckoned for Paige to follow her into the kitchen. "Iced tea?"

Paige answered quickly, "Yes please, thanks! And you know, Enya, you'll be happy to hear that May-vee's come a long way. She's made a few friends. She has settled down in a big way and I'm so thankful for that. She can be a handful, mind you!

"I think she's gotten in with some good kids. They really seem to care about her. Not like the love-'er and leave-'er pals she had here in Opalon. She doesn't say much about that time—her pregnancy and such. But she did say, when she first came to stay with me, that she felt lost and totally abandoned, especially by those she thought were her friends."

Enya nodded in affirmation, while pouring two tall glasses of iced tea. "Well, I'm sure she felt that—that abandonment—from me as well. She made the same mistake I did, getting pregnant so young, and I could see her whole future collapsing because of it. I wanted so much more for her. I know because I lived it myself—twenty years old and single to boot. It was such a long struggle to finish my university degree part-time after that, what with a tiny baby, and later a toddler, to look out for. And, thank God I did finish. It got me a good career in teaching, but I'm afraid I've blown it with my own daughter."

Paige walked on eggshells with her next words. No one needed to hear judgment, feel judgment, or be the judge. "May-vee was hurt, Enya. Really hurt. First, she was mad at me about letting it slip about who her father was. Then she was mad at the world for keeping her paternity a secret for so long. I'll regret that awkward conversation—when May-vee first found out who her father was—I'll regret it for the rest of my life. If only I could take it all back. But, I can't.

"So. Here we are. Both of us. Carrying burdens that are weighing us down. And what are we going to do? We're both living with our shame and big-time regrets. I honestly don't think it is up to either one of us to change or explain, or spin or soften any of this situation. I think May-vee just needs time—a whole lotta time—to come around to see the whole picture. Maybe, down the road, she'll come to us, to you anyway, and voice what is weighty and troublesome on her heart. They say time heals."

"How was she yesterday?" Enya asked anxiously. "Yesterday, July 31, would have been her little girl's first birthday. I'm sure it was a rough day for her. I can't imagine not being able to celebrate all of the little milestones with your own child. She's never even heard her baby's voice or cry, except for maybe in the delivery room, before the baby was whisked away in an incubator, to another room."

Enya paused, and looked down at the floor. "I feel so guilty. I made her give up her baby for adoption. It was my shame and my anger and my crushed hopes for her that changed her life forever. She didn't get to be a mom. She never held her own child. She never even saw her own baby. She must think I am the most awful person in the world to do that to her."

Again, Paige searched for the softest words possible. She knew her thirty-seven-year-old little sister was hurting badly and was terribly guilt-ridden. "She doesn't hate you, Enya. I know that in my heart. You're her mother. She doesn't like the situation she got herself into, nor does she like the outcome. I think she's more mad than hateful, if that helps at all. Hopefully she'll let go of her angers, and she'll move on with a new purpose in life. She'll find her stride again. There's a whole wide world out there just waiting for her. She's very kind. And street-smart—savvy. I'm sure she'll put all of this behind her and make good in her life. She'll not be lost forever. I hope and pray."

Paige continued, "And, as for the baby, May-vee said that she wants to believe that her little girl is living with a family who truly wants to love her and to give her a beautiful life. She said that believing in this is what gets her by, day by day. This is what gives her comfort, and hope, and the will to carry on.

"And yes, yesterday would have been especially hard on her. She was up and gone to work before I even got up. And I was out late last evening, picking up last minute things to pack, to come here. I didn't see her last evening at all. So, I'm sure she got through it. She has a close friend, Zahryn, who lives in town, in Moonstone Cove. I bet the two of them were together, drinking tea yesterday, talking it out, together."

Enya gasped and then lit into Paige with rapid-fire questions. "Zahryn? Inglis? Walker-Inglis? Connor's kid? Oh my! That's a little close for comfort! Does she know? Do they know? That they are sisters—half-sisters anyway? I wonder if Maeve said anything to Zahryn about their dad? How did Maeve and Zahryn come to meet? How'd they become friends?

"Oh my God! Poor May-vee! Shouldering all of these secrets, all alone! Connor, he is—he was—such a great guy! He's changed a lot of people's lives though, with his flirting and his fooling around. He needed to keep his zipper done up. It started even before he married Rose, you know. I wonder if Rose ever even knew, or if she went to her grave still believing in her husband's faithfulness and love?

"Oh! I'm asking so many questions that will never, ever be answered."

Enya quickly changed the subject, and turned with a small, sly smile to her sister. "Paige, do you remember when we were little kids, Great Aunt Maisie would tell us about *the secrets and the legends of the men in the mountains?* I know she didn't tell us everything, because we were way too young to understand. But, she did say over and over to us to 'watch out for the dark-eyed boys. They don't know their fathers. None of them do. And they don't know discipline. They are all kind of wild. They've never had a father in their homes and they all walk a bit on the wild side.'"

Paige replied, chuckling. "Yes, I do remember. And, I'm sure there is some truth to her stories. She was full of little pearls of wisdom. And you know what? I think you're right! She *is* the one who first told us both about the Sullivans—about the dark-eyed boys. They're from a town in the upper Ben Lonrach called Sullivan's Gate. The main bridge over a creek there was built by a farmer named Jack Sullivan in the 1800's. The guy who comes to the pub these days, to Pints—well, he is Jack Sullivan's great nephew. His name too, is Jack Sullivan, but he only ever goes by Sully. 'Ol' Sully' folks call him.

"And, Ol' Sully was a drinking buddy of Connor's until Connor died so suddenly. A generation apart they were, but they were tight, tight, tight. Thick as thieves. Aye, they were both dark-eyed and there was a dark side to both of them, Connor and Sully. Not all as plain as they seem."

Paige stopped to sip on her iced tea, and then continued with her recollections. "A little wild they were, in the sauce—in the booze. Especially after Connor's wife died in childbirth. They'd been literally sowin' their wild oats all around these parts for years. There's a whole lot of kids out there by different moms. They say it's Sully's Secret—Sully's Secret Charms. They might as well say it though—it's Connor's Charms as well! There's a good lot of boys and girls who don't know their daddy, who only know their mama's love."

Enya was listening to her sister, fully aware of the dark-eyed men. Her mind wandered to a few she knew, but she then quickly tuned in again to Paige's tale.

Paige said, "I don't know why they did it. I don't know how they got away with it! The moms usually moved away to another town to have their babies, and raise them. Some gave their kids up for adoption. Some raised them on their own. Story is, there's hundreds of them. The dark-eyed boys and girls. To some, this is truth. Like, for Connor and you, and your sweet May-vee. To others, it's just fantasy and mystery—and nonsense. And for most, it's just a legend. We live in the supposed "Mountains of Secrets." And us Celtic folks, we do love our legends!" Paige smiled and let her words lift into air. Her words drifted on, away, away, away.

Enya sat quietly. She paused momentarily from listening to Paige, and this time she allowed the heaviness, the reality of the legend, to swell in her heart. She broke into tears.

Paige put down her iced tea and strode over to console her sister. She held her tenderly. Enya's shoulders heaved again, and she melted into Paige's arms. She broke out in a tsunami of tears, of guilt and shame, of grief and inadequacy—and self-imposed self-worthlessness. She had not shared her emotional pain with anyone for so very long. The tears came down. She sunk into Paige's loving embrace.

They didn't say a word. There was nothing to say in the moment. Enya's tears fell down like a mountain stream finding its way to the sea.

The sisters stood together as one, in a locked-in embrace. They both knew the story, word for word. They knew the characters—all of them—intimately. They were now just the audience, spectators watching, powerless to change anything. They held on tight, wondering if the tumultuous storm would ever pass, and if it did, where on earth would they find the strength to face the aftermath? Would there be more such fearsome storms ahead?

They held each other in love. They shone their Lights together, in their darkness. Light and sisterly love would help them find their way.

Fighting Words

"ZAHRYN, MY DEAR," THE school secretary beckoned, "the principal will see you now." She opened the big oak door wider to allow Zahryn to pass by her, into the office.

Zahryn stepped into the scary room. She had been summoned to the principal's office—called out of her very first class of the day, Tuesday—and escorted to the principal's office. She had never been called there before. Ever.

Zahryn was quite tall for her twelve years, but everything in the scary room seemed to be bigger and taller. The built-in bookcases to her right were floor-to-ceiling height. They were filled with oversized manuals, binders and books. The school itself was old, with high and lofty ceilings.

The ceiling in the office was also vaulted and domed and way, way, way up there. In her panic, in her fear, Zahryn imagined that their voices would sound hollow or distorted, and echo in the room. But the books covering the walls served to buffer and absorb the sound. Their voices actually sounded quite normal.

"You asked to see me, Mr. O'Shea? I mean, Sir?" Zahryn posed her statement as a timid question. She was shaking and her tummy was churning and her hands were icy cold.

"Please come in Zahryn. Mrs. Johnson, would you please come in with Zahryn, and close the door? Please, both of you, take a seat."

Zahryn turned and looked nervously at the school secretary, Mrs. Johnson, who smiled and motioned to Zahryn to sit in one of the large old oak chairs in front of Mr. O'Shea's big oak desk. The tall straight-back chairs were prominently grained on the armrest. There were no seat cushions.

Zahryn sat down, sitting up tall. She pushed herself back, all the way to the back of the chair, allowing her feet to rest flat on the floor. Her hands landed in her lap, clasped tightly. They were still cold. Mrs. Johnson was calm, and she sat down quietly, in the chair beside Zahryn.

Mr. O'Shea sat back briefly in his big brown leather chair. It looked comfy—cushy, anyway. He slowly loosened his tie and then leaned forward in earnest. His elbows and forearms rested on his grand oak desk. "How are you doing these days, Zahryn? Are you enjoying being in First Year Junior?"

Zahryn looked startled. She struggled a bit with her words. "I'm good. School is good. First Year is good." is all she got out.

Mr. O'Shea continued, "Are you happy, Zahryn? I mean, are you every-day-kind-of-happy? Is anything or anyone bothering you?" He knew that Zahryn was a very good student, that she liked school and liked people, but he was concerned about an incident that had happened just the day before.

A boy student named Delaney had come to him yesterday to complain about Zahryn's behavior in the schoolyard at recess.

Zahryn looked puzzled. She was unsure why she was being called into the principal's office to talk about her happiness. She simply said, "No. I'm good. I'm happy."

"Well then, Zahryn, I am concerned. A student told me you kicked him in the shin yesterday. Hard. So hard that he cried. He admits that he called you a name, but that you kicked him intentionally hard, and just stood there and stared at him when he was crying. Can you tell me what happened?"

The principal's facial expression showed his genuine concern, not judgment or contempt. He simply wanted to hear both sides of the story before saying anything further. He remained leaning forward on his desk, eager to hear her words.

Zahryn mustered a stronger, louder, voice. "Did he tell you WHAT he said to me? He did not call ME a name! He called MY DAD a name! And my dad is dead. And the name he called him sounded really bad. And I don't want to hear anything bad about my dad. He's my hero and he's gone. He died. And, he's not here for me to ask him what the bad word meant!"

Concerned, and still needing to know the whole truth, Mr. O'Shea said, "Well Zahryn, what did Delaney actually say to you?"

"He yelled at me—he came right up close to my face and he shouted, 'It's a good thing your dad is dead because he was an f-ing man-whore.' Maybe he said man-o'-war. I don't know what either of those words mean, and I'm not sure I even heard him right. But he used the f-word in a mean way so the other words are probably bad words too. I'm not going to let anyone call my dad bad names. So, I kicked him in the shin. And yeah, I hurt him. But he hurt me first!"

Zahryn's mouth went dry, remembering the kick. Her right big toe hurt, in the moment, in the remembering. She stared straight back at Mr. O'Shea, waiting to hear about a punishment.

Mr. O'Shea sat back for just a moment. "Are you sure that's what Delaney said?" He asked in a kind voice.

"Yes! Would you please tell me what it means?! What is a man-whore? Or a man-o'-war? My father was a kind man, and wanted nothing to do with war. War made him angry. All the countries fighting over the years just made him sick. He liked peace. He used to say that there's always a better way to settle things than by going to war."

Mr. O'Shea looked directly at Mrs. Johnson, who had remained silent throughout the conversation. She did not offer any comment. He took in a slow breath, and spoke with encouragement in his voice.

"Well Zahryn, you do have good reason to be upset. No one should ever speak or shout unkind words about another, especially after they die. And people—kids especially—sometimes use a word in a sentence before they even know what the word really means. The f-word is one example. And both man-whore and man-o'-war are not particularly nice words either. They are adult words. And Delaney should not be speaking of things of which he has little or no understanding. Nor should he be doing any name-calling.

"You all learned a rhyme when you were in kindergarten. Do you remember?"

Zahryn piped up immediately, "Sticks and stones can break my bones, but names will never hurt me." Is *that* what you mean Mr. O'Shea? That *I* need to learn a lesson—that name-calling can't hurt me? Well it did! It did hurt me! It hurt my father too. And if Delaney were to say it again, I'd kick him again!"

Mr. O'Shea desperately wanted to avoid explaining the meaning of Delaney's words to Zahryn. He stood up abruptly saying, "Zahryn, please stand up."

Zahryn almost leaped to her feet, fearing that her plaintive words, her vocal outburst, were going to cost her. Mrs. Johnson rose beside her, in solidarity, and placed her arm around Zahryn's shoulders.

"Zahryn, I totally appreciate your honesty today. We adults, we call that 'candor.' I appreciate that you told me the truth—the facts—and, exactly how you feel about the facts. And I can tell that all of this has upset you.

"I'm not going to punish you. I am going to call Delaney to the office, and I will have words. I will have some very special teaching for him. He needs to know that he has truly hurt you. He needs to be more considerate of other people's feelings.

"In future, Zahryn, please choose to use your words, not your foot. If someone makes you angry, take a breath, a deep breath, and remember that name-calling rhyme that you already know so well. Then find a way to simply walk away, without hurting them back. You don't have to hurt the ones who hurt you. That's not the way the world is supposed to work. You're a big girl now. You can do this!"

He looked at Zahryn with direct eye contact. She had taken in his every word. Defiance had left her visage, and wisdom now registered in her big, sage-green eyes. She was indeed wise beyond her years, yet still very young, and so very naïve.

"Thank you, Mr. O'Shea for not punishing me. Sorry for kicking Delaney, but, he deserved it."

"You're welcome Zahryn. We're done in here for now. Mrs. Johnson, would you take Zahryn back to her class? Thanks.

"And by the way, Zahryn, if anyone asks you why you were called to the office, you do not have to tell them anything. You do not have to tell anyone what Delaney said or did. That's between you and Delaney. My lips are sealed. Mrs. Johnson's lips are sealed. No one needs to know. Are you okay with this?"

"I'm not telling anyone. I don't want to bring any shame to my father's name. He's my hero, and I still love him!"

On that, she turned and left the office, with Mrs. Johnson following to escort her, closing the door behind her.

Chester O'Shea sat down on his big chair, letting out a loud, heavy sigh. He swiveled the chair so he could face out the floor-to-ceiling window.

He knew that sadly, young Delaney had the power with his feisty words, to open a giant can of worms in the school, in the community, on the island. The mountains of secrets remained as yet, unrevealed. He himself only knew some of the secrets of the Ben Lonrach—the elephants in the adult rooms of Moonstone Cove. He knew that his forthcoming disciplinary words in this Delaney mess, in this man-whore mess, would need a certain diplomacy and a sure-fire degree of tact. It would require discretion and *savoir faire*. And prayer. He quietly bowed his head and prayed.

Lowland Delights

IT WAS 10 A.M. on a Friday morning in Glasgow, leading into the last weekend of Autumn Reading Week. Gaelan turned his car key and the engine sputtered a bit as it came to life.

Zahryn buckled her seatbelt on the passenger side and said, "Gaelan, thanks for inviting me for a drive! Where are we going?"

"Stirlingshire. Ever been there?"

"Yes—as a child. My father took me to Aberfoyle and to the Stirling Castle. It's pretty all around there."

Gaelan smiled. "Well, I thought maybe a daytrip—Balloch on Loch Lomond, Aberfoyle, Stirling, and back to Glasgow. We'd have lunch at the castle, and then we'll follow our noses through the roads less traveled. The scenic route. You game?"

"Perfect!" said Zahryn. "This will be fun!"

"So, Zahryn, It's about forty-five minutes to Balloch, on the western shores of Loch Lomond. Wanna go for a boat ride around the Loch—maybe an hour or so? Then find our way to Stirling for lunch?"

"Sounds great, Gaelan. It'll be sunny all day. I've got my wool cape in my bag. It will keep me warm on the boat."

They drove in silence. Gaelan's Mini Cooper had a small but cozy interior. They were both really tall people and their shoulders were touching as they drove the twisted country roads. The terrain was clearly lowland and wide open. The roadside views were of shared paddocks for goats and kids, grazing meadows for Highland cows—hairy coos—and scattered small farmsteads. They slowed down as they passed through tiny villages, burghs and steadings. Evidence of old croft stone fences lined the lands. And sheep—so many sheep!

The topography began to roll a bit as they approached Balloch. The countryside was picturesque, even pastoral—straight out of a wordsmithed passage in a Celtic romance novel.

They saw the sign for the boat tours and the docks. Zahryn said, "Don't you just love seeing the ancient Gaelic town names listed alongside the modern town names on all of the road signage? It gives me a real sense of the ancientness of this place—of times of yore and yesteryear."

"The Scots are really proud of their heritage. Their language. Their faith and their beliefs. It's been a stormy and storied past here in the UK, what with Viking and Norse and French and Roman influences—invaders. Everyone came here looking for new land, a new life, and a new world to conquer and claim as their own. I'm so glad that the ancient peoples—the Druids, Picts, Celts, and Gaels—were *eventually* able to maintain and celebrate their cultural identity through the ages. What about you, Gaelan?"

Gaelan had been listening to Zahryn, but more than anything, he was tuning in to her passion. Her awareness of person, place, and time in history. *No wonder she's studying the Humanities. She 'sees' people,* he thought. *She's interested in them as a whole—personalities, historical context, relationships and community spirit, through all time.*

He answered her slowly. "I haven't thought about it much, Zahryn. I'm a numbers guy. But you are a people person, for sure. And you are so aware of the bigger picture for people, places, and times. Were you always like this, or is this truly your studies bringing out the best in you?" He turned and smiled at her beauty only briefly, as he drove into the parking lot at the dock.

"To be continued on board, Gaelan. Let's find out where to get tickets, and when the next boat goes out."

The next boat would be leaving at 11:15. After buying their tickets they sat on a bench on the dock, waiting to board. Their boat was approaching the dock, bringing its first-of-the-morning tourists back to land. Gaelan and Zahryn watched in silence as two-dozen folks disembarked. It was a perfect day to be out on the waters. Sunshine. Clear sky. Gentle breezes—a friendly north wind. There was only a little chop out on the water, not enough to make for a rough ride.

A crew member beckoned. They handed over their tickets and boarded. Taking the steep ladder stairs, they climbed to the upper deck, to the bench overlooking the bow of the boat.

Gaelan said, "I hope you'll be warm enough, Zahryn." She had chosen to wear layers—the perfect autumn attire—a long oatmeal cable-knit sweater over a turtleneck, leggings and lace-up leather ankle boots.

"My cape is wool. I'll get it out of my bag. I'll be toasty. Thanks for asking, Gaelan."

She glanced over to smile at him and he quickly looked away. He said to himself, *If she only knew how much I really like her. She is amazing. She is pretty. She's smart. She cares about people. I hope she didn't see me staring at her just now like a besotted geek. I've got it bad.* He felt himself blush deeply.

For the next hour, they sat side by side and simply gazed. They pointed at castles, ruins, and farmsteads. Sandy beaches, tiny hamlets, and villages on the shores. Ben Lomond loomed in the distant north. The composer who coined the lyrical phrase, "On the bonnie, bonnie banks of Loch Lomond" had certainly been there. Bonnie banks they were indeed!

The tour boat did a one-hour full circle tour and was heading back to the docks when Zahryn spoke. "Thanks for bringing me out here, Gaelan. We hardly know each other, but I feel like we've known each other forever. I feel free when I'm with you. You let me blab on and on about people and history—Celts and Gaels—and you don't cut me off or put me down. You're open to my thoughts, and I like that. Thanks for being a great guy. Thanks for being you!" She smiled broadly as she spoke.

For the first time, Gaelan gave her full eye contact the whole time she spoke. This time he was not compelled to look away or look downward. He was drawn to her very being.

Gaelan said, "I don't have words like you, Zahryn. As for me, I like being with you too. We have fun."

With that, he leaned closer to her, face to face, and said, "*You* are fun!"

Zahryn looked at his face so close to hers. He was handsome. His scruffy unshaven facial hair today made him look relaxed and playful—more than she'd ever noticed before. He was wearing his favorite tweed flatcap. He looked so cool. They were cool. They were cool together.

The boat horn blasted, bringing them back to reality. The boat docked smoothly and the deckhands deftly secured the boat with hefty lines and knots and their nautical know-how.

"It's 12:30 now. We'll head up to Aberfoyle, and then over to Stirling. It's just an hour's drive and we can do lunch in Stirling Castle. You good with that?" Gaelan asked.

Zahryn nodded, and they headed back to the car. Zahryn took off her cape before climbing in. They sat close, again, and toured in silence. The scenery was breathtaking. Sheep and coos and ancient dwellings whizzed by on the roadsides.

Gaelan's stomach growled loudly, breaking the silence. They laughed. They were both hungry! Lunch would be soon enough.

Zahryn offered up a question. "Gaelan, could you ever see yourself as a modern-day shepherd—a sheep or goat farmer? Like, you'd have your whole day everyday devoted to the health and safety of your flock. And you'd be tuned into the rhythm of the herds—mating cycles, lambing and kidding seasons, and all that goes with providing pastures that give good nutrition to the animals. It's a whole different world out here!"

Gaelan tilted his head, thinking, pensive. He had no immediate answer.

"It's simple but complex," she continued. "It's tough, hard work, but its good wholesome living. It's about being part of the village, the sheep community, the family. It's about being a part of the whole—a small part of something big. About being connected in rural and village life. I kinda like this. I don't need the big city—except I guess for the university. I love the country. The pastures. The shores. The mountains. The great big sea all around us."

Gaelan had collected his thoughts and he said, "Yup. Me too. My hometown, Doran's Brook, is kinda like this. Sheep. Goats. Cows. Long-haired Highland coos. The shores. The rock-lined pastures. There's nothing like the village life."

They drove through Aberfoyle, a quaint village on the River Forth. Looking to the north, they saw the changing elevations leading to The Trossachs Glen. Gaelan so wanted to take Zahryn farther north, through the Duke's Pass and into The Trossachs National Forest. It was lush. It hushed with ancient Celtic history. *Another day. Another day for sure!* They drove on in silence, sensing all of the wonders and the mysteries of rural and olden-day Scotland.

As the terrain became gradually more rolling, Zahryn raised her voice with excitement, "Gaelan, Can you imagine the fun we could have up here one day, renting a couple of off-roaders—ATV's—and just taking time to explore this area? It's so rugged. It's calling to me!"

Gaelan answered quickly, "Oh yeah! For sure! This is a perfect area for ATV-ing. It's almost a household requirement to own one, to get around in these parts." He smiled at the thought of yet another fun-filled adventure with Zahryn.

On entering the town of Stirling, they saw the famous Wallace Monument, across the valley in the wide-open space. It stood high on a rocky outcrop, stark against the blue sky. They could see that the monument was in sad need of repair, as multiple scaffoldings circled its base, awaiting the next season of renovation.

Gaelan chuckled. "Hey, Zahryn, did you know that the Wallace Monument is affectionately called 'The Gateway to the Highlands'?"

"No, I didn't," Zahryn replied.

And, putting on a fake, and exaggerated noble accent, he asked, "Did you know that of Stirling Castle, it is said, by the historians, "He who holds Stirling, holds Scotland." Zahryn and Gaelan both laughed loudly at the absolute silliness of his little poke at the noble class.

Gaelan then dropped the phoney and resumed his normal speech. "Over there is the castle. There's a lunch and tearoom downstairs. I wonder what's for lunch?" Gaelan said as he drove toward the castle. It too, like the Wallace Monument, stood prominent in the skyline, high upon the imposing rocks. It was so visible from anywhere in Stirling. The antiquity was palpable.

They drove up a lengthy drive into the heights, and parked in the castle parking lot. It was a most breathtaking scene. They walked toward the castle, noting the grandeur of the sprawling terraces, courtyards, and gardens in the October air, in the brilliant mid-afternoon sunshine. They passed through an ancient stone archway, across a stone path, and up stone steps to enter the castle through the grand wooden doors. A sign pointed them to the tearoom downstairs.

Zahryn said, "I feel like I've walked into another century. The air here smells older. The stone walls have been here for centuries—if only they could speak and tell their stories." Zahryn just let that thought wander off into the castle air.

The stairs in the stairwell were uneven and curved, and they had to watch their step. Small wall sconces lit the way dimly, causing shadows to appear on the steps in front of them.

"Be careful Zahryn. Don't break your neck on these stairs! We'd be late for lunch!"

Zahryn chuckled. She liked his humor. They navigated the stairs successfully and found themselves in a whole different era, like they had walked through a time-traveling tunnel, back through the ages.

The tearoom glowed in soft candlelight. Servers were clad in long, dark colored dresses, with long white aprons, and they were serving lunch and tea to their guests at small square tables. The tables against the one wall had old wooden benches, the backs of which rose high up onto the ivory stucco walls. The ceilings were lofty, with grand arches at both ends of the room. The room was almost filled to capacity. Zahryn pointed to an empty table in the front of the room. She asked Gaelan, "Should we wait to be seated?"

Just then a server beckoned them to follow her. She was a middle-aged woman with auburn hair pulled neatly back in a bun at the nape of her neck. She said, "Hi! My name is Erinn. I have a quiet table in the corner, or, one right here, up front."

Zahryn replied, "Hi Erinn. Thanks. Let's do the corner. It's quiet and we can chat."

As they sat down, Erinn handed them the menus, saying, "Potato soup and fishcakes are today's special."

Zahryn said, "I guess I don't need a menu then! The special sounds great!"

"Make that two, please!" Gaelan added, and they both handed back the menus. "That was easy!"

Both Zahryn and Gaelan took a moment to settle. Sweaters came off. Chairs were turned and angled outward so as to see both the tearoom and each other with ease. Zahryn took a moment to refold her cape and sweater and place them in the bottom of her deep handbag. Her olive-green turtleneck beautifully set off her ivory skin and curly auburn locks. Her sage green eyes deepened in the flickering candlelight.

"There. I'm settled. Thanks so much for bringing me here. It's good to get out of the city. We've done a lot already today, and it's only two o'clock!" She beamed at her cool friend.

"You're welcome!" he said. "It has been fun! But don't expect this every weekend now—you know—student's budget and all!"

Zahryn said brightly. "Yup! Got it! No problem! Sir!"

Gaelan continued, "How 'bout we change up our plan a bit? I saw a really cool old pub on the way here, back in Aberfoyle. Why don't we take our time here at the castle, and then drive back the way we came. Then we can stop for a pint in Aberfoyle, and head home from there? That way, instead of following our noses blindly at night on a road we've not yet traveled, we'll be on semi-familiar roads in the dark on the way home to Glasgow."

"Sounds good," said Zahryn, admiring his practicality and safety-mindedness. He was looking out for them in his own sensible and practical ways.

Erinn arrived with soups in hand. "Fishcakes are coming. Do you want crackers with your soup?"

They both nodded yes and she lifted a bowl of crispy crackers from her tray onto the table. "Himalayan salted tops," she said, then demurely moved on.

Steam was rising from the soup and they continued chatting, allowing the soup time to cool. Zahryn took time to crumble her crackers into her soup.

"What made you decide to choose the University of Glasgow, Gaelan? Was it your first choice?"

"Well, it's kind of embarrassing. Everybody said I should 'go local' for my first two years of university, and maybe 'get noticed academically' during that time. And then they suggested I apply broadly for bursaries and scholarships to the bigger schools—Cambridge, Oxford, Edinburgh—you know, for Math and maybe Commerce. So I did, and here I am.

"My marks are great and just this fall, I have started to apply for the bigger schools. My problem is me. I have to decide what I want—and not be swayed by what everyone else wants for me.

"Those who know of my IQ score and my math smarts are kind of leading me—kind of pushing me into a life of academia. A long journey in school to a PhD in Math, followed by a work-life married to academia. I would have a secure career for sure—maybe even a tenured post at the university—focused on the minutiae of Math. I would be always on the cutting edge—leading edge of Math, in a highly competitive world. I would be publishing a lot. I wouldn't have much of a life, beyond algorithm, theorem, and proof. My life would be driven totally by the pursuit of academic excellence.

"Or, I could listen to my heart. I could just get a basic Commerce degree that would credential me to work in many fields. I could have a nine-to-five, Monday-through-Friday workweek that affords me a comfortable lifestyle, and my free time would be my time. I'd be able to enjoy the outdoors and all that life has to offer. My work-life balance would be wonderful. I could breathe. My choices and my passions could be the center of my life, not my IQ! And not Math!"

"What do *you* want Gaelan?" Zahryn interjected. "What are you leaning toward? Not what your mom wants for you. And not what the profs want—you know—those who have noted your brilliance and identified your genius as an asset to their school. And not the elitist establishment either, those who only see IQ narrowly, as a career pathway predictor. What do *you want* your education to do for you, Gaelan?"

Zahryn stopped to sample her soup. It was tasty and still quite hot. As she set her spoon down again, she studied Gaelan's expression. She noted that he had been paying full attention to her question. She didn't interrupt his thinking. She gave him time to work through it.

"You know Zahryn? You just gave me space to explore my chaotic thoughts and to get the big picture. You let me put words to my disorganized feelings and gave me permission, through your very direct questions, to think it all through for myself. I'm seeing that I can make life-choices for myself based on what I want out of life. You're empowering me to choose!

"I know I'm smart—but do I want my whole focus, my whole life, to be centered on that? Maybe I just have to spend a lot more time in this very question: What do I want my life pathway and career pathway to look like? Then I need to ask myself just this. Basic Commerce degree versus PhD in Math?

"I think that there is a lot more life and living out there for me to explore and experience, and, I think I would miss out on an awful lot if I stayed the course in academia for a PhD. Bursaries and scholarships are tempting and they do stroke my ego. But, do I really want to go there? I should try to decide by Christmas. There are a lot of submission deadlines for scholarships coming up. Maybe I'll apply and maybe I won't. Maybe you'll help me to decide?"

Zahryn had sampled her soup while listening. "I think you're already well on your way in making your decision, Gaelan. Think of it this way. Look ahead down the road. If you gave yourself completely to the PhD route, would you be able to get back to nature—to the shores and out on the water—even impromptu daytrips like today? Would you be free, totally free, to do any of these things that you so love to do?"

Gaelan immediately said, "No way. Not a chance. There would be the constant pressures of timetables, schedules, and deadlines, tutoring, organizing TAs' workloads, and timely publication of my critical works. Endless tedium. Perpetual focus. My time would never be my own. My life would be all math and no play."

Gaelan stopped putting his words out there, for a moment. He thought, *In just a few directed questions, Zahryn has opened my eyes to my true inner conflict. She's helped me to name it and clearly identify it. And then she gave me the go-ahead to muse it into reality. She's good!*

Gaelan said in earnest "Zahryn, Have you ever thought about counseling, or career advisory roles—guidance or advocacy roles? You get the whole picture. You see the person and their needs. And then you give them clear choices and the confidence to make those very choices. You are amazing. You are helping me so much!"

Zahryn smiled. This was not the first time she had been complimented for her people-sense, and for her pure clarity of thinking. It was her gift. She had a Light that could lead others—that would lead others to find their own Light for their life-journey.

"Here are your fishcakes. I hope you're hungry. Chef is making them pretty big this afternoon!" Erinn said and placed the plates on the small table. "Will you be having tea after your meal?"

Zahryn looked at Gaelan. "Of course! We've come a long way to the castle. We wouldn't miss it. We're not in any hurry today."

She looked slyly at Gaelan and asked Erinn, "Is there somewhere else we could have our tea? Is there a wee room, like a library or a nook with comfy chairs, where we could just sit back, curl up, and enjoy our tea?"

Erinn answered, "Yes, my dear. Sometimes we do this. We open an old library down the hall for small groups. We could, since you've asked, open it for the two of you!"

Zahryn's jaw dropped. "That's wonderful! Will you take us there when we finish our meal?"

Erinn nodded in agreement, and went on her way. Zahryn reached out and squeezed Gaelan's forearm. "A private sitting room for tea at the castle! This is lovely. Sometimes you just won't know the answer until you speak the question!"

Gaelan couldn't help but turn his full attention to Zahryn. Her hand on his arm, her assertive query, her exuberance and delight—all of these qualities engaged him deeply and drew him in. He was totally gobsmacked by this lovely life-force sitting across the table from him. *She's a keeper, I'll say. A real keeper.*

Zahryn took her hand back and picked up her fork. "Let's eat!" And they enjoyed every morsel. There was both a locally sourced, homemade tartar sauce and an imported Canadian Lady Ashburnham mustard pickle on the plate with the fishcakes. They sat back and savored both of the delectable garnishes. The fish was tender and sweet. A wholesome and savory meal at the castle.

They set their forks down on their empty plates. Erinn dutifully cleared their dishes and cutlery and she bustled away to the kitchen. In a few short minutes, she returned, saying, "Come with me. Tea is ready!" They picked up their things and followed her down the wide corridor to a small, unmarked room right at the end. She opened the stately library door.

Inside, the grand walls rose up tall to meet the lofty gallery-arched ceiling. Even though they were in the true basement, the windows looked out over the lower, beautifully landscaped garden terraces. Zahryn took a moment and allowed her mind to wander—to wonder about the beautiful garden views from this room in the summertime. She vowed to return one day, in the summer. And she sighed.

The large wrought iron and etched glass wall sconces held delicate white-light candle bulbs. The late afternoon daylight streamed in through the giant floor-to-ceiling windows—leaded, beveled glass windows—giving the space an ambiance of finery, whimsy, and calm.

The walls on the one side of the room had many oversized, framed canvases depicting the stories of Stirling of yesteryear. There were lion-crested coats of arms, lovely noble ladies, hunting dogs and legendary unicorns, ancient military battle scenes and more.

A second wall was completely covered in bookcases, which were laden with leather-bound books. A third wall had a massive fireplace. Four upright brass stands with silken ropes and tassels kept guests a safe distance from the ornate mantle and its precious treasures.

A rustic burgundy tapestry-covered settee was nestled beneath the tall window. Three other deep-seated, velvet chairs formed a semi-circle in front of the settee. A richly carved mahogany tea wagon stood against the south wall, with a silver tea service on top. These were remnants of the finery of days of olde. The bone china tea cups sat poised beside the cream and sugar silver pieces.

"Oh my! Gaelan!! This is too good to be true! I just wanted a little private space for our teatime, and look at this! It's like a page out of a princess' fairy tale! I feel like a princess!"

Erinn spoke quietly, "I'll leave you two now. Your tea is on the teacart. I'll return shortly to see if you need anything."

They sat down in the teal velvet chairs, placing their tea cups on the ornately-carved table between them. Time and time again, they returned to the tea wagon to fill their cups.

When Erinn returned and offered to refill the teapot, Zahryn and Gaelan both declined as they were reaching their fill. Erin quietly stepped back and walked away down the hall.

Zahryn got up and brought the teapot over. She filled both of their cups and set the pot right where they could reach it. They both drank their tea black. No fuss. No muss.

"I guess it's not proper to keep the teapot right here. But, neither Martha Stewart nor Her Majesty Queen Elizabeth are here with us. I think it's okay to break with teatime etiquette, don't you? It's just you and me!"

Gaelan answered, "No problem. Do what works—whatever's easy."

"I am full!" said Zahryn emphatically. She placed her hand on her tummy that looked lean even in her current state of fullness.

Gaelan sighed. "I'm full too. We can just relax and drink tea. No schedule. I'm good with that."

Gaelan gazed up at the lofty ceiling, to the wrought iron chandelier. It was oversized. Everything in that library seemed grand and oversized. He felt physically small against the noble backdrop, but he had a growing inner sense of largeness of self—of person—of his very being. And inwardly he gave gratitude to Zahryn for these positive changes in his own self-perception.

Gaelan settled in to his chair. "So, it's my turn to ask you Zahryn. How did you know? When did you know what you wanted to study, and where? You're from the Southshore Islands, and I'm from the Hebrides. What made you want to leave your mountain island lifestyle to come to Glasgow to study?"

"Well" she started, "That's not too hard to answer. There's no university in the Southshore Islands, so I had to come to the mainland to study. And, the Glaswegians are wonderful folks. Historically hard working, kind, and down to earth. My dad always told me that a Glaswegian made for a better friend than a snooty Edinburgher! That sounds kind of prejudicial, but I think maybe he meant that he preferred the overt human-kindness of the working-class folks of Glasgow over the nobility and the scholars of Edinburgh! He once said that he'd hire a Glaswegian any day, for their amazing work ethic. They really do know how to work hard, and get the job done!

"And, I guess I've always wanted to work with people. Studying people and relationships seemed like a natural choice for me. A basic degree or credentials in psychology and sociology will at least get me some interviews in the 'serving-humanity-sector.'

She went on with fervor. "You know, you can choose to see relationships and life simply, or, you can look way deeper and view all relationships and life through the lenses of personality, motivation, and issues of control. For example, all relationships, and even every conversation, can be analyzed by looking at who is in control, who wants to be in control, and who has lost control and is seeking to regain control."

She stopped abruptly and looked at Gaelan straight on. "There I go again. Analyzing. Framing. Naming. You didn't need a Behavioral Psychology 101 lecture today! It's teatime!" She smiled broadly.

"Hey, Zahryn! It's okay! I asked! And you answered with passion and zeal. I like that in you. You have a fire—like an interior turf fire that is constantly blazing. I love listening to you talk."

Zahryn put her hand up to stop the compliments. "Stop, Gaelan. You're making me blush! Really, I'm just being me. And yeah, I like people. And I like being me. I guess I'm turning out okay after all the darkness in my life."

She sat back in her chair and reached behind her, gathering all of her locks to pull the mass and lengths of curls around in front of her. There, the horizontal sunrays simply danced and enhanced her natural loveliness, giving her rich golden highlights in the moment. Auburn tresses. Olive-green turtleneck. Teal velvet chair. Jewel-esque tones of exquisite beauty. Gaelan had also sat back, and was watching her intently, smiling.

"And you know, Gaelan, if I was just a little more academically-driven, I too could have to face a big decision—a possible future of academia. I could really be interested in taking some post-grad studies in Geopoetics, here at Glasgow U. It's a really cool realm of broad-based conceptual thinking that incorporates geographical, cultural, artistic, philosophic and spiritual influences on life as we understand it. My 'humanities brain' is truly drawn to the program, but I'm afraid my actual energies are shying away from such depth and intensity and focus." She paused for effect and then said slowly, "But . . . I'm thinkin' a straightforward four-year MA Honors Degree in Social Sciences will be good enough for me."

Zahryn reached to pour more tea. She poured the last few drops into Gaelan's cup. "Enough of my geopoetics dreaming. Tea's all gone. And, I'm so full, I couldn't drink another drop. How about you?"

"I'm good." Gaelan replied slowly. "Wow" he offered softly, in awe of Zahryn's dreams. He was still trying to wrap his head around the world of

Geopoetics. "We both have so many options and opportunities. And for sure, we'll make these big decisions at the right time.

"But for now, maybe we'll just chill. We'll stay put until the sun goes down—another half an hour or so. We can stay and watch the shadows come alive in the fading light!"

Zahryn tilted her head to the side and smiled as she looked at Gaelan. "Well, that sounds just perfect." She was enjoying seeing this thoughtful side of him. She was learning that he was not just a numbers geek. She could see he had a soft heart. In her eyes, he was not a hopeless romantic by any means but most certainly he was alert to details, to moments, and to place and space. She quite liked being with him.

The tearoom took on an energy of its own as the last rays of sunlight retreated into oblivion. It was well past the equinox, and the sunset in late October came early.

Zahryn said, "You're so right about the shadows in the dark. They seem to be dancing, or playing. There is movement of light all around us, responding to an unnamed force or presence in our midst."

Gaelan chuckled. "Like, from the drafts in the basement of an ancient castle?"

Zahryn didn't miss a beat. "Or the energies and the flows of life—past and present—flowing in, around, and through us?"

Gaelan spoke a little louder. "You mean ghosts?!"

"No, silly! Like an eternal realm—a flowing energy linking all of us to the past, to all time, to eternity." Zahryn looked away, through the waning light beyond the beveled glass.

Gaelan caught himself. "I'm not sure I follow . . . ."

Zahryn regrouped. "Well, I know for sure that we are all connected somehow, through something, to the past. Our wisdom—our insight and our knowing—is deep. I think that there is an energy, a flow, a fluid motion of the past through to the present, that keeps us grounded, and connected, and knowing."

Gaelan said quietly, "Zahryn, Sorry, you're losing me."

Zahryn continued, "Maybe I'm not explaining myself very well. We are all connected—interconnected through time and eternity. We are all re-lational beings and we are in relationship with everything in our midst. The dancing light and shadows simply reminds me of this flow. And I feel it too."

Zahryn took a long deep breath, and looked into Gaelan's baffled eyes. "I'd better stop before I confuse myself. Sometimes I can take a simple no-tion and just run with it. Sometimes things become crystal clear, and some-times like right now, not so much."

Zahryn paused again. They sat in silence—in the stillness. Inlonracance filled their souls. While the word "exuberance" is an outward showing, a visible expression of energetic joy, inlonracance is a subtle inner shimmer, a dancing inner Light that rises to full expression only inwardly, in times of pure joy and deepest inner contentment. Both Zahryn and Gaelan were inwardly alive in their own inlonracant Light.

After a time, Gaelan said, "Maybe we should move on." Zahryn nodded. Silently they collected their things and made their way back to the tearoom. Gaelan paid the bill and said to Erinn, "You are one fine hostess, Erinn. You helped to make our time at the castle extra special, and I cannot thank you enough. Your service is thoughtful and kind. Thanks for everything—Thanks so very much!" He reached out and shook her hand.

Then Erinn quietly bowed to both of them. "You're so very welcome, my dears. Have a safe drive home now. Mind the partiers, the hooligans on the road. It's Friday night and all!" She stood in the doorway and watched as they made their way up the steep and winding stairs. They stepped out into the fresh October evening.

They drove in silence, shoulder to shoulder, back toward the charming village of Aberfoyle. The country roads were in complete darkness. And the starshine was blazing in the moonless sky. Gaelan wished he had a sunroof, so as to see straight upward into the night.

The streetlights of Aberfoyle bathed the little village with a warm and welcoming light. Their soft glow could be seen against the darkened horizon as the Mini Cooper approached from the east. They were almost under the first streetlight.

BANG!!!

Zahryn called out loudly, "What was that?"

Gaelan answered, "I don't know! Holy God! I think a tire blew." Gaelan pulled over quickly to the shoulder of the road and hopped out of the car. He was right. The passenger side rear tire had exploded. It was totally shredded. The Mini was stopped in its tracks.

Gaelan called out, "Are you okay Zahryn? That was a loud bang and it sure startled me!"

Zahryn replied, relieved to hear it was just a flat tire. "I'm okay. But Wow! Why here or now? We didn't drive on any rough roads or cross any treacherous breaks in the road, or crevasses, or potholes. We didn't hit anything, did we?"

Gaelan answered, "No. We didn't. I would have known that for sure. Well, let's lock up the car. We're already here in Aberfoyle. We don't have to walk very far to get help."

Zahryn asked, "Do you have a spare, or a jack, or both?"

"No, and I sure wish I did. It's Friday night and nothing will be open tonight." He looked unsure. He looked over at Zahryn, wondering what on earth they would do next. He felt a little uneasy, even a little guilty about the mishap.

Zahryn offered, "Let's go to the pub, like we planned, and talk about our options. We can't do anything out here. We can work something out. We'll find our way."

Gaelan marveled. "You're so calm and level-headed, Zahryn. You think it through. I hope you'll start to rub off on me. I like the way you just move on, take things in stride, and deal with whatever comes your way."

Zahryn explained, "Maybe I've come to look at life, not as a chain of obstacles or problems, but rather, as a series of opportunities through which I can grow. I choose to see my glass as always half-full."

Gaelan listened attentively. "Well, whatever Zahryn, yes, we'll figure it out. Let's go." They locked up and strode quickly toward the center of the village. The streetlights were indeed lit, but the shops were all in darkness. Every last one of them. A bakery, a local artisan gallery, a grocery store, a bookstore, a woolens boutique, an antique store—all with lights out for the night.

All lights were on at the pub, across the street, and half of the town seemed to be gathered there. They could hear the laughter, music, and Friday night sounds as they approached.

Gaelan led the way into the pub. Zahryn followed closely behind. Once inside, they realized it wasn't as crowded as it had sounded from outside. "Bar or table?" he asked.

Zahryn pointed. "Over there to the booth—let's go there. No, wait! Maybe the bar. We can ask the bartender about tires and stuff."

Gaelan smiled. "Good thinking." He led onward to the end of the old wooden bar. He turned just as Zahryn stepped up close to him. Their eyes met, only briefly. His eyes were worried. Hers were sparkling with excitement.

Gaelan hailed out to the bartender, "Och Aye! A couple o' pints over here, Buddy! Thanks!" He nodded and smiled in acknowledgment.

They sat on the tall bar stools, shoulder to shoulder, facing inward to the mighty taps. Gaelan turned to speak to Zahryn. "What a great little place! I'm sure many a tire problem or an ornery goat story has been shared, or solved, or celebrated right here in this place!"

Zahryn was grinning with the energy of the room. "Yup. Right here. No doubt. And we'll solve our tire situation too. No problem."

The bartender plunked down their pints just as Zahryn started to speak again. "Hey bartender! What's your name?"

"Emmett. What's up?"

Zahryn spoke first. "Well, Emmett, nice to meet you! Great little place you have here!"

Emmett beamed at the obvious newcomers to town. In his eyes, tourists and strangers were always welcome at the pub. They kept things interesting. The door was open and the taps were flowin' for all.

Zahryn continued on her quest. "We have a few questions, Emmett. First, does anyone here in town sell tires?"

Emmett straightened up. "Yes. But they're closed. Open at ten tomorrow morning. Ronan's Garage. What? You got a flat?"

"Yeah. It's flat alright." Zahryn replied. "Second question. Is there a guesthouse here in Aberfoyle? I guess we're going to have to stay the night."

Emmett knew the town well. "Yup. Just down the road. Across the road just after the bridge. Buchanan House. Want me to call ahead for a room?"

Zahryn looked at Gaelan with total confidence and said, "Yes please! That would be great!"

Gaelan's eyes were wide. Zahryn had a plan. She could see no quick fix to get back on the road so she became quickly decisive and made their needs known to Emmett—someone who had already kindly offered to help them. This was the heart of Scotland. Helping spirits. Helping hands. Ready and willing to help those in need. Lucky for Zahryn and Gaelan, here and now!

Emmett was making a call from his cell phone when Gaelan spoke quietly to her. "Are you okay, Zahryn, with staying overnight, with me? I mean. Like. I didn't expect this or plan this or . . . ."

"It's okay, Gaelan! We don't have a choice, do we? We could call a friend to come up from Glasgow to get us, but we'd still have to deal with our flat tire tomorrow, here in Aberfoyle. We could get a tow to Glasgow, and that will cost as much as a room at the guesthouse. So. Let's enjoy the pub. And deal with the tire tomorrow. Deal?"

Gaelan was fascinated. Her conquering spirit and sense of adventure gave her all she needed to see the whole picture and make some practical, workable choices.

And before he could even nod, Zahryn continued. "I'll pay for the room. You've treated me all day to a country drive, a boat ride, and lunch at the castle. And, now you have to buy a new tire. The very least I can do is cover the room. Done!"

Emmett came back smiling. "Buchanan House has one room. They are still on the line. Do you want them to hold it for you?"

"Yes!" they both called out together, in synch. Zahryn giggled. "Emmett, We'll stay here still for a bit, at the pub. Maybe tell them we'll get there by 11-ish? You said it's just a short walk."

Emmett spoke into the phone. "Can you hold it till 11? They look like decent folks." He smiled at Zahryn and Gaelan.

Gaelan called out toward the cell phone, "And, thanks so much, 'Buchanan'!"

Zahryn and Gaelan spent the next two hours sipping their pints. During the second round, Zahryn commented that she was still pretty full after soup, fishcakes, and tea—so much tea! "Who knew what this day would bring, eh, Gaelan? What a great day! And so what if we blew a tire! We've had a great adventure in Stirlingshire—in Buchanan country—and now we have even more craziness to add to the story! Thank goodness Buchanan House has a room! Can you imagine sleeping overnight in the Mini-Cooper? Ha!"

Gaelan laughed too. "No! An overnight in the Coop would be crazy for sure. Aye, Buchanan! Slàinte!" And they clinked and chugged and set their empty tankards down, in perfect synchrony.

Gaelan spoke again, this time to Emmett at the taps. "We're done, Emmett. Hey, here's for the pints." He handed him cash with a good-sized tip. "And thanks for helping us out, eh? Thanks for putting in a good word with Buchanan."

Emmett stuffed the cash into his front apron pocket. He called out, "And thanks for this! Nice to meet you both! You have a good time, okay? Go see ol' Ronan in the morning. Tell them Emmett sent you. You just might score a deal!"

Zahryn was standing now, right behind Gaelan. She called out, "Right! And thanks Emmett. You've been a great help! Bye!"

Zahryn and Gaelan left the pub, feeling carefree. Tomorrow was another day to unfold, in its own time. But for now, the night was theirs. Tonight the adventure would continue.

Zahryn spoke first, once they got onto the street. "You know, Gaelan, we didn't even ask about the room. We said 'yes' right away without asking. We'll have to take whatever we're given because we don't have any other choice. But, right now, I need to put some boundaries out there. And, I don't mind saying so. Okay? No hanky-panky. I'm not ready and I'm sure you're not either. We're together overnight because of a tire, not because we chose to be together romantically or otherwise."

Gaelan said, "Perfect. Thanks, Zahryn. You called it right, again. Let's just wait and see what Buchanan House has to offer."

They walked in silence over the ancient cobblestone road. It became a loose gravel track, just before the little bridge. Zahryn wondered about the age and stage of the old stone bridge. She asked quietly as they walked, "I wonder if this bridge is hundreds or thousands of years old? And how many people have crossed over safely, and crossed over confidently, over all the years?" Unsure if Gaelan had even heard her, she just let those questions waft away into the night.

Just over the starlit bridge, a short lane led them to the well-lit veranda of the Buchanan House. The four wooden steps creaked loudly under their weight. The wooden veranda housed quite a few antique rocking chairs of varied heights and styles of craftsmanship. Four wall-sconces lit up the front of the grey and white painted two-story building. They felt welcomed.

She pushed to open the large country door, causing an overhead bell to ring. They stepped inside and Gaelan closed the door quietly behind them.

The host met them in the foyer. "Hi! I'm Malcolm. Malcolm Buchanan. Come in my friends, come away in! You must be from the pub. Emmett described you, young lady, to a T. You're every bit as lovely as he said!" He bowed his head to her, in appreciation of her wholesome beauty.

Zahryn blushed, and Gaelan smiled inwardly. *Yup, She's lovely alright!*

Zahryn blurted out, "Thanks so much for holding the room for us, Malcolm! We're stuck! We have a flat tire."

Malcolm grinned. "Well, I'm happy to have you. Always happy to have a full house. Let's just do a little paperwork and we'll get you up to your room."

In all of ten minutes, Zahryn's credit card and contact info was shared, documents signed, computer updated. Malcolm told them that breakfast was served from 7–9:30 a.m. A hot breakfast even!

They received their key and went up the stairs to the second floor. "Room Four," Malcolm had told them.

"Here it is." Zahryn called out softly. Gaelan used the key to open the door, and they were pleasantly surprised.

The room itself was quite small, but it was big on charm. The loo was just inside the door, off to the left. Handsome grey tweed full-length curtains covered the windows on the wall straight ahead, and two grey and white tub chairs were casually placed in front of them.

And off to the right was a double bed, angled artistically into the corner of the room. A single bedside table was on the left side of the bed with an ornate glass Turkish lamp perched upon it, giving the room a touch of finery and charm. The oversized grey cloth headboard seemed to tower over the white quilt-clad bed. A grey and white tartan throw was draped over the bottom third of the bed.

Gaelan spoke up. "Hey, this is pretty nice, Zahryn. I can take the wool blanket and a pillow and crash on the floor. You can have the bed."

"No way, Gaelan! We're adults. We're sensible. We'll share the bed. I've already named my boundaries. You can't spend the whole night on the floor. That sucks."

She looked and saw him smiling. As nervous as he was, he was pleased at her invitation to share the bed. "Okay. Thanks, Zahryn. Thanks a lot!"

Zahryn dropped her large handbag on the chair. "I'm going to wash up a bit. See you in a minute. Maybe you can turn up the thermostat—it's a little chilly in here, don't you think?"

Gaelan went to check the thermostat. Zahryn washed her face. She then took some time to gather her long locks into a loose low ponytail, using her favorite scrunchie. She pulled her ponytail forward, allowing all of her curls to cascade down over her left shoulder, in front of her. She walked over to the right side of the bed. Unhurriedly, they both removed their multiple outer layers of clothing, and climbed into bed in t-shirts and turtlenecks, jeans and leggings, and bare feet.

Zahryn set her phone on the floor beside her. "I'm not setting any alarms for the morning. We'll get up when we're ready." Gaelan reached over to switch off the bejeweled table lamp on his side of the bed. The room was in total darkness.

"Bed is comfy," she said, lying flat on her back.

Gaelan too, was on his back to her right. "Yeah, it is. Look Zahryn, you know, this is a pretty tight fit. This is only a double bed. Do you have enough room? I mean, I want to respect you and your boundaries. But this is a pretty small bed for two really tall people. I can hit the floor, no problem."

"No, Gaelan. No way. We'll make it work. We've been shoulder to shoulder all day in the car, on the boat, and in the pub. And now here. I'm good. Just don't hog the covers!"

With that, she turned onto her right side to face him. Her ponytailed tresses tumbled, descending into the small space between them. "You know Gaelan, you are one special guy. We've had one amazing day that you put together for us and it's been really fun! And so what if our luck changed, and the tire thing happened. We got to have an even longer time together at the pub because we didn't have to drive anywhere tonight. And, we can—and we will—work our way through our first night together. It's our story. Our adventure. Our fun."

She wanted to feel close to Gaelan. But safe. She reached over and placed her left hand onto his chest. Her heart rate accelerated as she touched him. "Thank you for being you, Gaelan. You are a one-of-a-kind guy and I am pleased to call you friend!"

Gaelan's heart was pounding. He appreciated her simple touch. He felt so very shy in the moment and he knew he was blushing in the dark.

With his heart bouncing off the walls of his chest, he rolled toward her, to face her, placing his hand on her shoulder. Almost instinctively, he softly gathered her to him. "You are special, Zahryn. You are the special one. And I am the grateful one."

Face to face they lay there, in silence, barely touching the other. Their breath was mutually warm and tidal to their cheeks, drawing them even closer into the moment. Their excitement was never expressed, verbally, physically, openly.

Two Lights shone in the darkness. Two souls lay as close as their boundaries would allow, in tenderness, in gentleness, in wonder and in awe—in their shared intimacy of the moment. Touching, together, they fell into blissful sleep.

Voices in the Heavens

NOVEMBER 5, 2022

"Hello Zahryn, it's Abba speaking. I am here with you. Come walk with me. Come talk with me, and share with me all that is heavy on your heart."

"Oh Abba! God! It's so good to be here with you, where I can walk with you here in the gardens, in the meadows, on the shorelines, even in the mountains. Out in the open—and free. I am well here, and I am able. My earthly body no longer weighs me down. And I no longer need my UTV!

"I had hoped I would find you, that you would find me. I lost my way, and you have found me. And so, here I am now, seeking your forgiveness. I chose to leave my earthly life on my own terms, in my own time. Surely, most surely by now, I have known enough darkness and suffering. I chose to go one last time up into the mountain heights and I took my life. I intentionally overdosed with all of the palliative care meds I that had on hand. And I had a few Mary Jane edibles too. It was like, my last hurrah—my last mountain mellow! And then I just I slipped away, peacefully. It was a hard choice to make, but I felt it was my decision to make. Please, please, please forgive me God. I'm happy to be here with you, now."

There was a warm and blessed silence between them.

"I do have something more to say, God. I have lots more to share with you. I've been working through a lot of deeper things. Deeperlings. And so, here I go. These things—this wisdom and these deeper truths—I now know. I intuit them. And in them, I delight.

"I am love. I am Light. And my Lovelight shines for all of the world to see—in heaven, on earth, and everywhere in between. On earth I suffered loss—many great losses. But I was always loved. Unconditionally loved. And I continued to find even more love, all along the way.

"I lost a mom, I gained a mom. I lost my dad but I was always loved by a granddad I never even knew. I found a sister and a brother to whom I felt so deeply connected. I had old friends, and new friends, and a wonderful Anam Cara. Two Anam Cara! And, I had religion and spirituality

114

and ancient Celtic Wisdom—I had all of these to help me to know and to experience your love. I am truly blessed. I am grateful for all of this love. I was graced by love. I am humbled in love.

"But, I'm in a brand-new space now, in a whole new realm, and I must soon find my place. I want my love and my Light to define me—to continue to define me. And so I ask you God. Let me river on in this new place, ever ready to face whatever comes my way. Let me be Light. Let me be love. Let me shine brightly for all of those in need, that they too may know the wonders of love and Light, in their own way, here and now. In the Light of now.

"Please God, hear my prayer—not just the words of my prayer but the intentions of my whole self."

And God said, "It is so, Zahryn. Indeed, you are shining brightly. You always have and you always will. You are what you ask.

"Turn around Zahryn, more love awaits you, my child!"

Zahryn turned around and she paused for a moment to take in the sight—the wonderful sight. Zahryn spoke tentatively at first, in almost a childlike hush. "Mom? Is that you, Mommy? I mean, Auntie Rose? Dad? Daaaaaaaaa-deeeeeeeee!!!"

And, God smiled. God's blessed Light was all around them, in them, and through them. Reuniting all. Their own special inlonracance arose within, filling them, sustaining them, nurturing them. An ethereal iridescence began to glow, and to shimmer, warming them, and bathing them in pure sparklescence—in the wonders of God's Holy Lovelight. Love was their bond. Love was their connection. Love, was their everything.

Putting Two and Two Together

SATURDAY MARCH 27, 2010

IT WAS A LIMINAL time—a transitional time indeed, in Moonstone Cove in late March. The March Break was just over, but Easter was still down the road. The spring equinox was the week before. The skies were brighter and the days were longer, but the cold winds could still chill to the bone.

Zahryn had graduated with her BA the year before and had moved back to her home in Moonstone Cove and had settled in. She had easily become reacquainted with old friends from school, church, and her community.

"Hey Zahryn, thanks for meeting me here at the pub. My Auntie Paige works here, but she's not working today. Want a booth?" Maevyn pointed to the row of booths on the eastside wall.

"Well thanks for inviting me here, Maeve. We always have a good time! A booth is good. Sure. Wherever."

The girls sat in a rustic wooden booth. There was a coat of arms in a stained-glass window right above them, which cast bright green, gold, and red light onto their table. Sitting there, they had a really good view to the bartender and around the whole room.

Maevyn said, "I'm so glad you're back in Moonstone to stay. I missed you a lot when you were away at university. And, I see that Gaelan's living in Moonstone now too! I've seen him here at the pub a few times. He seems nice—pretty easy-going. We've never actually talked though."

"Yeah," said Zahryn. "His stepdad's company has moved their geologists' whole families here to Moonstone to work on a big government grant project. It's really nice that Gaelan lives nearby. We can stay friends."

Maevyn lowered her voice to a whisper. "Loaded statement, girlfriend! Kinda like you can still keep an eye on our bro for us!" They both grinned and giggled.

Both girls enjoyed being around Gaelan. They both felt good being near him. But their lips were sealed—their secret bro remained a secret.

Zahryn then spoke with concern in her voice. She needed to hear that Maevyn was okay. "So, Maeve. Tell me how you're doing. Are you feeling like you're finally part of this community? Are you feeling settled, feeling at home even, here in Moonstone?"

"Thanks for asking, Zee. I was in a pretty dark place and it really meant a lot to me to have you as a new friend who accepted me for who I was, just as I was. I was a girl with a past—damaged goods I guess—and you helped me to get back to being me. Carefree me. I still get sad and all, when I think about my little girl. But you helped me move on. I'm good now, thanks to you!"

Wanting to take the focus off of herself, Maevyn glanced over at the bar. She noticed the giant shiny brass taps, capped off with tall ceramic handles. She smiled as she mused *I wonder how many kegs and casks have flowed through these taps, over the years?*

"Hey Zahryn, Want a beer?" Maeve offered.

"Yes! A Beer! Please! Draught is good!" Zahryn reached over and grabbed Maevyn's hand. "I'm glad you're good. Your dark clouds have all blown away."

Maevyn smiled and went to the bar. She spoke to the bartender, Murray, then returned to their booth. She looked over to a wee gathering place in the corner. A wood carved sign hung overhead—"The Snug." It was a two-meter square, glassed-in nook with cushioned benches on three sides, and a large round dark wood table in the center. An older man was sitting there, alone. He had a pint on the go, and an empty tankard was on the table.

Dark hair. Dark eyes. Darker complexion. His eyes were soft as he stared out into the pub. Wistful? Wanting? Wondering?

Maevyn sat down across from Zahryn in the booth. She spoke quietly. "See the man—the older guy—in the Snug? Do you remember me telling you about our dad's bar-buddy, Sully? That's him! He's got to be in his sixties or seventies by now. He was quite the ladies' man around these parts, back in the day. Lots of stories and secrets. Auntie Paige joked that half the children in the primary school here in Moonstone, in any given year, were all fathered by Sully! Probably not true, but it's the stuff of legends!"

Zahryn's eyes grew really wide. She looked intently, directly, at the legend. Her dad's friend and confidante. Connor's mentor, and maybe even his dad! The original travelin' man, Sully, himself.

Though his story was larger than life, he was slim, with a wiry frame. Tall, yes, but much smaller in stature than his grand and storied persona. She couldn't help but notice his eyes. As black as they were, they were soft and kind. Approachable. Not cold and distant or shady.

Zahryn blurted out, "Should we talk to him? Like, really talk to him and tell him who we are and what we know?"

Murray arrived with two drafts in hand, and plunked them down on their table. "Would you young ladies like a tab?"

Maevyn answered. "Yes. Please. One bill, my treat. I think this is going to be one special day! Thanks, Murray." He left and returned to the bar.

Maevyn turned to Zahryn. "Let's down this round. Liquid courage! And then we'll order another one before we go over and talk to him. Deal?"

"Deal!" Zahryn laughed and they picked up their drafts. "Sláinte!" The girls started to drink, first sipping, then gulping, then chugging. Maevyn finished milliseconds ahead of Zahryn, and they both set down their tankards hard on the table. Clunk. Clunk.

"Murray! Another round!" Maevyn called out loudly. Notably surprised, Murray acknowledged the request and nodded, from behind the taps.

Maevyn's dark eyes were flashing and wild. Her mind was toying with a juicy thought. *Perhaps Connor WAS actually Sully's son—them both being so dark-eyed and all, and they were so buddy-buddy throughout their lives. Connor's own "known parents"—Donovan and Leah Inglis known to him as Dad and Mom—were currently living in London. They had left Connor long ago when he was just eighteen. They moved to London when he went away to university, when Leah's health was failing. She needed medical care in a big city hospital.*

Maevyn really let her imagination run away for a moment. *Maybe, just maybe, when Leah was younger, she had a once-upon-a-time-fling with Sully? If so, Sully would be Zahryn's and my granddad! Oh, this is too big!!!* As crazy and far-fetched as this thought was, Maevyn kept it to herself.

Maevyn and Zahryn threw their heads back and laughed. Long curly auburn tresses and black silken locks danced behind their shoulders, in their robust laughter. They were caught up in the moment—in their palpable and contagious *joie de vivre.*

Murray brought the second round. "Have fun, ladies!" He saw their playfulness and grinned. He caught on to their energy and felt their fun. Maevyn said, "Hey, thanks, Murray. Sláinte!" And she raised her beer as if to toast him. Maybe she was flirting, just a little. He nodded, smiled, and headed back to the bar.

Maevyn turned back to Zahryn. "Hey, Zawi! I heard your Auntie Tagyn call you that a while ago and I guessed that your initials spell ZAWI. How cool! Zahryn-Ava Walker-Inglis. Zawi is a great nickname! Ha! Can I call you that?"

Zahryn laughed. "Hey, sis, call me what you want! Zee, Zawi, Zed, Red. It all works. Did anyone ever give you a nickname?"

"Yeah," said Maevyn. "My mom had a couple of pet names for me." Maevyn went quiet for a minute. "She used to call me May-May, and May-vee. And sometimes just Em, like the initial M. And then other times, she'd call me Twig or Toadie. I guess I jumped around a lot like a toad when I was really little, or something like that."

Zahryn laughed loudly. "That's adorable! Maybe we'll introduce ourselves to Sully as Zawi and Twig!"

She looked into Maevyn's eyes. They connected knowingly in the moment. Their sisterly bond was relatively new, but their roots ran deep. They knew in their hearts that they were sisters. They felt it.

Always the instigator, Maevyn said, "Are you ready?"

"Yes!" Zahryn said with conviction. They picked up their draughts and walked over to the Snug, giggling.

"Hi there! Is your name Jack Sullivan?" Maevyn spoke with a boldness that really looked good on her.

"Yes. Hello! Jack is my given name, but nobody calls me that." He held out his hand. "Sully, call me Sully. They each shook hands and Maevyn asked, "Do you mind if we join you?"

"By all means set yourselves down. Lotsa room here."

Sully held up a closed fist high in the air, and hailed out to Murray. A raised closed fist was code for a round of whiskey shots at that table.

Maevyn and Zahryn had barely sat down in the Snug, and the shots arrived. The girls still had beers in hand. Seeing their surprise and wonderment, Sully laughed and said, "It's okay! Don't worry. My treat. It's an old habit of mine. Pretty ladies all get whiskey, on my tab!"

The girls eagerly picked up their shots, then Sully as well. They all downed the whiskey and slammed their glasses down. Sully was smiling freely. Maevyn noted the vibrance of the whiskey, and nodded with approval. And Zahryn . . . well, this was her first-ever shot of whiskey. She tuned into the warmth in her throat and in her chest. She noted the flavor that dominated her whole mouth—her whole focus. She gasped loudly then giggled nervously.

"So, what's up, ladies? What's on your mind?" Sully was curious.

Maevyn led the charge. "I could be really sly and introduce ourselves using our nicknames, or, I could just say our real names . . . ."

Sully quickly cut in, smiling, beaming. "I know your names. This is a small town." He looked directly at Maevyn. "You're a not-so-newcomer in town and your name is Maevyn—Paige's niece. I know Paige well. She's worked here at this pub for a really long time."

Turning to Zahryn, he said, "And you, young lass, your name is Zahryn. Such a beautiful name and a beautiful person. Connor was your dad, and I knew him well, before he died. He told me your name means Radiance, or Radiant Light. It's so sad about your mom. She never got to meet you."

He stopped, noting their absolute shock about his knowledge of their persons and their stories. "Sorry, I'm not trying to shock you or scare you. I haven't been stalking you. It's not like that at all. It's just that I already know lots about both of you, and that must be strange for you to hear, seeing how you don't know me at all.

"Let me start again. I'm Sully. I've been coming to this pub most of my adult life. I know people and things. And as much as I like people, I'm kind of a private guy. But you young ladies, you can ask me anything you like."

Zahryn spoke first. "What's my middle name?" She spoke almost defiantly.

"Well, that's not too tough. Connor told me your nickname, and that it came from your initials. Zawi he called you, and if my brain isn't too pickled, I'll say your middle name is Ava. Zahryn Ava Walker-Inglis. Zahryn means Light. Ava means Life. 'Light of Life' is a beautiful name!"

Zahryn blushed deeply, and her mouth dropped open immediately. "So you do know my dad really well, if he told you my middle name. This is unreal! We thought we were coming over to ask questions of a complete stranger, and, you're not! You already know us and our families."

Maevyn chimed in. "And, what's my mom's name? You know my Auntie Paige, and you know I'm not from here. Who is my mom and where am I from?"

Sully settled back on his bench, and brought his draught closer to the edge of the table. His fingers traced the edges of the tankard handle. "Well, Maevyn, your Auntie Paige told me how she accidentally let the cat out of the bag one night, talking to you about your parents. She was mortified. She honestly did not know that you didn't know Connor was your dad—that Connor and Enya had had a fling and you were born. I'm not telling you anything you don't already know—Paige told me. So yeah, your mom is Enya, and you're originally from Opalon."

Maevyn, emboldened in the moment, grinned, and said, "And right you are! So. Now, us two girls, we look like we have egg on our faces. We must look so naïve. But, we do have one question that we haven't asked yet, and, I'm not sure if you'll even want to answer it."

Sully quickly chimed in, thinking he knew the question to be asked. "You don't even have to ask the question, Maeve. The answer is yes. You both have a brother in Doran's Brook. Yes, Connor had a son, too. And his name is . . . "

"Gaelan!" Zahryn shouted. Now it was Sully's turn to be surprised. He had no idea *how* these girls could have known this. Gaelan was raised in Doran's Brook, in the Hebrides, nowhere near the Southshore Islands. And, as far as Sully knew, Connor's son, Gaelan, was Connor's best kept secret.

"So you girls know? Now I'm feeling a little shocked. How long have you known he's your brother?"

"A while." Zahryn found her voice. "I met him in university, and, with a lot of help from Maeve and my friend Saorise, we figured out where to find him—what classes he was taking."

Sully settled back a little. "So, you're okay, you two? Knowing all of this? Does Gaelan know you are his sisters?"

"No!" both girls blurted.

Zahryn continued. "No way is he to know because it would open a huge can of worms with his mom and his stepdad. They are all living here in Moonstone now. His stepdad's company relocated all of them from Doran's Brook to here. Some things must remain secret. It's not our story to tell. Gaelan is smart and happy and he's going places with his career, and he doesn't need this info to complicate his life. Let sleeping dogs lie."

Zahryn leaned back on the bench, trapping her tresses behind her. She stretched out her long legs under the table. The beers and the whiskey were hitting her quickly. She didn't want to end up saying something she would regret later. Maybe they had already said too much.

"I see," said Sully, tapping his fingers on the now empty tankard. He let a couple of minutes of silence go by, before he continued. "So, you said earlier you have one more question for me. Did I answer it already or do you still have a question to ask me?"

Once again Maevyn found her bold heart, and her voice. She sat forward and leaned toward Sully, looking hopeful. "You can choose to answer this question or not."

Sully nodded, and waited, keeping his eyes trained on the dancing dark-eyes of this spirited young woman.

Maevyn spoke slowly. "It might be a crazy rumor or a tall tale told by someone with an overactive imagination, but, here goes nothing."

She looked at Sully, directly in his deep dark eyes. They were receptive, interested, curious, even hopeful.

"Sully, are you Connor's father?" Maevyn let her voice trail off, and she held her breath.

"Yes Maevyn, I am."

Maevyn was quivering. No words were coming. She looked over at Zahryn who looked like she had just seen a ghost. Maevyn spoke again. Slowly. Very slowly. "So you, Sully, you are our granddad?"

She could hardly believe she was asking this question. She took in a long deep breath, and braced herself for the answer. Maevyn reached out for Zahryn's hand, and together they gripped firmly, palm to palm, fingers tightly clenched.

Sully looked relieved. This was his story to tell. "Yes. I am granddad to both of you. I have watched both of you from afar, knowing this. And, I have loved you from afar, knowing this. But it has been the hardest secret to keep, all of these years. Townsfolk talk a real lot and they don't have much good to say about a good-for-nuthin' love-'em-and-leave-'em kind of guy like me. They have no time for me or my kind. So, I kept my mouth shut. Connor, my son, was the only one I ever confided in, and if word is out about Gaelan, then I guess Connor must have blabbed. It sure wasn't me."

Sully stopped. The moment lingered. The space between them was soft and warm. There was a feeling, an air, a mood of relief—of release. The truth was revealed at last.

Zahryn's color returned. She was truly overwhelmed. Then she reached out her hand to Sully and said, "Hi Granddad! Hey, Daideó!"

Sully did not reach over to shake her hand. Instead, he stood up tall and he leaned forward, with both arms reaching out wide toward both young women. "My sweet granddaughters, I've hoped for this moment for twenty-some years. I want a hug. Group hug."

Zahryn and Maevyn were more than ready for this. They could not have possibly known earlier in the day, that they would be meeting, and hugging, their newfound grandfather, today.

They all moved closer to the door of The Snug, where there was more room to gather in close. And, they hugged. Their own inlonracance fueled their spirits. Love was found between these newly acknowledged family members. Love was the connection. Love and joy lit them all from within.

Then Sully collected himself and stood back from his beautiful grand-daughters. He said, "And I want to tell you something else. Something I really think both of you should know. It might help you to understand a few things and why they happened the way they did." He sighed and reached out to hold one hand of each granddaughter, as they themselves were still hold-ing hands. Full circle. He inferred gentleness, tenderness, in this gesture.

With a quieter voice, he shared some historical truths. "Your father, Connor, was a sensitive young man. Overly-sensitive, I'd say, for a guy his age. He had a really big heart where his family was concerned, but, he got hurt so very easily. Tough and strong on the outside, but a vulnerable softy on the inside.

"His parents had to move away to London for medical care, and he never got over that. He drifted. It simply broke him to be alone, at eighteen all on his own, when they left. His words—he felt like they 'left him up a creek with not even a broken paddle to steer his own canoe.'

"And I believe I am quoting Connor now, in these next few words. He spoke to me from the heart more than once about his true feelings. I can almost hear him saying this to me, a long, long time ago.

"Connor has said in earnest, 'Is there anything wrong, with just needing to be needed? Needing to be wanted? Touched? Held close? Isn't it just a basic human need to belong, to feel safe and loved?'"

Sully shook his head and said, "I remember Connor saying that it was an awful thing to be abandoned by your family. I think he wondered if there was something wrong with him or if he'd done something wrong. It's awful to be alone, you know.

"One time, Connor said to me, 'Sully, if I ever have a family, I'll be there for them. And they will know this. They will always know this. As long as I have breath, they'll know we are family—strong and together and needing to be together, as a family.'"

Zahryn, just then, broke out sobbing. An inconsolable sob. This was all so much for her to take in. These words resonated deeply, reminding her of her loving father. She could practically hear her own dad's voice in Sully's words when he spoke.

Impassioned, she cried out loud, calling out to her departed father. "I love you Dad. I always will. I needed you Daddy, and then you were gone. And I needed my mom too. I never even knew her. I will always need you—both of you! I miss you so much Daddy and Mommy. God, this hurts so much. I need you, Daddy!"

Zahryn then let go of both of their hands—Sully's giant man-hands and Maevyn's petite young-woman-hands. She hung her head intentionally, allowing all of her tresses to tumble in front of her. She hid behind her cascading locks, safely burying her face in her own hands as her tears rained down.

Sully and Maevyn heard her every plaintive word. They could see Zahryn's grief, and they simply reached out to hold her. They drew her in close. They were powerless to change anything for her, in the moment. She needed to let her feelings out, to express her heartfelt losses, to give voice to the pain she had silently borne for so long. All they could do was help Zahryn to weather this storm—to be there with her in her darkness—to let her know she was safe in sharing her feelings—to let her know she was not alone.

Their hug continued until the tears fell no more. And in that moment indeed, they were not alone. Love had found them. And love would lead them on.

PART THREE

Be the Love—Unconditionally

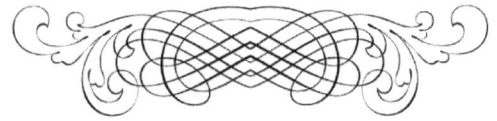

Still Unspoken, in the Light

APRIL 3, 2010

Barely a week later, Zahryn knew she needed to talk. She was restless. Scattered. She needed to find Gaelan. She just needed to be near him. She had been wrestling all week with so many feelings about him.

She simply delighted in confirming that he was her brother! She was so drawn to him. She desperately needed to connect deeply—deeper—with him. But, she knew she had to be careful.

So she had phoned him at the end of the week and arranged to go hiking with him on Saturday morning. It would be safe. Just the two of them. Just casually chatting, casually sharing, while trekking on the mountain trails. She didn't need to tell him everything. She just needed to be near him, to feel close to him, to be with him.

"Hey Zahryn! Do you know why this hiking trail is called The Cairn Trail?"

"Actually, I do, Gaelan. You see, these trails in the Ben Lonrach are all ancient trails, cleared and marked by the original peoples—the Celts, the Druids, and the Picts. And, in the last fifty years or so, as more money was given by the government to improve recreation sites in the Southshore Islands, all but one of these trails have been physically widened and graded for safer travel for the average hiker.

"But this one, the Cairn Trail, is still in its original form. Steep. Twisty-turny. A tough go for sure, but no rock-climbing equipment is needed. There are no modern trail signs posted here, only these ancient Cairns. The trail is often forked, and the way up is clearly marked by these original piles of rocks carefully placed to point the safe way up.

"And," she continued, "you cannot access this particular trail from the park's parking lot. That's why we drove farther east to get to the Cairn Trailhead."

"Makes sense. Good to know. Be sure to show me a Cairn when you see one so I know what I'm looking for!"

"No problem, Gaelan. You can't miss them. Some of them are quite tall. Like, as tall as us!

"Let's go. It's already 9 o'clock. We should be done by noon-ish. We can decide later whether we'll have our lunch up there in the heights or back at my home. No matter what, our lunches are here, in my knapsack."

They set out together keeping a good pace, walking side by side, into the fog, into the mist, finding their way into the obscurity of the weathered heights.

Zahryn looked skyward and said, "It's a little foggy out this morning. Darn! I sure hope it clears a bit. The views of the Celtic Sea are pretty spectacular from up here. I'll be sad if we don't get to see everything from the heights."

Gaelan replied, "Well, we'll take what we get, I guess. Beggars can't be choosers. It was very kind of you, Zahryn, to invite me on such short notice for an impromptu hike here, on Easter weekend. When you called me yesterday, you sounded pretty excited about getting together up here! Is something going on?"

"Hey, Gaelan, ya know, yeah, I do have a lot of stuff going on. Thanks for asking. I am feeling a little conflicted this week, for sure.

"Just last week, I got to meet a really cool guy at the pub—at Pints. I was there with Maevyn. This guy knew my dad a really long time ago, and they apparently were pretty tight. Sorta-like confidantes. Birds of a feather, you know? And I instantly felt really, really close to him—uncanny close. Almost like there was a bond we shared because he knew my dad so well.

"He spoke highly of my dad. And, I liked getting to know a bit about the guy. It was nice to feel close. Like, family-close. Almost kinship-close. And then, it just made me feel sad all over again, because my dad is gone. I miss him, Gaelan, and the old guy Sully misses him too. Dad died thirteen and a half years ago. Where does the time go? Anyway, a lot of people in this town, not just little ol' me, felt the loss of my dad. I guess I never really knew just how connected my dad was.

"But, not to dwell on the dark side, this is where my conflicted feelings come in. It's springtime! It's Easter weekend! I should have exhilaration and joy and anticipation in my head, and in my heart. And I do! But, I oscillate with being sad for my dad, and full of joy for the season—back and forth like a bloody yoyo. Happy and blah. I'll get over it."

And then she blurted out loudly in lament, "And I miss my sweet Master Madigan too! It's been two months since he died, and I miss my little buddy. I miss my secret confidante, my unconditional listener.

"See! I'm just a bouncing yoyo! Up down up down up down. Enough already!"

Gaelan had been listening intently. It was hard for him to hear her heartfelt words. His own heart hurt with hers. Rarely had he seen this side of Zahryn, wound up and unsettled.

His mind had wandered for a second when he heard her mention the words—Old guy Sully. His mom had often spoken of an older acquaintance, "the mustache man" who traveled throughout the UK in his work. He would visit Doran's Brook quite frequently. As a child, Gaelan had met the man once or twice, a long time ago. "Mr. Sullivan from the Islands" was how he was introduced.

He then recalled another tidbit, something about his mom Kelly's parents once upon a time having known Sully's parents. They were all originally from the mountainside town of Sullivan's Gate. He wondered if this was the same Sully. But he did not go there. He turned his thoughts back to the present moment, to Zahryn's heart.

He spoke to her thoughtfully and gently. "Well, that must have been a great visit, Zahryn. Just sitting down with a friend of your dad's and speaking now as two adults—just that alone would be kind of therapeutic for you. What do you psych people say? Cathartic? Or something like that?" He smiled inwardly at his own growing people perception.

He went on. "Just sharing stories and some old-time remember-whens—these alone would be bonding. They'd make you feel connected, for sure. I am so sorry that they made you sad, though. You're such an upbeat person. I'm sure it won't bother you for very long."

His gentle voice trailed off as he looked at her fondly. Their eyes met for a fleeting moment. And then, he saw Zahryn's eyes actually began to sparkle and twinkle and come alive as her playful spirit was returning, in the moment.

"Look at you go, Gaelan! You get it! You get me! You listened to my story and you looked deeply into what I said and how I was feeling. You are not all numbers and equations and calculations! Not anymore!

"So Gaelan, you can see why I called you—and why I was anxious to get out here in the mountain heights with you. I just needed to clear my head and feel like my old carefree self again. Get reconnected to things that are important to me. Like, with nature and my ancestral draw to the land. Like, with you.

"We're both done with school now and we're finding our way in the working world. I just wanted to make sure that we stay connected. Hiking can do that for us, you know, a common interest. Something we can always do together because we enjoy it so much.

"Your friendship is so important to me, Gaelan. We need to be intentional about finding time for us. Work can eat us up—life can eat us up—if we let it. You're the one who first talked about work-life balance. Are you glad you chose the Commerce route, instead of a PhD and Math academia?"

"Yeah, I am glad, Red. I think I made the right choice. I'm so fortunate to be able to work from home. I crunch numbers all day on the computer and keep the company's accounts accurate and accessible. Year-end was December so that was a pretty busy time and tax season is over now. I'm in the clear. Life is good. My time off is my time—me-time. And I'm glad to spend it with you too.

"I've never been here in this part of the Ben Lonrach. It's rugged. You'll have to be my guide. I'll have to trust you, Red!" They smiled and continued hiking over the steepening trail.

The ground itself was quite variable—some rocky outcrops, some gnarly tree roots at the surface of the earth, some downfallen foliage, and patchy grasses even. They saw their first Cairn, only three minutes out on the trail. The Cairn stood about two meters tall, in an obvious fork. The upward path would always be the correct choice. So, upward and onward they went.

The fog lingered, and that was somewhat frustrating when they arrived at some lovely lookout vantage points. They *could* see the sea waters directly below, but no sky, let alone a distant horizon, was visible at all.

They came across a beautiful, ancient, free-standing stone Celtic cross. It stood maybe five meters tall in the foggy air, about five meters from the edge of the cliff. Zahryn said it was about 1500 years old. She had read that in a trail guidebook, once upon a time.

She said, "Some folks call this the St Mungo's High Cross. And then, of course, other's dispute this, saying that it is so obviously Irish in origin. No matter what, it is just beautiful, even on this dull and greyest of days."

Gaelan pointed upward, to the cross. "Look at the details. After all these years, you can still see most of the remnants of the carvings etched into the stone. This one has weathered amazingly well, here in the heights. Some crosses are toppled over due to wild weather and exposure to the elements, but this one is still whole and stunning."

Zahryn said, "The ancient Celts worshipped out of doors, where they could sense both the power and the presence of God. I'm sure there were regular gatherings here, at this very lookout, a few thousand years ago. That's why the cross is here. They must have felt close to God, here.

"The Celtic people felt so connected to God and to Creation. Interconnectedness is such a huge theme in their teachings, in their ancient wisdom. Every life, every living form in all of Creation is part of something greater—Divine, Holy, Sacred. They are all parts-of-the-whole, of life. Everything that has life is of God—not made by God—but of God. Therefore, all life is Sacred and all of Creation is interconnected by the inherent Sacredness of all."

Gaelan spoke softly, almost reverently. "Wow, Zahryn, you sure know your Celtic stuff. I really like hearing you speak about connectedness. It feels good just thinking, just knowing—and maybe even believing—that we are all part of something greater than ourselves. That we are all connected in ways that we might not even comprehend yet. Not just by DNA and such, but by what you call, an ancestral draw. By our roots. By our own intimate Sacredness."

"You got it, Gaelan! Interconnectedness is not a theory, or a concept. It's simply a way of seeing all of life. It's a way of being! Look here at you and me. We are not known to be brother and sister but we could be, by the depth of our beautiful connectedness. Gaelan, you even feel like a brother to me.

"We're both physical beings. Our physical needs are met by physical things on and of this earth. Like food. Water. Air. Our homes—our shelters—are built from materials of the earth. Our relationships—familial, friendship, communal, church relationships—all of our relationships connect us heart to heart, soul to soul, Light to Light."

Zahryn continued giving direct eye contact to Gaelan as she spoke. "We—you and me—we are connected through school, through our common interest in the outdoors, and through our like-minded views of humanity. And, we are probably connected in more ways than we know. We are brothers and sisters in Christ, living a life of love and Light and service to others—a Christ-like life—we are connected deeply through the family of Christ.

"We very well might or might not have different moms and dads, but we are indeed brothers and sisters of the faith, of the heart, through all of time and eternity."

Zahryn paused, still looking directly at Gaelan. Her sage green eyes were fervent and intense with passion, yet somehow, her gaze was still soft and tender.

In Gaelan's eyes, and in his humble opinion, she was full of wisdom. She was a believable teacher, an inspiring mentor, and an amazing tutor in life.

She spoke inwardly, in awe. *We are standing here in the heights, at the foot of this stunning ancient Celtic Cross. I have just delivered a most meaningful message that holds so many hidden truths. So many inferences of our own real personal connections. He is taking in my every word. But this is as close to the truth as I dare speak. This is as much as I can share with him. Bring on the blackbirds. Bring on the lennons. This is us.*

Gaelan spoke softly. "I learn so much from you and I'm starting to sense something that I've never ever been able to put my finger on—something I've never been able to put into words.

"I feel so drawn to you. I cannot explain it. It's like we know each other really well, even though we only met in university. You're kinda like a second sister to me. I feel like I have a much longer, deeper—even higher connection with you. Like a spiritual connection.

"I'm not good with words, like you, and I'm not good with expressing my feelings. But, I will say, I love listening to you and I love being with you. When we're together, I grow in so many ways. I can't explain it. We're just good together."

Zahryn loved Gaelan's earnest attempts at self-expression. He was indeed, evolving. He even voluntarily offered up the "sister" word! Zahryn shivered in goose bumps. Gaelan had admitted many times before that he was better analyzing numbers, not people, and that he had a lot to learn about self and self-expression. Yet here he was, here and now, openly attuning to—and affirming—his relational self.

She stepped closer to him, saying, "I just want to hug you! Can I?"

And with that, Gaelan scooped her into his arms and they hugged. She nestled her face into his shoulder and neck, and discovered the prickly bristly stubble of his weekend unshaven skin. It didn't matter. Connection and compassion mattered. They did not need to speak. They felt comfortable, cared for and valued. They felt blessed. Time stood still.

Zahryn with her eyes still closed, began to cry, softly. She was so overwhelmed by what she had just intimated to Gaelan. They were family! They shared a father and a grandfather too. This was so real now. She had only confirmed all of this last week at the Snug, with Maeven and Sully.

All of this lay heavy on her heart, and there it would remain. Unspoken. But, she was able to infer their greater connectedness and he had just responded so positively to all of her words.

Gaelan whispered to Zahryn, "You're crying, Red. What can I do?"

"Just hold me, Gaelan. Just hold me like you are doing right now. You get me, and that is so special to me. You are special to me, Gaelan, more than you'll ever know."

And Gaelan held her. He held her close, sensing a closeness beyond words. With both of his hands resting in the small of her back, he pressed still closer into her lanky frame, not wanting the hug to ever end. He reached upward with one hand, and stroked her long tresses tenderly. He discovered—he knew—he wanted her. He buried his face in her hair and breathed in her scent deeply. He held her with his heart and soul. His heart was full, so—very—full.

Zahryn stopped crying. She released one hand to wipe her tears. "Now I need a tissue. Where is my bag? I'm sure I packed a few."

With that, she pulled away from Gaelan. She bent down to search her bag, and found her tissues. What happened next was almost a miracle—an amazing suspension of disbelief!

"Oh my God! Zahryn!" Gaelan called out with excitement. "Look up! Look to the sky! This is fantastic! This is unbelievable!"

Hearing the excitement in Gaelan's voice, she quickly rose up. She and Gaelan stood at their fullest height, lifting their faces to the incredible vista in complete wonderment. They both looked upward at the sky, then outward toward the horizon.

All of the fog had rolled away. All of it! The southern horizon was now completely visible. Sky meet water. Water meet sky. Bliss meet blue. Blue meet bliss.

The Celtic Sea below and beyond, was a deep teal blue color hosting a dazzling parade of white Light sparkles in the brilliant morning sunlight. Soaring high above them now, was a grand grind of lennons—a flock of blackbirds—hushed in their approach, graceful in their presence, and richly mystical in their very being.

Zahryn thought, *No broken wings here. Blackbird sky! A moment of waiting, anticipating. A sweet moment of undeclared love. Metaphor of true awakening on a deeper level. The moment has arrived! I feel like I too, have arrived! And I too can fly! Soar! Up, up, up, and away! On the breath of God, and rise some more!*

In the vastness, God's Holy Lovelight most surely lit them, held them, and nurtured them. Into the heights, their Lights, their unspoken love was lifting. Into the heights, their insights arose, winging away, away. Lovelight had set the mood and Creation followed suit, matching it, moment by moment, with all of its splendor.

Gaelan and Zahryn stood side by side, leaning on each other. Zahryn reached for Gaelan's hand. In the mountain heights, high above the shores, their hopes and visions and dreams—their joy of togetherness and unspoken love—all of these now lay out so clearly before them in the Light, across the waters.

Gratitude

JUNE 15, 2022

IT WAS A FAIR-WEATHER day in June. Warm enough to want to spend time outdoors in the fresh air—intentional time with a dear friend—with a best friend who had always been with you, through thick and thin.

"Thanks, Saorise, for helping me to get out of my wheelchair and onto your porch swing. We've spent many hours together out here, at your parents' house, over the years. Cartwheels on the front lawn, or playing games in the backyard, swinging from the willow tree branches, and, drinking many fine pots of tea here on this very porch! And," she paused with sparkling pleasure in her eyes, "oatmeal cookies!"

Zahryn reached over to grab a freshly baked homemade oatmeal cookie from the plate, then continued to speak. "You and your family have been so very kind to me as far back as I can remember. Your mom is like a mom to me—maybe even like the mom I never got to have. She always had a cookie or a sandwich, or she offered us a drive to the park or to the movies—she was always there for us. I sure have some great memories of all of you—your family—of all of us through our thirty-five years on this earth."

Saorise was now married, to Ryan, and they were expecting their third daughter. She too had fond memories of Zahryn, her lifelong friend, her church friend, her Anam Cara.

Saorise smiled and said, "Yeah, Zahryn, we've got it good. We have had a village helping us to grow up. Nice neighbors, good teachers, wonderful church leaders and church family members. Long-term friends. And now, I have my husband and my children too. Life is so good. We are totally blessed. And, I know that neither one of us takes any of this for granted. We have our whole lives built on strong foundations of love and faith and hope."

Saorise continued, "I still don't know how we came out on this side in such fine form. You especially, Zahryn! You met so many challenges early on in your life. Illness, your parents' deaths, your own disability—and you met all of this darkness by merely shining your Light. Never once did I see you

134

fall down and dwell in your darkness. You never uttered "Why me?" or "Not again!" You've even evaded Covid for a whole two and a half years, knock on wood! You've been smart in being so careful, wearing your mask all the way through this whole darn pandemic!

"You channel your energies to look to the bright side and you move forward with optimism and hope, and contentment. The world needs more Zahryns!"

"Thanks, Saorise. You are so kind with your words. And you know me so well. I love all of this positivity, I really do, but I did come here today to share some hard news with you. And I guess there's no easy way to tell you, so I just I will. Please bear with me."

"You're scaring me, Zee. What is it? Are you okay?" Saorise turned sideways on the swing to face her friend while she spoke. Zahryn was struggling to say her next words.

"Saorise, my time is up. My post-polio symptoms are advancing very quickly now. Starting next week, they are setting up home oxygen for me. I'll have to start using oxygen pretty much most of the time because my numbers have gotten too low. I can still stand up to transfer from my wheelchair to a chair, or to a car, or to my UTV, but I am getting weaker, especially my legs, and I need a lot more help.

"As I said earlier, it's so nice here in this moment, just to be out of that wheelchair for this visit, and to sit with you on this porch swing. A simple pleasure for me, for sure!

"I saw Dr. Gordon last week. My blood-work and my oxygen numbers are not good. I may only have a few months—maybe only four to six months. They're not sure. He's going to line up the palliative care team so they'll be ready at the right time, and I might go to the Hospice here in Moonstone or over in Pearl Haven. We'll see. That's still down the road.

"But there's a couple of things we need to talk about . . . . "

Saorise didn't wait for Zahryn to finish her sentence. She was shocked at the news. She said, "Oh Zahryn, I'm so sorry. I had no idea this would all be so soon! We've talked about it before—you know—that your PPS would become a terminal thing for you, and your life would be shortened. But, oh my God! This is happening! This is so fast! How are you doing? How are you feeling about all of this?"

Zahryn smiled her beautiful smile. "I'm actually okay, Saorise. I've known about and accepted my end-of-life story for a long time now. It's like a scene simply playing itself out until the final curtain falls. Really, I'm okay. I made a pact with myself a long time ago that when my time on earth became limited I would do my very best to still live—*to consciously choose to really be living*—while my body was slowly dying. I would try hard to find joy in each day, and in each moment. I would speak my mind and share what was on my heart and be grateful for the life I had. I'll appreciate what I do have, not resent what I won't have. I want to cherish what I still have left."

Saorise was listening to every word. Zahryn was pouring out her heart. Zahryn had come to visit, with the intention to do just that.

Zahryn continued, "I know it all sounds so surreal and maybe overly optimistic, but, you know, it has been so much easier living with a 'come what may' attitude and a 'glass-half-full' approach. It makes coping with all of this so much easier. And, it's easier on my family and friends. I'm not sucking them down into a deep dark hole—a black pit of despair. I'm not dragging anyone down, anywhere. My life is what it is right now, and I am making the very best of it. Every minute counts.

"I do have one teenie-weenie misgiving though, Saorise. It's not really a full-on regret, just a fleeting feeling that I get now and then." She paused to collect her thoughts. "I see you, married and pregnant—again! You're happy and contented and you're bringing yet another new life into the world. A part of you and a part of Ryan! And you are such wonderful parents already to your twins, Neve and Nella. Parenthood looks so good on both of you!

Saorise leaned forward and smiled ever so sweetly. She graciously nodded and received Zahryn's words of praise.

Zahryn went on, "I made a conscious decision about ten years ago when I was twenty-five—when I first learned that I had developed PPS and that it would severely limit my life. I grew up without a mom and that was so tough. You know—you lived it with me. So, when I learned that PPS would likely shorten my life, I decided to not pursue any lifelong relationship with anyone—like a marriage with children—so that I wouldn't be setting up a husband and little ones to suffer the losses that I did. No one should go through that. Ever.

"And it took every ounce of courage and conviction that I had, to tell Gaelan way back then that we could only ever be friends. I couldn't allow myself, or him, to fall in love—to share in an intimate relationship. It only would have caused him pain and grief in the end.

"And here we are today, Saorise. You are absolutely glowing with your pregnancy—with your growing family. And me, well, just a wee bit of me is still wishing that things could have been different for me. Yes! I made these conscious decisions, and I still stand by them. But, oh my, what I wouldn't give to have had a baby of my own—to know that a part of me would live on in my child. Kinda like a wee legacy here on this beautiful earth." Her voice trailed off.

She gazed beyond the porch railings, the yard, the street, as if into the real beyond—into the future. Zahryn so wanted to know that her life had meaning and purpose. That it would continue to have meaning and purpose long after she was gone. She loved the names Zoe (Life) and Gavin (God-send) and as she peered away into the beyond, she could actually visualize her own wee ones, Zoe and Gavin, playing and cavorting in the sunlight on the rugged mountainside. It was a beautiful vision, a wholesome scene—it was a dream that would remain just that, a dream.

Saorise leaned in to hug Zahryn. They spoke no words. Their hearts understood. Their souls shared. Their Lights shone brightly. Saorise thought the world of Zahryn, and could only marvel in the moment, in the wisdom of her words, in her insight into her whole situation, and at Zahryn's glowing aura of peace. Saorise was in awe of the largeness of Zahryn's love and the very grace of her selfless thoughts. Zahryn was content with her chosen approach. Her faith truly made her strong.

Saorise pulled back from the hug. "I hear you Zahryn. I do. You've had to make some super-tough decisions in your life, and wow, intentionally distancing yourself from intimate relationships must have been so hard. It's just so natural to fall in love, with the right person. And wow. You and Gaelan. You could have been married and had a family together by now! And you would have been a wonderful wife and mom—I know it!"

And sensing the weight of the moment, Saorise steered the conversation in a new direction. "Zahryn, I think you'll love what I'm about to tell you. And it's a perfect time to share this exciting news with you!

Saorise's grin stretched from ear to ear. Her speech quickened and she spoke in fervent tones. "Ryan and I have been talking about baby names, and we both want to honor *you* when we name our third daughter. Your name Zahryn, you know, means Shining, or Radiant, and so does the name Ailee! We'd like our daughter to shine as brightly as you do!"

Zahryn placed both of her hands over her heart. She was overwhelmed with joy. She said, "You would do that? You and Ryan? Oh—My—Goodness! I don't know what to say! That's so beautiful, Saorise, to be remembered in a name. A tiny part of me WILL live on in little Ailee!"

"AND . . . " Saorise continued, "we'd like YOU to choose Ailee's middle name! We know you'll choose something lovely. Something symbolic. Something so perfectly 'you'!"

"Oh, that won't be too hard! Not hard at all!" Zahryn knew right away. "Could you call her Ailee Lennon? Lennons are blackbirds, and a flock of blackbirds is said to fill the sky with beautiful love! They are so full of love! Her whole name would translate to Shining Love! Oh my! Ailee Lennon Sullivan—so many L's—such cadence and flow! Do you like this name for your precious wee girl?"

"Oh, Zahryn, I love it! I really love it! And I know Ryan will too! Especially knowing that you chose it, and, knowing the deeper meaning of the name! You're brilliant Zee! I love you so much!"

They hugged again and the world was warmed by the love in their embrace. Hugs make the world a softer, sweeter, safer place. In that moment, their world was indeed, softer, sweeter, safer, if only in that moment.

This time, it was Zahryn who pulled away first. "Saorise, you've made my day with all of this. I'm so happy! I'm blown away. I'm honored. This feels oh-so special.

She sat for a few moments, simply enjoying the little joys of her world. She could feel the love. Then reality set in again and she spoke again, this time in an assertive tone.

Zahryn said, "I hate to change the subject, but my energy is limited, and I did come here to discuss another important thing with you. I want to give you time to think about your answers. This is a sensitive matter, so, here I go."

Saorise looked at her beautiful friend. *What more could be weighing so heavily on my friend's heart? Isn't facing the news of her own imminent death, enough?* she wondered. *Isn't just talking about it all with such grace and dignity and integrity enough? What else could be such a "sensitive matter" in her life right now?*

Zahryn boldly continued. "I know my own feelings about MAID—Medical Assistance in Dying. It's not new, but it is in the headlines again while politicians, medical professionals, and religious leaders weigh in with their pros and cons and the ethics of it all. Human euthanasia, assisted suicide, death with dignity, end-of-life planning. There are so many names for it.

"Do you have an opinion, Saorise? Have you thought about it? Can we talk about it?" Zahryn had stopped swinging the porch swing. She allowed her head to rest back on the swing's padded headrest. She was tired.

Saorise noticed this. She noticed all of Zahryn's cues—verbal and non-verbal—and she tried to read Zahryn's current stance in this sensitive matter as well.

"Well," she said slowly, "I have mixed feelings. If a terminal patient knows that death is unavoidable and that the suffering into death would be a difficult journey, then I do believe that the patient has the right to decide which is best for them—the natural pathway or MAID.

"But then," she continued, "my faith is very strong. And I know that God is the Creator and the Giver of all life. I'm not sure how I feel about 'playing God' and making such a decision—such a controversial decision—in the face of God.

"But you know, Zee, what I think shouldn't matter to you. This is your journey. You know what you can cope with, and you know what your faith asks of you. You have an amazing prayer life—an indulgent interior life with God. You yourself are the one to know how to deal with all of this." She stopped and let her words and their inherent sensitivities simply float in the airspace between them.

After a while, Zahryn piped up, "I'm totally okay with MAID, especially in my own known and very predictable story. But, in fact, I'm not going to ask for it. I do believe that a person has the right to end their own life on their terms, at the right time. But because of the negativity and controversy and unclear legalities, I'm not going there. I'm not choosing MAID. Besides, it's way too hard on family and friends when there is a chosen, carved-in-stone date for the death of a loved one.

"And, I meant what I said, I'm going to live my best life while I'm dying. My UTV will help me to get out and about to the places that I love. I can still get to the park and the mountains and the shorelines. I'm as good as I can be. Just wait till next week and see what the new portable oxygen does for my energy level!

"My mantra throughout my adult life most surely served me well. 'Be the River. Be the Light. Be the Love. Across the Waters.' And it will continue to lead me and empower me in the time I have left. God gave me these words one day, at Riley's Beach, just when I needed to hear them. And, I will live out the rest of my life in their fullness, in their truth, in their Light."

Zahryn paused. She took in several slow, deep breaths. She reached over to hold both of Saoirse's hands in hers. "Saorise, promise me this. Please help my Auntie Tagyn with my funeral arrangements when the time comes. You know all of my favorite hymns and Scriptures—Isaiah 43 and Psalm 139, for sure. And about the faithful woman in Matthew 9, where her faith had healed her, and made her strong. And make sure my favorite Celtic blessings are sung and spoken by all, for all."

She stopped to catch her breath. "And, I want you, Saorise, to give the eulogy. You know me. You know my heart. Please share my story—share the goodness, not the darkness, of my days here on earth."

She leaned over for another hug, and Saorise gladly gave her friend what she needed—a warm, encouraging, love-you-forever hug.

"Of course, Zahryn, of course I will," was all Saorise said. They held each other. They became one in their hug. Love was their bond. Light lit them from within. Eternity danced before them.

Saorise whispered an ancient Gaelic blessing softly into Zahryn's ear, almost chant-like . . .

Deep peace of the running wave to you
Deep peace of the flowing air to you
Deep peace of the quiet earth to you
Deep peace of the shining stars to you
Deep peace of the gentle night to you
Moon and stars pour their healing light on you
Deep peace of Christ, the Light of the World to you, my friend.
Amen.

Two friends—one with all doors opening widely in marriage and motherhood and mirth—and one with all doors slowly closing all around her. Two lifelong friends, two soul friends—Anam Cara friends—leaning on each other in love, in trust, in faith, in hope. Two hearts full of grace, full of gratitude. Two friends sharing the Light of their love—a Light that would show them their pathways—onward, forward.

Loads Lifted

JANUARY 9, 2010

THE SUN WAS GLISTENING—DANCING on the snowbanks all around. The wind blew cold and blustery outside, but they were warm and toasty inside the car. The mood was light and breezy, mirroring their souls. Zahryn and Maevyn were enjoying reconnecting, spending time with each other, after Zahryn had returned to Moonstone Cove, having graduated from Glasgow U. They were both working, so evenings and weekends were theirs for fun, for chillin', for finding their way, together.

Zahryn spoke softly from the driver seat to Maevyn beside her. They were driving from Opalon home to Moonstone Cove. Side by side, in sync.

"Now that wasn't so hard, was it, Maeve?"

Maevyn responded earnestly. "Yikes! Zahryn, It took me six years! I never would have done this Zahryn, without your help. I would have stayed hurt, and angry and resentful—probably forever.

"Forgiveness is a really big deal, and I think you have to be pretty mature and you have to be very much self-aware before you can even begin to forgive.

"I was so young when I got pregnant. Sixteen. 2004. And in my own immaturity, I felt my mom wrongfully judged me. I felt that her judgmental words literally and viciously attacked me. They cut me down. They put me down. I was down so low, I just couldn't get up. I felt she just didn't care about me. And what I couldn't see then is that I was totally blinded by my own anger. I was so conflicted.

"And you helped me to see that, Zahryn—all of that. You helped me to understand myself. You are so good at helping people understand who they really are. You should be a shrink in a fancy treatment center where every mental health patient gets well and can live out their best life. I can just see you writing the center's new vision statement: " . . . And Mental Wellness for All."

"Ah, you're too kind," Zahryn said, trying to deflect the compliment. "You did all the legwork. You learned what forgiveness is, and, you needed and wanted it, badly. You took the steps to forgive both yourself and your mom. You did the work. You championed a new life-skill. And you succeeded!

"Your mom was so happy to see you, first of all, and that hug after you told her that you had forgiven her, well, that hug was everything! And then, when your mom heard about your journey to forgiveness, and all the work you did yourself in coming to understand forgiveness—well, she softened. She really did. You did something *for her, for both of you,* that was truly life-changing. I'm so proud of you, Maeve!"

Maevyn cut in, "Well, I'm still the thankful one. You, Zahryn! You make such a difference in so many people's lives and you've made an incredible difference in mine. Six years ago, I was the new kid on the block. I was so lost to life and living. I was consumed by my darkness, thinking that nobody could or should or would help me. And you literally rescued me, Zahryn, from a really dark place.

"I didn't tell you any of this back then. I just couldn't. It was all too painful and too shameful. I was considering suicide. I was going to drink myself into oblivion and find my way off a cliff somewhere. I had a plan but no firmed-up details."

Hearing Zahryn's great big gasp, Maevyn kept talking, hoping to soften her story. "And today you know, I say a big 'Ouch,' Zahryn. Just by mentioning the word, suicide, and just my very saying all of these dark words now, after all this time, it really, really, really hurts me, still. I was in such a bad place.

"But you Zee, you brought me back from the deep black hole and you showed me what living a good life is all about—you showed me what good clean living can really look like. You gave me a second chance when everyone else thought I was a loser. I've come a really long way thanks to you. You saved me."

Zahryn listened to every dark detail of Maevyn's heartfelt admission, but she held back her words. *Maevyn had never mentioned suicide! Ever!*

Still driving, she reached out to hold Maevyn's hand. She squeezed it tight. She spoke from her heart. "Maeve, May-vee, you never, ever, told me—you have never, ever mentioned suicide or suicidal thoughts, or a suicidal plan. I wish you had! I only knew, and felt, that you so desperately needed a friend. I knew that in my heart, loud and clear. So I brazened my way into a friendship with you, and I'm glad I did! You might have died. That's awful!"

Zahryn added slyly, lightening up the conversation a bit, "And, on that note, I never would have known you as a sister, or that Gaelan is my brother! Or that Sully is our granddad! See? What a WIN-WIN for both of us Maeve! I love you. We're so good for each other!"

They drove on in the wintery January weather. Eventually Zahryn pulled her car into Maevyn's laneway in Moonstone and turned off the engine. She spoke seriously. While turning to face Maeve in the passenger seat and looking directly into her dark, dark eyes, she said, "I'm feeling good, you're feeling good, and we've got lots more talking to do. Lots more. I need to hear the rest of your story. You need to fess up, Em. The hard stuff. The real hard stuff. The suicidal stuff. You can trust me. We're not done yet. We still have some issues of yours to deal with.

"Suicide is not a passing whim, nor is it the stuff of casual conversation. It can haunt you. It can break you. And I need to hear your story. I need to hear it all. I need to know that you are going to be safe. Truly safe. And I need to know for your future that you have a safety plan. This is so so so very important.

"I'm not here to judge, Mae-vee. Only to listen the best I can and to hear your heart. Oh Maevyn, thanks for opening the door."

Maevyn nodded. She was ever so grateful for Zahryn's blanketing receptivity and for her unconditional support. She simply said, "Thanks Zee. Thanks so much. I do trust you."

Then Zahryn shifted gears in her voice and in her body language. "But for right now," Zahryn's eyes twinkled as she spoke, "We need to lighten up. Let's go inside and see if we can make some of those yummy brownies! It's been a big day. We can just kick back. Chill. And, you should feel really good about your time with your mom today."

Maevyn smiled broadly and squeezed Zahryn's hand, hard. "Yes! Let's do this! Let's go!" And off they went. After slamming the car doors closed, they ran up the stairs together, sharing freely, as only two sister-besties could do.

Owning Up

JUNE 20, 2005

ZAHRYN WAS JUST ONE week away from graduating high school in Moon-stone Cove. She was leaving the grocery store on foot, on her way home from school, carrying a carton of milk. She was hoping to bake and cool a custard by evening to take to Saorise's mom who had just had oral surgery. Dental-soft diet. Doctor's orders. Zahryn wanted to return some small kindness to the woman who on many occasions, had helped her in the most thoughtful and caring ways.

Zahryn stopped at the long bench on the sidewalk, just outside the grocery store door. She wanted to see if the two-liter milk carton could fit into her oversized handbag. It did.

Just as she was re-shouldering the bag, a voice from behind her called out softly, "Hi, Zahryn."

She turned and looked at the boy standing there with distant familiarity. She had gone all through primary and secondary school with this handsome young redheaded lad, but, for her own reasons, she had kept her distance. She had chosen not to befriend the one who had spoken so harshly once upon a time, about her father.

"Hello, Delaney. Nice day." She spoke with an edge in her voice.

"Hello, Zahryn. I've been really hoping to talk to you before we graduate—before we all go our separate ways off to colleges and universities and traveling. And now seems as good a time as any."

"Well, Delaney . . . ." she started.

Delaney cut in. "Zahryn, I've had a long, long time to think about what I said to you way back when we were Juniors—and why I said what I said—and what Mr. O'Shea told me—what he taught me. I was pretty stupid back then. Would you please hear me out? Can we talk?"

Zahryn kept walking, in her long-legged stride. Delaney walked quickly beside her. "I'm listening," she said.

Delaney pursued with his words. "Can we sit somewhere? Just sit and talk for a few minutes? Just a few? I really need to do this, Zahryn."

Zahryn pointed. "There's a small picnic table out in front of the ice cream shop. How's that?"

Delaney hesitated. "That's kinda too busy. Too many people. Maybe out by the bridge, down by the stream? Maybe we could just sit down for a few minutes, by the water?"

Zahryn said, "Sure. It's not far. Let's go. But only for a few. I've got stuff to do."

Delaney smiled as if relieved. "Great! Thanks!"

They walked side by side, striding out quickly in the June air, in an awkward silence. The main road curved and the old stone arch bridge came into full view. When Zahryn saw the bridge, her mind wandered. She remembered something Auntie Tagyn had once told her about old bridges. *Ancient bridges do so much. They stretch over water and time, and times. Bridges are metaphor, indeed, for trust and encouragement, hope and new beginnings, forgiveness and moving forward. Bridges help keep us going on our path.* Zahryn sighed in the comfort of Auntie Tagyn's reflective words.

Delaney said nervously, "There it is. We're almost there."

They walked down a steep embankment of gorse bush and wildflowers. The bridge to their right enhanced the mountain stream with its antiquity. Those stones had been carefully hand-placed by the Roman builders of yesteryear, forming three charming arches over the braids of the meandering stream. Grey lichens and green mosses gave the bridge color and life.

As there were no benches or rocks upon which to sit, they remained standing, gazing at the stream with its clear waters sparkling in the afternoon sunlight.

They stood looking upstream at the open meadow just above the brae, where the world-famous giant oak tree, the Caomhnóir Síochána, stood in all its gnarly grandeur and glory. It lived up to its name, Guardian of the Peace. Its oversized broad green leaves cast great shade for tourists and hikers alike. It spoke grace and murmured peace. It towered in strength.

Delaney turned from the beauty of the landscape to face Zahryn—to look directly into her eyes. He needed to unload his emotional burden, one that he had carried for far too long. "Zahryn, I know I hurt you when I called your dad that name. I was stupid. So stupid. And Mr. O'Shea told me it was an awful thing to say. I was just starting to want to be cool, and pretended that I was tougher than I was. I thought swearing loudly and using words that were offensive would make me sound cool, or tough, or, like I knew what I was talking about. People say FUCK all the time and HOLY

SHIT and those swear words really have nothing at all to do with what they are saying. How can shit be holy, even?"

Zahryn did not allow herself to be distracted by his light-hearted question. She did not laugh. She sensed the true seriousness of his words, and she listened intently. Without even speaking, she veritably redirected him. She gave him time and space to refocus on his intention, and not on his humor.

Delaney took a deep breath in and continued bravely. "Back then, I was pretty impressionable, and I was hearing new slang and swear words all the time, and I didn't really know what I was saying."

Delaney paused. Zahryn remained attentively silent. "So, Mr. O'Shea called me to his office and he talked to me like a nice guy. Kinda like a father figure, I guess. And he taught me what that word really meant. And then he asked me about my own dad, and he asked me how I would feel if someone said bad things, truth or lies, about my dad."

Delaney took in a deep breath and let it out slowly. "I love my dad. Like you loved your dad, Zahryn. And yes, it would feel awful, it would feel terrible, if someone said bad things to my face about my dad."

Zahryn started to speak, but Delaney kept going. "Please let me finish, Zahryn, while I still have some courage. You know, I probably would have done way more than kick a shin, if someone had said that about my dad. I probably would have beaten the crap out of them. I guess I got off pretty lucky with just my bruised shin—and my bruised pride."

Zahryn nodded in response to his sharing. She appreciated his honesty.

Delaney carried on, "But Mr. O'Shea told me something else. He used some big words that I really didn't understand back then, but I get it now. He said something about needing to be an upright, self-respecting, and decent kid *before* I could be an upright, self-respecting, and decent adult. And that that all comes with being more aware of my feelings and of other people's feelings—and their rights as human beings.

"I'll never, ever, forget his words. And I know now that I cannot be a self-respecting decent human if I never apologized to you or if I never asked you for forgiveness. I'll always hate the person I was and the words I spoke and the dumb reason I said what I said.

"I'm sorry Zahryn. So, so sorry. For hurting you and being mean-spirited and not caring about you. I'm not that kid any more—I'm not that guy. I want to do right by you, and by Mr. O'Shea. I'm saying sorry, and I mean it. I hope you'll accept what I'm saying. It's taken me years to find the courage to tell you all of this and—there. Well. I've said it. You didn't deserve any of this. I hope you can find a way to forgive me."

She turned and glanced first at the ancient stone arch bridge, and then over at the grand old oak tree. She sighed. The symbolism was rich, powerful—deep. Building bridges. Living in peace.

Zahryn said quietly, "You're forgiven, Delaney. I forgave you a long time ago. I couldn't carry the hurt for very long. It was only hurting me, so one day I just let it go. In forgiving you, I felt so much better.

"You hurt me, Delaney. You really did. But, you were taught a really big lesson and you're happier and more humble—you're more human—as a result of your learning."

She reached up to give him a brief hug, and then broke away just as quickly. "Thanks, Delaney. I hope you're feeling better already. All is good. I gotta go. Custard is calling. Bye!"

And she left. She picked up her bag, shouldering it, and strode away, up the braeside, onward.

Delaney remained by the moving waters, watching her walk back up and across the bridge until he could no longer see her. He felt finally freed in the framework of her forgiveness. He felt he could move forward, bridging the gap that had been holding him back all those years. His own troubled waters stilled. He breathed in deeply and took notice of the fresh scent of the gorse flowers in bloom on the steep brae. The scent filled his lungs and he smiled, enlivened.

He glanced once more upstream at the grand old oak, the Caomhnóir Síochána, and spoke softly, upward, into the calm, "Thank you Zahryn. Thank you Mr. O'Shea. Thank you, God."

Secrets by Firelight

AUGUST 27, 2006

AUTUMN APPROACHES. SCHOOL BELLS toll. Hopes arise. Dreams unfold. Plans are made and they fall in to place, one at a time. August is still considered the lazy days of summer, yet the anticipation of the fervor of fall, and the craziness of schedules, courses, and classrooms—these all stir inevitably. Yet in the lateness of August, there can still be calm. It can still be still.

"Come here, my sweet Master Madigan. Up. Up here in my lap." Zahryn patted her thigh, inviting her dog. Without hesitation, Madoh scrambled up her leg, up onto her lap. Her teenie weenie Westie, all of twelve pounds, nestled in so easily. Master Madigan was indeed a lapdog.

At the midnight hour, in the dwindling fireside light, she stroked her precious boy. "Well Madoh, here we are once again. Summer's almost over and I'll be leaving soon to go back to Glasgow—to go back to university with my friends." She paused and sighed audibly. "I wish I could take you with me! You are the bestest little buddy ever, my Bestie Westie!"

Zahryn smiled. Master Madigan was now eight years old. Zahryn had always confided in and shared many heartfelt stories with her four-legged pal. Secrets too. Master Madigan slept on her bed with her every night, snuggling right in beside Zahryn. Auntie Tagyn had, over the years, snapped many a sweet photo of the two—long auburn locks swirling and co-mingling reposefully in the tufty white fur. Such a pretty sight! Wonder and whimsy all wrapped up and cozied up in the stuff of the duvet, in the puff of percale, in the fluff of dreams. Sweet, safe, secure they were.

Zahryn sat with Madoh in her lap. They were both facing the faltering hearth-fire. Darkness had mantled the mountain over the last hour of evening. The stars were shining brightly beyond the windows, but in that moment, Zahryn could not see them. The tiny remnants of glowing embers drew her full attention, her focus.

Speaking to her lap BFF, Zahryn surmised, "This will be one incredible year, Madoh. If I play my cards right, I just might get to meet my brother.

I might get to know a young man who doesn't even know I'm his sister. Wouldn't that be just awesome?" The silence hovered and literally breathed, in the wonder of the moment.

"I've already met a sister I never knew I had—a sister by another mother. And now, a brother by another mother! What do you think of all of this, Madoh? Will this be fun for me?"

Zahryn's sage green eyes danced in the waning firelight. She stopped stroking Master Madigan's back, and with two hands, she gently rolled him over in her lap. Belly up. Paws up. Face up. He simply lay there contented, placid, in stillness.

"Ahhhhhh, my sweet little boy, look at you! So trusting. You've just molded yourself into me like you were part of me. Complete acceptance. Not every relationship is like you and me. Open and trusting. Unconditional and loyal. Yes, we are special, we two."

She let her voice trail off into the evening while gazing into the depths of Madoh's dark, dark eyes. She laid her hand upon his chest and felt the sure rhythm of his beating heart. No words were necessary. Simply presence. Simply contentment.

Moments like this could go on uninterrupted, forever, as far as Zahryn was concerned. She was energized by her one-to-one relationships and she was strengthened by them—strengthened even by her tender ties—her love bond—with her little Madoh.

Zahryn lowered her voice, almost whispering, "I hope that my first meet-up with Gaelan next week won't seem forced or even contrived. Saorise found out that her cousin Gaelan and I will be in the same Stats class. That's so cool! I hope I'll be able to sit beside him in class and we can just casually chat—you know—about anything. I hope he'll like me. I so want to meet him, and just get to know him.

"I'm probably playing with fire in wanting to know him. My brother. My half-brother. I've been alone with no siblings in all of my growing-up years, so I'm really excited in finding out more about him. That would be so cool, having a brother. That would be even cooler if we could relate to each other like family.

"Oh, if we could just be friends, and be close. I'm a starveling for personal connection—for family connectedness—for brotherly love. I've been alone long enough. Way too long. I want to not be alone, but, to be with. To belong."

Zahryn traced her long slim fingers in figure eights around Madoh's eyes and lightly across his tufty forehead. 'Round and 'round and up and down—even down his little snout to his nose. He loved her gentle touch and he closed his eyes, basking in these pleasure-filled moments. Zahryn went even deeper then with her thoughts about Gaelan.

After a few moments of silent, heartfelt reflection, she spoke ever so softly to her sweet boy. "Oh Madoh! I simply cannot be the one to tell Gaelan the truth about his father. Our father. I have absolutely no idea what Gaelan's mother Kelly has told him—or even what she has told his step-dad—about who Gaelan's father is! I have no business in disrupting their family story—their family unity—over my selfish need to be Gaelan's newfound sister.

"Our brother-sister relationship must remain a secret. And I will guard this secret forever. I promise. It won't be easy but I will keep my word on this for all of my earthly days—until I find my Holy rest.

The last ember flickered and snuffed itself out in the old stone hearth. Starlight was now streaming into the windows behind Zahryn, from two sides of the room. She looked up and noted the white-light moonbeams and starshine. The stuff that ballads and poetry are versed upon. Zahryn's heart was full. The perfect peacefulness washed away all of her lingering queries.

Slowly, she picked up her tufty pal and raised his sleepy form to her chest, to her heart. She carried Master Madigan into her bedroom, laid him down, and crawled under the cool white sheet—their snuggles a given.

She fell asleep as she offered her bedtime prayer. She had spoken the words of her heart, the secrets of her anticipation and her joy! Madoh had listened. God had listened. She was now answering the call to dreamland, to the world of wink and nod, to the mystery of the presence and the grace, of God.

Blessed are those who slumber—who arise in the morning singing, with a prayer on their lips, reverencing their God. Blessed are those who know their God. Amen.

Emanant Love—Into the Light

SEPTEMBER 2, 1987

ROSE LOOKED AT HER husband, lying beside her in the bed. Her pregnant belly and a full-length body pillow kept them farther apart in the bed than she liked. Connor was sleeping on his side, facing her.

He looked so peaceful. Way more peaceful than she was feeling, right then and there. It was 5:30 in the morning and she had had yet another restless, sleepless night. Her hips were sore. Her back ached. She was up to the loo every hour to pee. Her poor bladder had absolutely no room to expand with a full-term fetus taking up residence in her pelvis, so close by.

Rose gazed upon the love of her life, Connor. They were still in their first year of marriage. They hadn't even had their first wedding anniversary! Not for another two months. Their whole first year together was spent in preparing their hearts and lives for parenthood.

They had just moved from their tiny flat in the heart of the village of Pearl Haven, into a wee cottage on the outskirts. It was a perfect starter home for a growing family. Rented, yes, but a home nonetheless, with a fenced yard and some gardens and a lovely veranda looking down the mountainside to the rocky shores.

Rose continued to gaze upon her man. Connor was a really good sleeper. And so was she, prior to her pregnancy. He always slept through the whole night and awakened in the mornings feeling quite rested, alive, and energized. He was most certainly, a morning person.

Their morning lovemaking on any given day, was pretty amazing. Their young bodies were ready, and responsive after a good night's sleep. They were both hungry for intimacy and touch. Their sex was sometimes tender, sometimes playful, and sometimes raw and rough, unbridled and wild.

In their bed, in the moment, Rose couldn't help but feel exquisite joy, just looking at her sleeping man. They had talked long before they were married, about wanting to raise a small family, in their lovely hometown of Pearl Haven—about how love and faith and hope would guide their parenting. They looked forward to seeing their life together come into full bloom with their growing family, in the tiny village.

And, just two months after their wedding, they had conceived. A beautiful dream had come true! They smiled when they had counted backward, and calculated the actual date of conception. New Year's Day! What an amazing symbol of a fresh new start, and of new beginnings! What a way to ring in the New Year! Their little one would be born in late September. September 25 was the due date.

And here, on September 2, in the quiet moments before dawn, she smiled, remembering the finer moments of their hot New Year's afternoon delight. She and Connor had returned to their bed after brunch, exhausted after a good night of partying with friends and royally ringing in the New Year. She had awakened late in the afternoon, in Connor's arms, enlivened and more than ready for pleasure and fun. And that they had! Her big O had brought her to the stars, to that place where only the perfect cocktail of love and lust and passion and play can propel you, soaring into the heights. In the moment, in the memory, she blushed. Her own internal warmth grew.

Rose shifted her weight and she rolled away from Connor, accidentally losing the body pillow to the carpet. Her sleep-deprived, aching body was now talking loudly—it was crying out to her, to move around. She needed to get up and she didn't want her restlessness to disturb Connor's blissful sleep.

As she swung her long lean legs over the edge of the bed, she chuckled to herself about how comical—how awkward she must look, just trying to get off the bed! With her knees wide apart and her feet firmly planted on the plush ivory carpet, she stood up slowly, in the dark. The bedside LED clock said 6:00 a.m.

"Okay." She spoke quietly to herself. "I'm up." And into the loo she waddled to empty her bladder. Again. While washing her hands she looked into the mirror, dimly lit by a stained-glass nite-lite. Her face was full and glowing. Her pregnancy fullness made her look especially pretty, bedhead and all.

Walking out of the loo, into the dark-ish hallway, she found her way across the hall to the study. She eased herself down onto the ivory tweed sofa, and, one at a time, she lifted her feet up onto the rustic wood coffee table. She placed both of her hands on top of her big-as-a-house-belly. She caressed her flesh, hoping that her wee one could feel her gentle touch.

"Hello little one! My sweet girl. Our little radiant light. You are so loved. I have wanted to be a mommy all of my life, and, in just a few weeks, I will be. Finally! I'll get to be your mommy. And I'll get to love you, and mother you—I promise to mother you well. I'll be complete. Your daddy and I will be complete.

"I can't wait to meet you! We are pretty sure you are a little girl. Pretty darn sure! There was not even a hint of any little baby boy parts in the ultra-sounds, so, sweet pea, our wee baby girl, we'll see you soon!

"I sure wish you would hurry up and arrive. This business of going-to-pee-every-hour is very tiring." Rose then twisted to her left, reaching over, stretching out, intending to turn on the table lamp beside her.

She felt a sudden, horrible pain, a sudden ripping, searing pain in her pelvis, and a large hot gush flooded around her buttocks and thighs. She looked down and saw bright red blood. A lot of it. She moaned loudly and called out Connor's name. She suddenly felt dizzy. So—very—dizzy.

"Oh no, this is not good!" she said out loud. "Connor! Help!" She didn't hear any response from the bedroom. She got herself up to a bent-forward standing stance, and she cautiously took steps toward the study door, holding onto the built-in bookcase to steady herself. Her bleeding was getting heavier, She could feel it. It was out of control. Her dizziness was getting worse and she found it difficult to see clearly.

She knew she was hemorrhaging. She was in danger. She started to gasp for air. She made her way into the hall. Across the hall. Into the bedroom. Her only thought was *I need to get to Connor!* Overcome by her dizziness, she slumped and fell forward onto the bed, in front of Connor and was only able to utter, "Help me, Connor. Help me, God."

Rose continued to talk inwardly to herself. She had no more energy to voice her words out loud. She spoke with encouragement to her own self. *Hold on girl. Connor's right there. Hold on. That's a lot of blood but Connor will call an ambulance and all will be well. All will be fine.*

And she continued speaking inwardly, to her unborn child. *You, my sweet child, will be safely delivered and your daddy and I will get to hold you and show you our love. And, you'll grow up here on the island, on the mountain. And you'll know joy and hope and peace and love. And every day you'll play with all of your friends in the warmth of the sunshine, under clear blue skies. And you will be loved. You will be love.*

Oh look—there's the sunlight now—the sun must be starting to rise—it's rising quickly—it's so bright—it's so white—this room is so full of beautiful radiant light—shimmering Light. Oh! This Light is so beautiful. This Light is shining all around me.

It's all too beautiful for words. . . .

Holy Moment—Holy Ground

AUGUST 27, 2022

IT WAS STILL WARM-ISH for August in the Ben Lonrach, but the winds were indeed changing. Darker, lower clouds and stronger winds from the north closed in upon the mountains. Both were clear signs of the impending change of seasons.

The giant, gorse bushes were no longer golden with their grand fragrant blossoms. They were very green, and a little dry. But the bracken ferns lining the roads and the forests took their turn and became the exquisite golden splash in the countryside, in the wilds, in the Southshore Islands.

The cedars willingly shared their wonderful aromatherapy. The waters of the brooks and the streams were seasonally shallower. They were silently running away, down, down, down to the sea. The heather on the hillsides wisped in the heights in a glorious purple-pink—a gasp-worthy sight for tired eyes, weary souls, and sagging spirits. It was still summer but the telltale signs of autumn were there. Yes, there's a time and a season for everything under the sun. And yes, just like the title of the folksong, there's a standing invitation to 'come by the hills'.

Aoife was standing beside her car near the grand cedars in the parking lot of the park, on the outskirts of town. She had lived in many small towns in the Ben Lonrach after her first encounter with Zahryn in 2014. Her journalism career had blossomed as she sought story and truth and ancient wisdom, while listening to the elders in the communities. She had gained perspective, delving into legend and mystery and folktales, looking for Light in the shimmering mountains. She loved her work. She loved putting her words and her modern slant to the wonders of the ancient Celtic Wisdom.

Aoife was now a mom, although she was still a single woman. Her mothering heart desperately yearned for a child and she had chosen to adopt a twelve-year-old girl in 2016. The pre-teen girl's own parents were adoptive parents—they had adopted her as a newborn. But tragically, she was orphaned a second time. Her beloved parents were both killed in a freak winter accident that had sent their car off the road, off of a cliff to their death in the frigid waters below. In her grief, in her unspeakable loss, the sweet young girl was going to need all of the love, encouragement and understanding that Aoife could give her. And Aoife had risen to the challenge. She graciously welcomed little Joy into her home—into her heart. In 2016, she took an extended parental leave from work to help Joy to settle down and to settle in.

It was a Wednesday, a quiet day in Moonstone Cove. Zahryn and Aoife had agreed to meet today. Aoife would hike and Zahryn would drive her UTV as far up the mountain as her energy would allow her. That was the plan. Zahryn was on oxygen continuously now, and fatigue was a large part of her every day. She still tried to spend time outdoors as much as she could. She was happy to be mask-free in the outdoors—Covid was still widespread and so highly transmissible. Zahryn had persisted in wearing her facemask in crowds and in public places. But, in the parks and on the mountain trails, her mask-free-moments were her freedom, her body, mind, and spirit delights.

Zahryn's days on the mountain were numbered. In her ever-positive outlook, she still wanted "to live" while she was dying—while her body became more limited and debilitated each day. Her will was strong, but her strength and her endurance were failing rapidly.

Zahryn was delighted when Aoife had called her earlier in the week to invite her to go up the mountain. It's where they had first met eight years ago, by chance, upward on the mountain trail. They had taken an instant liking to each other back then, and had nurtured a wonderful friendship since that very first time. Theirs was a connection, a bond of friendship that would carry them both, through thick and thin, through darkness and Light, through all time.

Zahryn drove up in her hot yellow UTV. Aoife watched her drive up to the gate, to the cedars. Zahryn was harnessed in safely in her coveted wheels. This vehicle was a godsend. It had become Zahryn's legs. It was her freedom dance. And Zahryn's face showed all of this. She glowed with happiness, an inner joy, a radiance second to none. Her inlonracance lifted her up and set her apart. Zahryn was happy. Zahryn was Light.

"Hey Zahryn, so good to see you! How are you?" Aoife noted Zahryn's color, or lack thereof. A pallor. A greyishness to her visage. She looked tired—weakened, but certainly not beaten or defeated by her disease. Aoife thought to herself, *I'm so glad she's wearing all of her harnesses and straps. They'll keep her safe on the mountain. I'm sure she couldn't ride at all without them, seeing how her energy is so diminished.*

Zahryn called back with a stronger voice, with more energy than Aoife had expected. "Hello Aoife, my friend! I'm so glad you called me and asked to join you here! I love these beautiful mountain trails and the lookouts, where fancy meets free. I love looking out across the waters. I so need to be here, and I'm happy you're here with me!

"How are you and Joy doing these days? You look fabulous by the way—so fit and strong!"

"Thanks, Zahryn. Joy is good, and I feel great. This outdoor air just energizes me" Aoife replied, inhaling deeply after she spoke.

Zahryn continued, "And, how old is Joy now? Does she like hiking with you?"

"Well, she's growing up so fast. She's a really good kid. She had her eighteenth birthday just a few weeks ago. On July 31."

Hearing this birthdate made Zahryn cringe inwardly with anxiety—with acute discomfort. Zahryn had recently put some pieces of a puzzle together, about Joy's real birth mother. Right or wrong, Zahryn said nothing. She withheld her words. Some secrets simply need to remain secret. Through her silence, she perpetuated—she lived out—'the Mountains of Secrets.'

Aoife went on. "And, yes and yes. She loves being up here on the trails and we do come up here a fair bit. But, she doesn't like going near the cliffs much, and I get it. She has nightmares still, about the crash . . . ." Her voice trailed off as she shuddered involuntarily. "Maybe someday, hopefully, I'll be able to teach her—to show her at the cliff—at the precipice—what you and I intuitively know here in the heights. It's a beautiful mindset—an approach to all of life and living, seen most clearly up here on the mountain. It's spelled out so perfectly in the words of your mantra 'Across the Waters.'

"Changing the subject, sort of. Guess what Joy asked me just yesterday?" Aoife's eyes were dancing.

Zahryn answered "Ha! The sky's the limit for that question! She wants to dye her hair purple—she asked you if she could go purple with your blessing!" Zahryn was just beaming at the thought of her playful, wild-guess answer.

"Well, wouldn't that be interesting! My beautiful black-haired daughter—my little blackbird—goes royal—royal purple! That could be a lot of fun!

"But no" Aoife continued. "Her question is way way deeper than hair dye." She pasued intentionally for impact. "She wants to change her name!" To herself, inwardly, she sang a familiar tune, superimposed with her newly minted lyrics *Blackbird-Skye. Free in the breeze with her purple wings she'll fly!*

"Oh my goodness! Aoife! Where did this all come from? Is she unhappy? What's stirring in her that she needs a new name? Is this a good thing? A whim? What's going on?" Zahryn's voice tones were escalating, her eyebrows were raised up to the max, and her eyes were wide open as her concerns tumbled forward as direct questions.

"Well, I listened to her reason and I'm actually inclined to agree with her, as radical as it seems."

"Well, why does she need to do this?" Zahryn asked again. She was still in overdrive, in wonderment. "Tell me!"

Aoife took a long slow breath in and began. "You remember she was adopted first as a newborn baby, and, at that time her adoptive parents named her Joy, because they were filled with joy at the news of becoming her adoptive parents. I think this part of the story is so touching, so beautiful.

"But, ever since her parents died, Joy says that her own sense of joy died with them. And she wants to leave that name behind her. She wants to not be reminded every time she hears her own name, that she is joy-less. Sooooo . . . ." she looked directly into Zahryn's sage green eyes.

"She wants to honor *me*—her new mom—the one who truly rescued her and brought her back into the world. So, since my hometown of Portree is on the Isle of Skye—drumroll please! She wants to feel like she is part of me and my family. She wants me to call her Skye! Skye Stewart!"

"Oh Aoife! That's deep. That's heartwarming. That's rich. She's obviously a sensitive girl, a sentimental young lady. She's just needing to feel like she belongs, that she is part of a family that is rooted or solidly grounded somewhere. What a total contrast!—her feeling more rooted and grounded in identifying with the airy, breezy name of Skye!"

Zahryn sat for a moment with her words, with her thoughts, with her growing admiration for Joy's choice of a new and meaningful name.

Aoife offered "And I think I'll let her do it. It'll be part of her healing journey. Heck, changing my name was a big part of my journey. I won't stand in her way." She smiled knowingly. "And, it's a perfect time to change her name, now, just as she's heading to university. Her curriculum starts in January so we have lots of time to to get the technicalities of her name-change looked after. So! Here we go!"

"Wow . . . ." Zahryn almost whispered. "A name change is a really big thing. Please tell her I admire her—a lot—and that I love love love her new name. Oh, I'm feeling so inspired right now!"

"I'm glad you like it Zahryn. Really glad. Your opinion and your support mean a lot to me. I'm still pretty new at this mothering stuff and it's nice to know I can bounce things off of you when I need to."

"Oh, Aoife" Zahryn spoke with encouragement. "You are already one fine mom! You've had a late start with your womanhood, and a bit of a rocky start in motherhood, but your heart is full of love and you are going to do amazing things as a mother of Joy—I mean, as mother of Skye! Your mothering spirit totally defines you. Mothering-and-you is a really good fit!"

Their eyes met. Without a word, Aoife stepped closer toward Zahryn and they hugged. A tender moment of sharing and caring. A warm and endearing moment between friends—between friends of the heart.

While still embracing each other, Aoife said "I guess we should get going . . . ."

Zahryn agreed. "Yes, let's do. Let's get going, alright? The UTV is too noisy for us to chat on the trail, but we can stop here and there and take breaks, tell stories, like we love to do!"

Aoife answered, "Okay. Let's go! Do you want to go ahead of me? Or behind?"

"Behind. You lead. I will follow. You'll know if I'm falling behind, and we'll take frequent breaks to stop and look—and to just be."

"Perfect! Onward!" And Aoife led them through the cedar gates onto the wide gravel trail, up into the heights, up into the clean mountain air.

Aoife approached the mountain stream just half a kilometer in to the journey. She asked Zahryn, "Want me to bring this cool refreshing water up for you to touch?"

"Yes," was all Zahryn said.

Aoife pulled her collapsible cup out of her packsack and filled it from the little stream. Although shallow, it still had a fair flow this late in the summer season. "Hold out your hands, Zahryn, and I will pour the fresh waters over them. Feel the cool. Feel the wet and the refreshment. Look at the glistening in your hands. Don't you just wonder where the water has been before? Let it make you curious about the stories it could tell you."

Aoife, who was also a lover of nature and the Celtic understanding of human inherent connection to nature, continued. "Water comes from the sky as raindrops, seeps over rocks and earth, collects in streams and ponds, hides in springs and aquifers. And it nourishes all life and living. Water connects us all. And this water has now touched you, nurtured you, refreshed you and delighted you. Maybe even it is teaching you something. You are part of its story now, and it is part of yours. This is interconnectedness in its finest."

Zahryn sat there, hands cool and wet, and dripping. She answered Aoife with powerful words. "Geopoectics in action. In our emerging eco-zoic age, we all need to respect all life—our interconnectedness—our place in this world. May this river—these waters—ever run clear." With that, she sighed and put her hands on the steering wheel. She was ready to move on.

Aoife took her cue and began walking upward into the heights. She was very aware of Zahryn's lagging energy and she would respect any request to stop and rest or turn around to go home. Zahryn's body was limited, but her will was strong. Aoife walked on, and listened for her next command. While moving forward both young women attuned—they fine-tuned all of their senses—to the sway of the trees, to the scent of the wind, to the sweetness of serenity all around them and within.

And after just a few minutes underway, Zahryn called out, "Can we stop here, by the arch? I have always been drawn to the antiquity of this place."

Aoife added, "Yeah, me too. I've learned, through my research and interviews this year, that the townsfolk don't really know why this arch is built right here. They think it is a Roman style of architecture, but the round circle of rocks at the base is clearly ancient Druidic. The Druids were here way before the Romans. They made rock-base cells—circular rock formations—in the mountains. They were probably the rock bases for wooden structures for the solitary hermits in the mountain. If so, this would have been a prayerful place. Likely a Thin Place.

"Perhaps we stand here on Holy Ground. The stories are vague. More like legends. But, isn't it awesome just to stand here, to sit here, in awe, in wonder, and feel the grace of the mountains? Again, I'm feeling so connected."

Zahryn looked down at her feet, and then at the ground that she was not walking on. She sighed.

Aoife said nothing. She let her mind wander into the backstory. *What was the history? The culture? The symbolism? The meaning? The truth? And, what wisdom did this ancient site hold for Zahryn and herself?* Her questions remained unanswered in the stillness. She looked at Zahryn, who nodded her onward.

Ten minutes later, Zahryn hailed out. "Let's stop for a moment at this lookout. It's only a small clearing. We cannot both be there at the same time. Step in, Aoife, and look out and beyond the water, to the horizon. The ocean is straight down—it's almost dizzying to look down, so, look out across the waters. Just imagine how many others have stood in this very place throughout all time. Imagine their awe and wonder. We're all truly different and yet, we're all the same."

"You're right, Zahryn. "The beauty of Creation stirs something deep inside every one of us. No one could stand here and not get caught up in the moment. Well, no one I know. I suppose all of the New York, Wall Street wise guys and the corporate business execs could hardly sit still in this place. Idle time costs them money—big bucks. It would surely just kill them all financially to simply stand here in awe and wonder!"

Aoife had been standing in the little one-person lookout while they chatted. She stepped back and chuckled at her commentary on the perceived and frivolous cost of wonder. For Aoife, wonderment was not a cost—it was simply priceless.

"Here, Zahryn. Drive up into the lookout. Your turn."

Zahryn did so, aptly maneuvering her UTV as far in as the space allowed. She sat and stared out in silence. These moments in the vastness of time and space were so precious to Zahryn. These were moments of eternity to be sensed and savored.

Aoife watched her friend sitting in stillness. It was then she noticed the Light. The day was cloudy, yes, but the skies were still bright. Yet, coming up from the ground beneath Zahryn's UTV was a peculiar sight.

There was a perceptible movement. A flow. Almost a shape-shifting flow. Of what? Was it mist? Was it dust? Was it Light? Zahryn always had a certain Light about her. Not like an aura but rather an emanance of Light from within. And mystically speaking, the Ben Lonrach Mountains—the shimmering mountains—were said to have their own Light. They shimmered and glowed as if they were adularescent. Like a moonstone that seems to give forth its own Light from within.

Aha! Aoife said to herself. *Is this possibly the origin of the name of their town, Moonstone Cove? Was she experiencing firsthand the interconnecting of the Ben Lonrach Light, Moonstone Cove's inherent Light, and Zahryn's Light?*

Saying nothing, so as not to interrupt Zahryn's special time, she held onto the mystery of the moment. She turned inward, praying silently, *Dear God of Light and Love, I am here. I am yours. Let me know you. Let me serve you. May I serve you well, using all of the blessings and the gifts you have given to me. My Kindest Shepherd, and My Gentle Pastor, please hear my heart—please hear my prayer. Amen.*

In another minute, Zahryn openly shared her own prayerful thoughts. She turned and spoke quietly, "God is with me. God is with us. God's Presence is so very palpable. The veil that separates the human and the Divine is thin. That which divides does not truly divide. The Light is bright. We are one. I wish more folks could know what I see, what I feel, what I know, here and now."

Zahryn looked into Aoife's eyes. They spoke no words. They knew. They both knew. Words could never describe the connection they felt in the moment, to each other, to Creation, to God.

Zahryn called out to Aoife, "I think I have enough oooomph in me to get to the next lookout and then, I'm afraid, I'll have to call it quits. I'm fading. The Rock of Hope, Crag Misneach, is my very favorite spot on the mountain, and I so want to get there today. Are you with me?"

Aoife knew it was another half an hour hike away, but she wasn't going to be the naysayer, nor was she going to put a damper on Zahryn's enthusiasm.

"Yes, let's move on!" Aoife led the way up the trail, setting a good pace. The noise of the UTV drowned out any sense of quiet, or silence. But that was okay. They would eventually get to hear the silence—the silence in the winds—when they came to rest at the Crag—when they came to rest in hope.

Aoife recalled the very first time she had met Zahryn and they had had their first deep conversation there at the Rock of Hope. It was like they were going back to their beginning. To their roots. Or, perhaps symbolically, they were going full circle. As she walked on, Aoife reflected silently on just how much she had learned from Zahryn. Her outlook. Her positivity. Her wisdom. Her faith. Zahryn had embraced and embodied Wholehearted Living as an intentional life-practice, as a chosen lifestyle, as a way of being, as a way of life.

Aoife segued for a moment in her heartfelt reflections. She knew that Zahryn always used the term 'across the waters' in her mantra, and as metaphor for her personhood, for her ideals, and her mindset. It is something Zahryn just knew—something she had known—intuitively for many, many years.

Aoife could also, at times, sense Zahryn's wisdom as it arose from the depths of her Sacred soul within. Zahryn's Light came up from that place. Aoife was exquisitely aware that Zahryn was Light. Zahryn was love. Zahryn was loved by everyone she met. They warm up instantly in her Light. Zahryn was pure Light.

Aoife was beginning to breathe a little harder. The steepness was winning and the call into the heights was a tough one to answer. Five years older than Zahryn, her forty-year-old body was talking back to her in the heights of the mountain. But she pressed on. She knew that if Zahryn had the will to get to the Crag, then she could too.

And in another few grueling minutes, they arrived. Aoife was breathing heavily. So was Zahryn. She was now relying entirely on her harnesses to keep her sitting up straight in the UTV. Her oxygen tank supply was still good. No worries. But Aoife noticed Zahryn's color.

"Oh my, Zahryn, you are pale, paler than when we started. You must be tiring. I'm so glad we made it here, together, but, we really must make sure you rest before we head back down. Let's get out some snacks and water, and then let's rest. No time pressures. It's only 10:30. We have all morning and all afternoon still."

Out came the blanket. Zahryn chose to remain strapped in for safety's sake. Out came the food. Out came the sun! Both Aoife and Zahryn took off two outer layers of clothes to feel the warmth of the sun directly on their skin.

What a simple delight to spend time with a friend in the sunshine, in the mountains, overlooking the vastness of the wide-open sea. With time on their hands, and all cares given to the wind, they could simply be present in the moment—connected as one. Their shared-here-and-now was a gift. A blessed gift. A gift to hold in their hearts throughout their lives.

Zahryn spoke quietly after carefully swallowing a few bites of her crustless, finely minced ham sandwich. Chewing was becoming harder, as was swallowing. But she proceeded slowly, with caution. No need for any unnecessary choking. She remembered Dr. Gordon's cautionary words from last June.

"Aoife, could you do me a favor? I think we can do this together, now that I've had a wee rest and a bit of food. Do you remember what I told you when we first chatted up here? I told you that I thought Crag Misneach was a Thin Place. That it was one place in the world where I could feel God's presence, especially when I'm here alone. I'm drawn to this place for some reason. I think God has a message for me, or a symbolism, or a hidden meaning for me, here.

"I've named it the Rock of Hope because that's how I feel up here. Full of hope. Full of dreams and visions. Full of life. Well, I must say, I'm not feeling totally full of life. Not today anyway. This post-polio syndrome is really taking its toll on me. So, I want to try to feel something—something more today. And I need your help.

"Could you help me out of my harness and my leg straps? Can you take off both of my shoes, and help me to stand here, barefoot on the Crag? I want so much to stand on Holy ground. God has been present to me here before. And if I stand barefoot on the rock, in the heights, in the Light, I may be able to feel something new, or more, or extraordinary—something Sacred or Holy."

She turned her face upward to the wide-open sky, saying, "Please God, let me know your Presence. May my faith make me strong."

Aoife stepped toward Zahryn and untied her shoes and removed them. Socks too. Zahryn was barefoot. While unstrapping her legs and thighs, she said quietly to Zahryn, "Are you sure?"

Zahryn looked deeply into Aoife's eyes and said with conviction, "Yes, I'm sure."

Aoife then unbuckled the chest harness and waited to see what Zahryn's core muscles would do. Zahryn was actually able to remain seated, in quite an erect posture. And this was good.

Zahryn calmly instructed her friend. "I'll swing both of my legs to the ground. And when I'm ready, I'll put both of my hands on your shoulders, while you brace my ribs near my armpits. When I say "Up," please help me to stand.

"If you just stand there with me, I'll close my eyes and stay standing as long as I can. Then you can help me to just sit down. And then you can buckle me in again. Is that okay?" She smiled in earnest at her caring friend.

Aoife said, "Of course. I'm ready when you are."

Zahryn slowly swung her long legs to the side of the UTV. She set her bare feet on the ground, about shoulder-width apart. Zahryn placed both of her hands on Aoife's shoulders and Aoife placed hers as instructed. Zahryn took a few long slow breaths in and out. Her five-meter-long oxygen tubing ran up and over her shoulder to lay coiled on top of the portable tank behind her. She quietly said, "Up."

Together they stood. They stood tall together. Aoife watched Zahryn closely. Zahryn was determined, and she had a look of true conviction across her visage. She was solid. Hopeful. Full of faith.

Zahryn closed her eyes slowly. Aoife knew Zahryn was attuning to every little detail—especially to her bare feet on the warm solid rock. Zahryn breathed in deeply in the fresh mountain air. She felt the subtle breeze in her long auburn tresses and the warmth of the summer sun on her face. She felt the strength of Aoife's hands supporting her. She felt strong in the moment. Able in the moment. So very able. And then, she felt *something more.*

She felt strong in a way that was different. It was an uncanny feeling. It was like an external energy was coursing through her. A new vibe that was awakening her flesh. She felt renewed, empowered, and whole. She opened her eyes wide with amazement. She was standing face to face with Aoife. They were so close, they could feel each other's breath on their faces.

Zahryn spoke boldly now to Aoife. "Please Aoife, do not question me. Let me go and step aside. God is with me."

Surprised and overwhelmed, Aoife slowly let go of Zahryn and took a big step to her right. With no further ado, Zahryn straightened to her fullest height in the Light, and walked forward with strength, with confidence, with joy. Intrepid, she took three whole steps. She looked over her shoulder, past the cliff, across the waters and beyond.

The horizon was clear, and the rich blue of the sea was dressed in pure sparklescence from the midday sun. Time stood still. The sun stopped in its track. The moment simply breathed with Zahryn as she took it all in, deep, deep, deep. This moment would last forever in her heart. She was grounded. She was with God. She was full of hope and full of Light and life at Crag

Misneach. All would be well. Her inlonracance empowered her. Here and now, in the moment, she was living her life to the fullest, with joy.

Zahryn lifted her eyes into the blue celestial space. Thinking she heard a voice, her ears tuned in—ever-hopeful. And from out in the vastness a calm, deep voice spoke to her. "Your faith is your strength, Zahryn. Your Light is your gift. Keep shining, my dear Zahryn, keep shining."

Zahryn held each and every word in her heart. She cherished them. She stood tall, grounded in those life-giving words.

But her energy was slowly leaving her. She remained there gazing for only a minute, and then cautiously turned around to face her UTV. She took three more steps back to where she started. There, she closed her eyes and prayed quietly, inwardly. Gratitude overflowed in her heart and in her prayer. Peace like a river nurtured her soul. Joy lit up her countenance. Indeed, her faith made her strong.

Zahryn opened her eyes and spoke quietly. "I'll turn around now. When I'm ready to sit, please guide me onto the seat. And help me buckle up."

Wide-eyed, Aoife listened, obeyed, and awaited her cues. Slowly Zahryn turned. On cue, Aoife assisted her to sit, limiting the plop as she sat. Then she put Zahryn's socks and shoes on her and strapped her in securely.

Accomplishing all of this, Aoife plunked herself down on the blanket and flopped back to look up at Zahryn. The sun was directly behind Zahryn's head, haloing her, placing Zahryn's face in complete shadow. But Aoife knew that her friend was smiling, beaming broadly in absolute amazement over what she had just experienced.

As the running waves perpetually lapped upon the shores below, intrepid, placid, sure, so too did their thoughts turn to God—God of Light—God of Love—God of their hearts.

Crag Misneach was truly a Thin Place for Zahryn. She sat there, unmoving. Her heart was full. That welcomed and enlivening external-sourced energy was now all gone, but that didn't matter. Zahryn had stood and walked on Holy Ground in the presence of God of Love—her God of Holy Mystery.

After a time they packed up their things. Aoife and Zahryn went down the mountain without stopping, in silent procession. They would both have to take time to work through all that they had seen and felt and known and learned. Their time together on the mountain was precious. They came away, forever changed, newly enlightened, and full of hope. Blessed be those whose faith is vibrant and strong, for they shall live out their lives in the Light.

Best Laid Plans

ZAHRYN'S SYMPTOMS HAD ADVANCED rather rapidly over the last month, leaving her chronically breathless, and with air hunger. She was anxious, weak and in pain.

Palliative care advisory nurses, Carys and Fiona, had been assigned to Zahryn for her hospice needs, for her end-of-life care.

Nurse Carys addressed Zahryn's support team. "So folks, let's recap and close this meeting for today. We've had a good two hours together, creating a care plan that is thoughtful, thorough, and complete. We've shared so much today.

"Thanks, Tagyn and Zahryn, for welcoming us into your home. And thank you, Dr. Gordon, for supporting all of us here today. These are difficult times."

Carys continued in her encouraging words. "We will journey with you and help you to navigate the health care system to meet all of your needs. We are here for you, Zahryn. You have our card with our contact info.

"We've given you a Symptom Relief Kit—SRK—full of high-powered medications to meet all of your needs for symptom relief," said Carys. "And we've taught you and Tagyn how and when and why to use all of these meds. And we're leaving printed instructions."

Fiona added, "Please remember that we are only a phone call away. Please call us for anything you need or to ask about something you do not fully understand. And of course, please call us for support if you aren't feeling totally prepared for something in your palliative journey. You can do your daily activities as long as you feel safe. You'll know when you're ready for bed rest. Your body will let you know. Your symptoms will guide you."

Fiona looked in earnest, first at Zahryn, then at Tagyn, and back to Zahryn. "Please, also remember that a hospice bed might open up any day this week, and you'll be eligible to go. I think your chances are better forty minutes down the road at Pearl Haven, these days. But, you never know. A bed may open up here, in Moonstone tomorrow." Her voiced trailed and she allowed the silence to rest between them.

Fiona was a seasoned palliative care nurse. She was kind and compassionate beyond words. She knew the phrase "knowledge is power" and she always did everything in her power to ensure her patients and their families had enough knowledge—that they were well informed for their journeys. She paused, and looked over to Dr. Gordon for support.

He took the cue. "Look Zahryn. I'm going to send Carys and Fiona on their way back to the office. You have their contact numbers." He nodded, and they picked up their things, leaving the SRK and the paperwork out in the open, on the living room table. Coats were on and they were gone.

Dr. Gordon came and sat down on a footstool directly in front of Zahryn in her wheelchair. Her lean frame towered above him. Tagyn remained in the room, in a rocker, over by the window. Tagyn could see that Zahryn was tired, physically and emotionally, and that she was trying hard not to show her fatigue.

Zahryn was quite obviously SOBAR—short of breath at rest—even with the support of her continuous portable oxygen. She wore her N95 facemask full-time on top of her plastic nasal prong oxygen tubing. Zahryn was wearing her mask during all of her waking hours now. She did not want to contract the Covid virus during her final days or weeks on earth. She did not want to die in an ICU on a respirator, in an isolation room, with no contact with the outside world.

On this day, Zahryn was quite pale. Grey, ashen. Her auburn tresses fell loosely around her shoulders, and down her back. She had no energy to bun them or even to ponytail them.

Dr. Gordon spoke slowly. "Zahryn, we've had a good run, you and I. For thirteen years you've been under my care, young lady. And for thirteen years, you have taught ME so very much, personally, about hope and perseverance and resilience."

In his own heart of hearts, Paddy Gordon knew that Zahryn had been a model patient, a personal example of grace and inner strength. Of optimism and glass-half-full living. She had taught him so much about open-mindedness and openheartedness—about self-understanding and self-affirmation.

And he had learned to be more trusting, through Zahryn. She was an incredible mentor to him, showing him the ways of wholehearted living—of humble service to others. His own understanding of humanity grew.

Dr. Gordon continued, "You Zahryn are a gift to me—truly a blessed redheaded gift! And I thank you for all of this. Thanks for being you."

Zahryn received his words silently and a small curl of a smile grew on her pale dusky lips. Her energy was low, but her spirit still shone. Her conquering spirit was still driving her forward.

Zahryn began again quietly. "You're such a busy man, Paddy! Are you still on call on Tuesdays for the coroner's office and doing two night shifts a month in the emergency room? You are so dedicated to medicine."

"Yes, you're very right. I am on call on Tuesdays for the coroner work. And I'm glad to do it. Dr Ure cannot work—or be on call—seven days a week. No one should have to! It's not that busy. And, thank goodness for small mercies, I'm not scheduled for any more overnights in the ER starting in the new year. I'm getting too old for those twelve-hour night shifts!"

They shared in a grin and a nod, in a moment of understanding.

Zahryn began again, quietly. "Dr. Gordon, we've never talked about Medical Assistance in Dying. I've read a lot about it. And I've spoken with my friends. They have their views too.

"For me, it is totally an acceptable decision to make, at the right time. God is a God of compassion. He will be with me—I believe this.

"But I am not asking you for MAID. I know it is complicated. Just know that I believe that leaving this life on your own terms is a good and right choice for many terminally ill folks. There, I've said my piece."

Dr. Gordon looked relieved. He knew that Zahryn was competent in her decision making, and eloquent and succinct in voicing her opinions. He also knew that Zahryn would be wonderfully cared for and guided by Carys and Fiona. The palliative care plan was now in place, as were all of the powerful SRK meds. All would be well.

"Zahryn, I don't know if we'll see each other again. Maybe, maybe not. And, if this is our last time together, face to face, I want you to hear this from me personally. "You are strong. You are so very strong. Your lungs are weakened by your post-polio syndrome, and you have managed to dodge the Covid virus for two and a half years now. And that in itself is testament to your strength and your diligent self-care.

"Quite a while ago, you told me your beautiful mantra, 'Be the River. Be the Light. Be the Love. Across the Waters.' YOU are all of this and so much more!

"Please know that I will hold you in my prayers. Whatever lies before you, I know you will meet it all with grace and hope and love."

He leaned forward for one more hug. They both knew it would be their last. Dr. Gordon slowly got up off of his knees, stood up straight, bowed ever so reverentially to Zahryn, and then walked over to Tagyn at the window. Tagyn stood up in front of her rocker. She chose to stand tall as a simple gesture of respect to the man who, over the years, had kept Zahryn alive and strong and so full of life. They shook hands, and nodded silently to one another. He stepped away and left quietly by the front door.

Zahryn was exhausted. All done-in. Emotionally flattened and drained. Auntie Tagyn spoke quietly and offered to her beautiful daughter, "Teatime, honey? Some cardamom tea?"

And Zahryn graciously said, "Yes please. Thanks, Mom."

EPILOGUE

Across the Waters

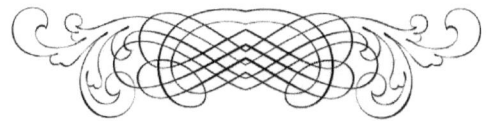

Across the Waters

THE ON-CALL CORONER THAT day was Dr. Gordon. He went to the morgue when staff advised him of a new female arrival. They handed him the hand-written note they had found earlier, on her person.

Receiving it tenderly, he said to the staff, "Thank you. I'm going for a drive. There's somewhere I need to be." He left the morgue and drove through the park in the noon-hour sunshine to the entrance to the Ben Lonrach mountain trails. He let his car windows down all the way to catch the rich scent of the cedars at the gate as he passed them by. Their fragrance would usually overpower the familiar salt-air scent, which was signature for coastal Moonstone Cove. And today was no different. He breathed in deeply, and sighed heavily. He parked his car and hiked upward on the zig-zagging trail into the heights, into the Light.

At the top, he walked across the clearing, to the rocky precipice. He quietly uttered the words, "Crag Misneach. Zahryn's Rock of Hope." He smiled inwardly. He sat down on the dry ground and gazed out across the waters, across the Celtic Sea.

Slowly, he unfolded the note and recognized Zahryn's handwriting. With both hands, he pressed the page gently into his chest. He almost knew, word for word in his heart, what he was about to read, but he read it out loud anyway. He lifted his voice into the up-drafting wind. He could hear her heart and her faith in the words. He felt the warmth of her Light.

Good morning, Dr. Coroner. If you're on call today as coroner, like you normally are on Tuesdays, then, Good morning Dr. Gordon, my friend!

Peace and Light be with you, Paddy. If you are reading this note that I tucked into my turtleneck in the wee hours of dawn this morning, then my plan has unfolded. With my broken wings, now I can fly. Blackbird, I. Into the heights. Into the Light. I have indeed left this beautiful world, willingly, in readiness, at peace. I have no regrets whatsoever in my short thirty-five-year life. Rather, my heart is filled with joy. I have truly lived. I have truly loved. And I have truly been loved.

They say it takes a village. Well, in my village, there are many fathers, mothers, sisters, brothers, aunties, uncles, and grands. There are friends and lovers, colleagues and kindred spirits. And what a mighty fine village they were!

Despite my many difficult barriers and my life-circumstances, I am free. I remain unlimited. My spirit is unbridled. My Light is unshaded. I have known love. I have known freedom. I have known a blessed inner peace. I have been gifted with many precious gifts, and I have shared them all, throughout my life, with those in need.

I have known God, and God knows my heart. God has been present to me—with me and within me—through all my days. And now as I leave my earthly journey behind, as I greet the saints of all time, I go forward in the grace, in the presence, in the love, of God.

I was born into life, amid clouds of darkness, and secrets, even mystery. I was borne through life on the wings of love and faith, on the power of hope, and in the grace of all human compassions. And now, I am borne by God into eternity, into my new home, into the next.

My life was good. So, so good. The ups were mountaintop highs, and the downs were roiling waters and dark black holes. But, I have always had a Light within me that shone in the darkness, that lifted me out of the depths to find my way with clarity, with insight, with vision. My Light empowered me to see, to truly see. My Light graced my very being, and gave me energy, giving rise to my conquering spirit. I am grateful. I am thankful. My heart is full.

I am Light. I am all of my visions and my dreams. I am my faith. I am contented. I want for nothing. I am at peace. I am where I want to be—where I need to be—where I hoped to be.

Please tell my village, my mother and sister and brother, and my grand-dad too, that all will be well. God bless all of you, who have so colorfully shaped my life. My Light still shines. Light into Light. Across the waters. Amen.

Dr. Gordon lifted his eyes up into the vastness and was still. A peacefulness enfolded him. He felt a presence. The thinness of the veil stirred his soul. God was with him. Dr. Gordon was sad, but he simply could not dwell in the depths of his sadness. Zahryn's joy of her earthly departure filled him—Zahryn's Light somehow lingered there. Her peace empowered him—she was free.

He said quietly, "Your beautiful Light, my friend, is not gone. It will never be gone. For you have shared it with all of us, and we will all carry your Light, moving forward, shining perpetually for all to see. God bless you, Zahryn. Keep on shining—keep on being Light. Light into Light. Across the waters. Amen."

The End

Closing Prayer

LIGHT INTO LIGHT

Dear God of Light and Love, hear my prayer.

They say it takes a village.
>   We all have mothers and fathers,
>   known and unknown,
>   natural or chosen,
>   present or absent,
>   earthly, heavenly, and ever-with-us.

We are all brothers and sisters in the family of life and living
>   —connected by our family ties,
>   our friendship bonds,
>   and our faith journeys.

We are connected by our lights—
>   our shared inner and emanating Lights of love and joy and hope.

We are part of something far greater than our solitary selves.
>   We are connected and interconnected—
>   here in our earthly home,
>   here in our spiritual realm,
>   here, within our very own Sacred Souls.
>   We are yours.

Blessed be our place and our time on this earth.

May we all—Be the River, Be the Light, Be the Love.

Light into Light. Across the waters. Amen.

Epitaph

Zahryn Ava Walker-Inglis
Zahryn Ava . . . Light of Life

September 1, 1987
November 1, 2022

River. Light. Love.
River on. . . . Shimmer on. . . . Ever-loving into Eternity

Acknowledgments

WIPF AND STOCK IS a lovely publishing experience. The staff in all departments are talented, insightful, and all of their work is so very timely. No task is too much trouble for them, and no question goes unanswered or is deemed irrelevant. Theirs is a well-oiled machine that time and time again creates quality literary treasures. I give thanks to Wipf and Stock for publishing my works so beautifully and so professionally, through 2021–2025.

Sallie Vandagrift is a godsend. She is a gifted editor who goes above and beyond with her clients to create the best possible version of her clients' written work. She aligns her vision with the author's. She's exquisitely articulate. She knows editing and the industry. That said, her insight is as broad as it is deep—and so very clear. Sallie is personable and works closely with the author, encouraging them, teaching them, inspiring them—even forming them. Sallie's eagle eyes can spot errors, flaws, and trends in the raw written work, and she makes targeted suggestions to correct and fix or rework and rebuild passages into reader-friendly literary beauty and flow. I give my heartfelt gratitude to Sallie for believing in me and in my work. This in itself is a most priceless gift.

I need to acknowledge my dear friend Molly Hosein. She watched and listened eagerly, intently, as my multiple fictional characters were developed and as plots were thickened, bent, and twisted more and more and more. Her smile told all when she spoke her exclamatory words, "I can't wait to know more about Connor! I'd really like to meet him!" Thank you, Molly!

And a special shout out goes to another longtime friend, Peter Sullivan. Without his sharing with me in casual conversation, once upon a time, about the ancient meaning of his family name, there would be no real twist in the plot of this book, nor would some of my fictional characters of Sullivan ancestry even exist! Thanks, Peter!

And I make special mention here of my dear lifelong friend, Lesley Thompson. She and I hold many mountaintop highs in our hearts—memories of exhilarating adventures, moments of knowing, and times of true grit and simple trust. We sought and found meaning and purpose and self-worth out there—way, way, way out there in the corners of Creation—in places that were only accessible by paddle and canoe—and with a good pair of hiking boots! Lesley knew to work hard, to play just as hard, and to rest well when the time was right. With gratitude, I sing out in full voice to you, Lesley, my friend for life, "Blue lakes and rocky shore, let's hit the trails once more. . . ."

My endorsers are very, very special people. They are Catherine Fletcher, Kristin Larsen, Barbara Brown, and Catherine Richardson. They all took the time, their valuable time, to read the unedited version of my manuscript one full year before it was published. They saw its literary merit even back then, and they got the messages—the deeply imbedded themes—then. They have been such wonderful cheerleaders for me, and their words of endorsement ring out like songs of praise in my heart. They truly lift me up. A writer's world can be a pretty immersive and solitary place, and it is such a blessing to me to have folks enter into this immersive world and walk along with me. Thanks just isn't a big enough word! Sigh. . . .

And I must lift up words of praise for my husband, Barry Constable. He generously gives so much space and time for my creativity to flow. He knows how meaningful my work is to me and he helps in any way he can to keep my written work full of inertia, moving forward, meeting whatever timelines and deadlines arise. He shares his marketing and computer skills to round out our shared skill set. I may already be grounded and centered, but he completes me, in my world.

And my final words of gratitude go to God. We are all differently gifted, called and chosen, and diversely abled. I am truly humbled by the gifts bestowed on me and on my life, allowing me to find my niche, my tiny target audience, and my literary platform—and enabling me to share broadly, through my writing, the wonders and the treasures of the ancient Celtic Wisdom. We are all Sacred. We are all interconnected in our lives. As we are all OF God, so too, we are Light. Thanks be to God.

> Blessed are those who walk alongside,
> encouraging, supporting, and believing in
> friends and colleagues and strangers alike,
> for theirs are hearts of gold, and gifts of love—
> in a treasured journey, together.

Suggested Reading

Constable, Janis. *Random and Nebulous—Nuancing the Psalms*. Wipf and Stock, 2021.
Constable, Janis. *Light Beyond the River—Encountering the Sacred*. Wipf and Stock, 2022.
Constable, Janis. *My Indulgent Interior Life*. Wipf and Stock, 2023.
Constable, Janis. *Wholehearted Me A—Z!* Wipf and Stock, 2024.
Newell, John Philip. *Sacred Soul Sacred Earth*. HarperCollins, 2021.
Newell, John Philip. *The Great Search*. HarperCollins, 2024.

www.ingramcontent.com/pod-product-compliance
Lightning Source LLC
Chambersburg PA
CBHW050401030726
47503CB00006B/1962